A Retribution of Soul:

Book 3 of the In-Between

Rebecca M. Senese

OTHER BOOKS BY REBECCA M. SENESE

The In-Between Series
Book 1: A Reluctance of Blood
Book 2: A Remembrance of Flesh

The Night Killers

Wreck the Halls: 5 Christmas Horror Stories

Oh the Horror! 5 Horror Stories

Bad Ends: 5 Horror Stories

*With a Bite: 5 Vampire Tales

*By Howl & Claw: 5 Werewolf Stories

The Color of Blood: The Chronicles of Richard Damon

Who Killed Santa? A Christmas / Mystery Novella

A Very Zombie Christmas

The Beginners Guide to the Recently Deceased

Daily Bread

*Forthcoming

A Retribution of Soul:
Book 3 of the In-Between

Rebecca M. Senese

Published 2013 by RFAR Publishing
Toronto, Canada
http://www.RFARPublishing.com

This is a work of fiction. All characters appearing in this work are fictitious. Any resemblance to real persons, living or dear is purely coincidental.

Trade paper edition designed by Rebecca M. Senese
in InDesign CS5.5

Electronic editions designed by Rebecca M. Senese

Cover design: Rebecca M. Senese
Image © ra2studio / CanStockPhoto.com
Interior Image © 100ker / DepositPhotos.com

ISBN: 978-1-927603-19-2

A Retribution of Soul:
Book 3 of the In-Between

Prologue

The glow of a new moon did little to illuminate the street but Alexa Hammond didn't need any light to see by. She crouched between the red brick wall of the dingy gas station and the blue, dented dumpster, hands on her knees as she watched the old highway in front of her. Over the buzz of the neon sign flickering the name of Todd's Gas, she could hear the pumping of blood from the clerk in the convenience store section of the station. It pounded at her brain with an urgency she found harder and harder to resist. But she had to, she knew it. She couldn't devolve like the others and just eat indiscriminately. Doing that was like its own neon sign pointing "vampire here."

She wasn't going to make it easier for the In-Between to catch her. She wasn't going to make it easier for *him* to catch her.

As always, that thought calmed her down. She'd survived this long without Constantine, her clan head, the vampire who had made her and trained her. She'd only been with him for a year before the disaster that was *him*. *He* had killed her Constantine, used Constantine's own ambition to control the book written by the first vampire against him, and in doing so destroyed the clan heads and all civilized vampire society. Now most vampires were little more than animals. Easy pickings for those freaks, the In-Between who hunted them. They were jealous, she thought, that they hadn't been turned completely into vampires but were stuck in that twilight in between human and vampire. Too bad their blood was poisonous to her. She would have loved to drink every last one of them dry.

Especially *him*. Especially Sebastian.

He'd loved her once, she knew, just a few short years ago when they were in college together. He'd been geeky and awkward and shy. She'd found him funny and charming in a way. Then he'd been bitten by a vampire, but instead of having the decency to die or become a vampire himself, he'd become an In-Between, and his stupidity had led to her becoming a vampire.

Not that she was sorry about that, oh no. She quite liked being a vampire, or she had when Constantine and the clan were around. Then she had a place, a family. Now she was alone, crouching between a dumpster and a two-bit gas station in the middle of nowhere. And it had taken her over eight months to get this far.

Without Constantine's influence, crossing the ocean from England had been a major undertaking. No more flying in a personal jet with the windows blacked out to protect her from the sun. Instead she had to travel on one of those horrible baggage ships, subsisting on the occasional drink from the crew. But she couldn't even take her fill. It would have been too suspicious. The crew had thought their boat haunted by a ghost woman anyway. If she'd taken too much and killed any of them, they would have searched the ship, breaking through any compulsion she planted for them to avoid the section she'd hidden in. If they'd found her and dragged her out into the daylight... well, she wouldn't be crouching here now.

She had certainly learned patience. Her vengeance was taking every last drop of it.

From the road, she heard the hiss of tires on asphalt. She poked her head out. A minute later a car approached. Would it turn in for gas? She hoped it would. She needed a ride.

The car sped by without stopping. She watched the red tail lights recede in the distance. If Constantine had been here, he would have been able to influence the driver from here and cause him to stop at the gas station. She didn't have even close to that ability and she might never learn it now, not with her clan head dead.

Because of *him.*

Her anger burned.

Even when she'd turned, she wanted to bring Sebastian across with her. They could have been together forever then. He would never have had to work up the courage to ask her out. But he'd rejected her and she left to be with Constantine. She'd even been willing to leave Sebastian alone. Let him live his own life with his own choices. Just as she wanted to live her own.

But then he'd interfered with Constantine's search for the book and used it to kill him and all the clan heads. Now she wasn't going to just live her life anymore and let him live his. Now she was going to end his in the worst way she could think of.

If she could just get out of this gas station.

Another hiss of tires on asphalt. She peered out from behind the dumpster, brushing her brown hair from her eyes. This time the car, a blue sedan with dirt along the bottom, slowed and pulled into the gas station, aiming for the unleaded pump. As it stopped and the driver's door opened, Alexa stood up. The driver moved to the pump and unhooked the gas nozzle. In the dark she could just make out the dark blue weave of his suit. As he turned his back, to hook the nozzle into his car, Alexa slid forward, moving with a gliding grace until she stood right behind him.

He was a full foot taller than her, with a well padded torso, arms and legs. Thinning brown hair had been combed over his head. As he turned to look at the gauge, she saw the double chin and the tortoise shell glasses perched on his nose. She tilted her head. He caught the movement out of the corner of his eye and started. The nozzle jiggled in the car.

"Careful," she said. "You don't want to spill any gas. It's expensive enough, don't you think?"

"Ah, yeah," he said. "Sorry, I didn't notice you there."

"That's quite all right."

"Um, you work here? I thought it was self-serve."

"It is self-serve," she said. She smiled at him and extended her will. "I am looking for a ride."

Behind his glasses, she watched his small brown eyes get that unfocused look as her command penetrated his brain.

"A ride," he said.

"Yes, I want a ride," she said. "You are going to give me a ride."

"I am going to give you a ride."

"Yes, thank you. Now finish and pay for the gas."

He started to pull out the nozzle before even turning off the pump. She flipped the switch before he extracted it. Only a few drops hit the ground. He turned in jerking movements toward the pump. She took the nozzle from his hand.

"Go pay for the gas," she said.

He crossed to the convenience store to pay. She replaced the nozzle and moved to the passenger's side of the car. When she opened the door, she found food wrappers and a map strewn across the seat. She tossed them into the back and climbed in.

The man returned a moment later, walking stiffly across the pavement toward the car. He hesitated when he reached the driver's door. His expression looked startled when he noticed her in the passenger's seat.

"I need a ride," she said again, concentrating at him. "You are giving me one."

"I am giving you one," he said. He climbed in behind the wheel and started the car.

"Close the door," she said.

He twitched and closed the door.

"Put on your seat belt," she said.

He did as she instructed. She sighed. Was she going to have to tell him everything step by step? Constantine never had to do that. He'd been so much better at this than her and he'd just started to train her how to do this before he'd been murdered. She supposed she should be grateful she could do it at all.

The car started and the man pulled out onto the street. Once he was driving he seemed more able to focus on the task. She stayed silent until she glanced in the back seat and saw the laptop case.

"Does your laptop have wireless Internet?" she said.

The man started. Confusion crossed his face as he looked over at her.

"Eyes on the road," she said.

He jerked his attention back to the road. "Ah yes, my laptop has Internet."

"Stop at the next coffee shop," she said.

They drove on for another ten minutes before a coffee shop appeared. As they pulled into the parking lot, Alexa noticed the lights were out inside. She peered at the hours sign. Only open until eleven. That didn't matter, as long as their WiFi was still operating.

"Park here," she instructed him. "Get on the Internet."

The man twisted in the seat and grabbed the case. He dragged it to the front and turned on the laptop. While she waited, Alexa repeated what little she knew: Sebastian Lockhart, grew up somewhere in Michigan maybe or Ohio, his parents were still alive and he had a younger brother named... Her lips twisted as she tried to remember. She was sure he'd mentioned it once or twice. Caleb? No, Callum. That was it, Callum.

That was all she had. It was going to take a little time to get the right Lockhart but she would do it, as long as he hadn't moved them somewhere. But even if he had, if she had the chance to find their home she was sure she'd be able to catch their scent. Even if someone else had bought the place and moved in. All she needed was the thinnest of scents and she'd be able to find them. It wouldn't matter where they went, she would never stop looking.

She had years.

Decades.

All the time in the world.

The man finished connecting to the WiFi hotspot. She took the laptop from him and rested it on her lap.

"Just relax," she said to him. He slumped against his seat as if he was a switched off automaton.

She pulled up a search engine and began hunting for Lockhart in Ohio and Michigan. Both states turned up way too many Lockharts. She had to find a way to narrow the field. Then she tried "Callum Lockhart." Still too many. There was no way she could search the list. Well, no, that wasn't exactly true, but it would take longer than Sebastian's lifetime and that wasn't what she wanted. She wanted him to feel the loss of his world crumbling around him just as she'd felt when Constantine had died.

She combined the name with each state and still pulled up way too many hits on each. She banged her hands on the edge of the laptop in frustration. Damn, if she only knew more details but Sebastian hadn't talked much of life before college.

Not much but some. Maybe all she needed to do was remember.

She tried to shy away from the thought but stopped herself. If she wanted revenge for Constantine's death then she would have to face it. She didn't think much about her life before she became a vampire. With every passing night, it became more and more like a strange dream she had long ago. Once in a while something would remind of her that time and jolt her back into memories, leaving her disoriented. Constantine told her it was natural for new vampires. It would go away in time, after five or six decades.

When he had first said that, she thought it was so long but now she knew it was a mere drop of time. Already she'd forgotten so much from that time before and it had been less than two years.

But if she wanted to find Sebastian's family, she was going to have to return to those memories. Her shoulders climbed up toward her ears at the thought of it. She would do it but she wouldn't like it.

She turned the laptop off and set it on the floor under her feet. She shook the man's shoulder.

"Hey, let's go," she said.

He stirred and started the car. At her instruction, he backed out and headed down the old highway again. She had him pull into an old motel for a room, making sure to get the one farthest from the office. She made him pay for three days and ask for a late checkout. When he parked in front of the room, she got out and entered, making sure to close the curtains. He wandered in after her, standing by the door until she instructed him to lie down on the bed. He did so, not even taking off his shoes.

The longer she Influenced him the more literally he reacted to her instructions. Soon she would have to tell him how to do everything as her Influence gnawed away at his functional mind. She didn't have the finesse with it the way Constantine had but even with him this disintegration happened. Eventually, the Influenced subject became useless for anything other than food.

And Alexa was feeling a bit peckish.

She crossed to the bed. He lay on top of the worn brown blanket that looked a muddy black in the darkness. Faint light from the parking lot lights outside filtered around the burgundy curtains. She would have to seal them securely before the morning and leave a note to the hotel-maids not to be disturbed.

She sat on the edge of the bed and reached for the lamp on the night stand. She liked to see what she was eating. A personal preference. Yellowish light splashed across the walls and reflected on the beige ceiling. She noticed a brownish stain over by the counter that held an ancient coffee maker. Someone hadn't liked their Mr. Coffee. Even from here, she could smell the staleness of the single serve coffee packets. Good thing she wasn't intent on drinking that swill.

She had another way to quench her thirst.

The man on the bed lay with his eyes wide open, staring upward at the ceiling as if it was the most fascinating thing in the world. Even now she could see the lack of awareness in him. It was her heavy-handed Influence. She just didn't have the light touch that Constantine had. He could Influence someone and keep them at top shape for almost a full two weeks before they began to erode. She couldn't even manage one night. She was going to have to get better at this if she was going to do what she wanted.

But it was too late for this one. He was already almost gone. At least he was still good enough to eat.

She reached out to turn his head toward the wall, exposing his neck. Ah, yes, the subtle sweet aroma of his blood, tantalizing her under the surface of his flesh. She smiled, exposing sharp fangs, and lunged, drinking deep and long.

She finished him in less than ten minutes, a veritable gorging. The body lay like an empty husk on the bed. She shoved it aside. It rolled off the other end and flopped to the floor. The empty space he left looked so tempting. She just wanted to lie down and sleep. But she couldn't just yet, not with that bit of light coming in from outside. In the daytime it could prove disastrous for her.

A quick search around the room gave her nothing to secure the drapes. She would have to go to the office. She hadn't wanted to, hadn't wanted to engage anyone else here but it couldn't be helped. Still, she should be able to wipe the attendant's memory of her presence without too much damage and could even implant a command to leave the room undisturbed during the day. That way she could be sure of safety.

Good, she liked that.

She left the room and stepped back out into the night. Crickets chirped an accompaniment as she headed to the office. The little bell over the door tinkled as she opened it. A single desk lamp on the counter was turned on. She heard a television playing through the closed door behind the counter. A glance at the clock on the wall showed her it was just after midnight.

She waited a moment but no one came in response to the door's bell. She slapped the bell on the counter. The sharp ring cut over the sound of the television. It turned down and then she heard footsteps. The door opened and a tall, thin man wearing a green robe came out. Reflexively, he tightened the belt around his narrow waist and tucked the lapels in around his chest. One hand brushed back the greying hair on his high forehead.

"Can I help you?" he said. "Sorry I didn't hear your car drive up."

"I need some duct tape," she said, giving her voice that special command tone. Immediately his features loosened. His eyes defocused. "You will not remember me. You will instruct your employees and any one else to leave room seventeen alone. You will not enter it yourself for one week."

"Yes... yes..."

"Get me the duct tape."

"Yes..." His voice sputtered. With a jerk, he bent beneath the counter. She listened to him rummaging under there then he stood with a roll of silver duct tape in his hand. She plucked it away from him.

"You have not seen me," she said.

"Not seen," he said.

"Go back to your television."

He turned and walked into the door. His nose bumped the wood before his fumbling hands found the door knob. Then he opened it and wandered through. She waited a moment until she heard the television again. Over it, she heard a woman's voice and the man answering but no one came out. She waited a little longer to make sure.

Nothing.

When she left, she opened the door slowly, making sure to not disturb the tinkling bell. It still gave a brief ring as she closed it, then she hurried back to her room.

She taped the sides and top of the curtains, making sure to cover every inch. When she turned off the lamp to test it, not a single shaft of light penetrated from outside. Perfect! Now she could relax.

Well, maybe not relax. Now she could remember.

She lay down on top of the bed, cradling her head on her arms. Anxiety twisted in her stomach. She didn't want to concentrate on that before time. That was another person, another life and it was one she didn't like thinking about. It felt too... weird. But she knew she didn't have any choice. If she wanted to kill Sebastian, she was going to have to remember as much as possible to find a way to exploit his weakness.

She swallowed her anxiety, took a deep breath and closed her eyes.

They'd met during the first week of freshman year. She remembered him as this tall, gawky guy who seemed uncomfortable in his skin, as if he'd gained his height within a short period of time and still wasn't sure how to deal with it. Later, he confessed he'd been this height since his early teens; his gawkiness had just been his usual self.

She was in the campus bookstore, looking for the text book on statistics. As she rounded the corner, a tall, young man stumbled forward, books tipping from his arms. She put out her arms to try to catch them and managed to snag one before the others toppled to the floor. He almost went after them in his rush to prevent their falling. Instead, he ended up on his knees, frantically gathering all the books together as everyone in the vicinity turned to stare. She noticed an endearing blush rise on his cheeks and turn his ears pink under his black hair.

As he piled the books on top of each and prepared to lift them again, she noticed she was holding a statistics textbook.

"Hey, is this the textbook for McDougle's class?" she said.

He glanced over at her. "Oh yeah, it is."

"I've been looking for this book," she said. "Can you tell me where it is?"

His eyes lit up. "Yes," he said. He turned back the way he'd come. "Down this aisle then over one more and it's on the top shelf above..." He tilted his head as he looked down at her. "You might not be able to reach it. I could get it for you."

She smiled. "That would be nice."

He pointed at his crooked book pile. "Watch those." Then he darted away, long legs hurdling him down the aisle. She almost expected him to trip over himself the way his legs flailed out. But he stayed upright and disappeared around the back corner.

She looked down at the pile of books and recognized a lot of them from her class schedule. Was this odd young man taking business as well? Maybe they'd have some of the same classes. He seemed pleasant enough.

The sound of footsteps caught her attention. She looked up to see him returning, textbook in hand.

"Thanks," she said. "Are you in first year business?"

"Yes," he said.

"Me too," she said. She held out her hand. "I'm Alexa Hammond."

He shook her hand with just the right amount of pressure. "I'm Sebastian Lockhart, fresh from Michigan and looking forward to warmer climates in the winter. Sort of, I guess."

She laughed as he bent to retrieve his books.

It was the beginning of their friendship, the beginning of the end of her life.

Alexa jolted upright out of the bed. Sweat covered her body. Yuck, she hated that, it was such a... such a... *human* reaction. She jumped out of the bed and bolted for the bathroom, tearing her clothes off as she went.

She leapt into the shower and yanked the tap on full blast. Under the scalding water, she rubbed her hands all over her body, as if she could wash the dream off. Sure, it had given her what she wanted, a memory of him mentioning Michigan which gave her a place to focus on, but it had also reminded her of how it felt to be human. She remembered first arriving at the college, the mix of excitement and anxiety. Making new friends, like Sebastian, who she came to care for, hanging out with him, laughing, joking around, smiling at how he always spilled food on his shirts and how he obsessively tried to hide it from her. Meeting Charlie, in so many ways the exact opposite of the frantic, neurotic Sebastian but complementing him, and the easy friendship between them. How comfortable she felt with them, always safe, always reliable, even as her feelings for Sebastian deepened over the years.

She shoved her face under the steaming shower, hissing at the hot water burning her skin. Enough! She didn't want to remember any more. That wasn't her any more, that person was dead and gone. Those hopes and dreams were meaningless. She didn't care about them any *more!*

Finally the scalding water pulled her back into her body, erasing the edge from her thoughts. When the water turned cold, she shut off the tap and stood dripping in the center of the bathroom floor. The human memories and emotions faded, leaving a simmering anger at the indignity of them.

With a snarl, she snatched the towel from the towel bar with such force one end of the bar came out of the wall. She scrubbed at her hair and then dried her body off. She moved into the bedroom and yanked her clothes on. She spotted the man lying on the floor between the bed and the wall. Even from here, she could tell he didn't have a drop left in him. She'd drained him dry. So why was she starving?

That damned remembering took up too much energy. She would have to feed again. She checked the clock on the nightstand under the lamp. Only twelve thirty. Not that long. She might be able to sneak into one of the rooms and feed a little off one of the other travellers.

But even as she thought that she realized that wasn't what she wanted. Not even close. She wanted more than a taste, more than even a feeding.

She wanted a massacre.

She thought that Constantine would approve.

She left the room and headed back for the office. She wanted a good idea of the number of visitors so she could come up with a plan. Opening the door slowly stopped the bell from tinkling and she slipped inside. In the darkness, she found the sign-in book, a quaint, old-fashioned check-in method that they still employed. From the book she could tell only half the rooms were rented, most around back, facing away from the road.

Perfect.

While she was here, she might as well get started.

She found the old man and his wife up in their bedroom, above the office. The man didn't make a peep as she sliced his throat open. The wife woke up as the splash of blood hit her in the face. She gasped, opening her eyes, her hands fluttering up in confusion. At the sight of Alexa straddling her husband, blood staining her top, mouth full of fangs smiling widely, the woman opened her mouth to scream. Alexa fell on her, stifling the scream as she wrenched the woman's head aside and plunged her teeth into the jugular vein.

The aborted scream ended in a gurgle.

When she left, Alexa tore out the sign-in sheet from the book and decided to start at one end of the motel and work her way back toward her room.

Using the master key from the office, she opened the first door and found a man sleeping alone in a queen size bed. He didn't even wake up as she ripped his head from his body. The next room held a man and woman. For sport, she killed the woman first, slicing up the torso with her claws. The man woke up, yelled when he saw Alexa and lunged for the door. She let him get two paces from it before she fell on him, dragging him to the floor as she broke his neck.

The next two rooms were empty. The following room was another single man. For fun, she turned the overhead light on, jolting him awake. At the sight of her fangs and the blood staining her shirt and smeared across her face, the man jumped from his bed and actually made it to the bathroom before she caught up with him. He slammed the door in her face and locked it. Fantastic! This was great fun! She giggled to herself as her claws dug into the crevices around the door and pulled. The bathroom had no exit.

He'd trapped himself.

Yanking off the door took less than half a minute. When she stepped into the bathroom, she found the man trying to squeeze his way out of the small window above the toilet. He managed to get his shoulder and head out but was stuck. She laughed when she saw him, then sliced into the femoral artery in his leg. He yelled for almost five seconds before she drained enough from him to shut him up.

She left the room, wiping her mouth. Hmm, maybe it hadn't been so smart to let him start yelling like that. Although none of the doors had opened yet, she could smell an increase in adrenaline wafting on the air. The few remaining people were awake now. She would have to move fast.

This was more fun than she'd expected.

But as she turned to leave and dispatch the last few she caught a glimpse of the clock. After one now. Hmm, she wouldn't be able to spend the day here, not after the mess she made. She'd have to finish up fast and find somewhere else.

No more time for games.

The last three rooms (two couples and a single) took her less than five minutes. She swept through like a scythe, cutting them down before moving to the next. She didn't even bother feeding much. She was already full and could barely force down a mouthful or two.

She circled back to her room and dug out the keys to the car from the man who'd given her a ride. That car had enough gas to get her far enough from here, she knew. She pocketed them and then returned to one of the other cars. She siphoned off some gas and spilled it through each of the rooms. Returning to her car, she lit a match and tossed it into the room.

Fire whooshed up. It tasted the gasoline and seemed to like the flavor.

She returned to the car and got into the driver's side. She backed out to the edge of the parking lot and waited, watching. Sure enough, the fire began to spread, sending arms of orange destruction to embrace the other rooms. Black smoke drifted into the night sky, blotting out the stars.

Alexa gunned the engine and took off. She'd find somewhere to hole up for the day. At least now she had a destination.

Michigan.

And Callum.

Part One: Retribution

CHAPTER 1

Even without light, Sebastian could see well enough in the early morning hours. Most of the lights in this parking lot had been broken or burned out, especially near the back alley. Rumors of something back there had caught the ear of the local In-Between, a man named Hanson, and an old friend of Jessica's. He'd called in a favor that she had to return and here Sebastian was again, dressed in the camouflage of black pants and a black long sleeved top, crouching behind a dented dumpster, peering around the corner into an alley.

All he wanted to do was get home but that had turned out to be easier said than done. Now with the clan heads gone, destroying any semblance of vampire structure, vampires roamed like animals, killing indiscriminately. Then when the police tracked them down, the vampires slaughtered them, leaving a trail of blood and destruction behind. The In-Between were stretched to the limit trying to stop them all. While the vampires were organized into clans, they hunted together. But now with the clans dissolved, all bonds had shattered and the vampires spread out alone. According to In-Between intelligence, the majority of vampires were in Europe, spreading down the Mediterranean toward Africa.

North America had to wait.

This last one, he thought. He'd finish this favor for Hanson and then he was heading home. He didn't care that it was somehow easier for him to stop the vampires than the others. He didn't care if they were stretched thin. He had to get home.

His eye caught movement at the end of the alley. He made a slashing motion behind him. A moment later, he heard the crunch of gravel. The figure of a woman, clad in the same black outfit as him, stepped forward. In the darkness, he admired how the fabric smoothed over her curves, the sweep of her dark hair pulled away from her face into a pony tail that fell to her mid-back. She didn't often let her hair hang free but he liked it when she did, when the soft brown waves flowed around her face and tickled his nose. He blinked the image away as she slipped near.

"How many?" Jessica whispered.

"Can't see," he said.

"Feel?" she said.

He pressed his lips tight together. Her hand touched his arm, her indication that she knew he didn't like it but it was necessary.

Dammit, it seemed necessary too many times lately.

He looked out at the alley entrance, willing them to move out, betray themselves without his having to do anything. Again he caught a hint of movement but they didn't come out. Did they somehow sense his presence the way he could sense theirs?

He never kept any of them alive long enough to find out.

He gave a nod to Jessica. She released his arm. He heard the gravel crunch again as she drew back. Her voice murmured into her walkie talkie, letting the others know to stay back until her signal.

Sebastian was going to Influence the vampires again.

He stared into the darkness of the alley. The familiar tones of Jessica's murmuring voice faded to a dull buzz in his ears. He felt the mouth of the alley expand, as if he were falling toward it. Then he was past it, feeling the scrape of feet on uneven asphalt, the heavy cloying stench of garbage and decay in his nostrils. In *their* nostrils. Three of them. He could feel them now. Still some remembrance of the clan in them. They clung together, whispering Xavier's name, their clan head, even though he had burned in an inferno six months before. They were loyal, they remembered. They would build up again.

The drive was strongest in one male. The other two, a female and another male, responded to the drive, desperate to bow down to someone. That first male retained just enough intelligence to be dangerous, just enough to maybe pull together a small clan of his own.

And he sensed the In-Between out here.

That's why he wouldn't show himself at the mouth of the alley.

But Sebastian could feel his desperation. The night was growing shorter. They probably had enough coverage for the day in the alley but that only worked if no one knew they were there. But with the In-Between staking them out... They would have to make a move.

Come to me, Sebastian thought. He gave it an extra push of urgency.

He felt the stutter in the vampire's mind, almost like a skip in his thoughts. He edged closer to the alley mouth. The others followed faithfully because that was what they did. They followed him, went where he pointed, killed when he commanded. Especially that one lovely young couple with the baby. The baby had the sweetest cry and even sweeter taste...

Sebastian jolted back. His arm hit the dumpster, upsetting his balance and he fell on his rump. Jessica darted forward.

"What is it?"

"A baby," he said. "They ate a baby."

"I'm sorry you had to hear that," she said.

"I can't connect back," he said. "They're close to the mouth of the alley. There's three of them."

Her hand squeezed his arm. "Okay. You wait here."

She turned away, muttering orders into the walkie talkie. Hanson and three others began to move. Jessica pulled out a machete and went after them.

Sebastian climbed to his feet, holding onto the dumpster. His head throbbed. He wished it was as simple as hearing the vampires and not what it was actually like; feeling them, almost being them. He had to get close into their heads like that before he could Influence them. Now he'd pulled out because he was squeamish about babies, leaving Hanson, Jessica and the others to go in without him.

Brilliant move, Sebastian.

A yell sounded from the alley. One of Hanson's men. Dammit! He looked around for a weapon but of course Jessica hadn't left him one. She didn't want him in on the fighting, not when he was their secret weapon.

Not so secret and pretty damned useless at the moment.

Okay, focus. Let the memories of their horrors wash by him. They didn't matter. Taking control did. He had to fight his own way and dammit, he was going to do it.

He stared at the alley and again felt the strange sensation of rushing toward it. Now he felt power and adrenaline coursing through him. The hunger to fight, to kill, to drink. Desire filled him, almost overpowering all other thoughts. He could get lost in it if he wasn't careful. Detach just a little, pull back... Now he could concentrate on the three of them. The female and two males. He focused on the lead male first, the one with the most coherent thoughts. The blood urge surged around Sebastian. He could feel his body tingle with it. Slow down, he thought. Time for rest. He let his own shoulders drop and felt an echo from the alley. The vampire slowed. His claws lowered from the attack. His head drooped.

Now Sebastian widened his focus, brought in the other two vampires. They were a bit more challenging because of their more animal natures, but in different ways, easier. He focused on them having fed, feeling bloated and lethargic. The memories of victims rushed through his mind. He tried not to pay attention but the images commanded it. Men, women, children. He tried to turn away, focus on the vampires, on making them tired. He could feel them weakening, feel their focus slip...

Then shock as one was decapitated. Sebastian slammed back into the dumpster. A shudder ran through his body. Yelling and screaming sounded around him but it seemed to come from a distance. Nothing to do with him. Pain shot through his head, pushing all sound farther into the background, muddying it into nothing. He felt hands on his shoulders. Someone in front of his face. But his vision felt doubled, here by the dumpster and in the alley. He was in both places. He was in neither place. Where was he? Who was he? Blood, pain whirled in his mind. Faces, so many faces...

He collapsed to the ground.

"You should have told me you were going to try again."

The anger in Jessica's voice cut through the haze of pain in his head. He blinked the blurriness from his eyes. She stood across the room beside the window, her arms crossed over her chest, her brown hair pulled back in a ponytail that trailed over her shoulder and halfway down her back. She still wore the same black outfit, now smudged with dirt. Her frown told him she was as much afraid for him as angry. When she noticed him looking, she turned away, staring through the sheer white curtains of the window.

He forced himself to sit up. His head objected, sending spikes of pain through his temples that radiated down his neck. He grunted a little and swung his legs over the bed. No one had bothered taking off his outfit, except for his shoes. His feet felt a bit numb. The single bed was too short for him. He was in the kid's room of the safe house, he realized. It was the one room they kept clear for any injuries, the hospital room as Joan called it. He wished they'd put in a longer bed or laid him on the floor.

He rotated his feet in circles, trying to get the circulation back into them.

"I couldn't just let you all go in there without helping," he said. "I'm supposed to be fighting too."

She spun to face him. "Fighting, yes. Getting sucked down in their deaths, no."

"I didn't get sucked down."

"I saw you," she said. "You were practically convulsing. If I hadn't realized what you were doing and come back, the others would have killed all of them and taken you down with them."

"That wouldn't happen."

"You don't know that. Nobody knows that. Nobody understands what the hell you *do*, they just want you to keep doing it no matter what it costs."

She stopped. He held out a hand to her. She crossed the room to take it and he drew her down to the bed beside him. As she sat, he put his arm around her shoulder and she leaned her head on him.

"You push too hard on this, Sebastian," she said.

"I just want it over with," he said. "The sooner the better. Then I can go home. Besides, this was the last one, right? Finish with your friend Hanson and then we can leave."

He felt her stiffen under his arm. Her head came off his shoulder but remained bowed.

He didn't like the sign of this.

"Jessica?"

"They want us to go to Rome," she said. "There's several nests operating out of there and they need help subduing them."

He was almost afraid to ask. "What did you tell them?"

She glanced at him. "What do you think I told them? I said you've done enough, you need to rest and you need to go home. I said we'd come back in a month and help out in Rome." Her head dipped again. "They said that wasn't good enough. They need you to go in three days."

He tightened his grip on her shoulder. He knew she'd tried her best but Nigel and the others had only one narrow focus. Finish off the vampires, and while Sebastian concurred with their efforts, he didn't agree with their attitude of doing it no matter the cost. Eight months he'd been focusing and Influencing vampires. He could feel himself on the edge and he didn't like it. He didn't like where it could lead him, he didn't like the exhaustion he felt almost all the time or the way he was getting used to constantly being in pain.

But he didn't much like the vampires either.

Dammit.

"What about five days?" he said. "We go to Rome for a week and that's it. Then we're done."

"It could take longer than a week," she said.

"Tell them I'll give them a week only, no more."

She looked back up at him. "Are you sure?"

"If they give me the extra two days rest, I'm sure."

She gave him a half smile. He knew she was as conflicted about it as he was; she wanted to stop the vampires too but she could see the cost to him up close.

"You get some rest," she said and kissed him.

He tightened his arm on her shoulder as he let the kiss deepen. Finally she broke away. Her tongue flicked out to lick his lips.

"You're supposed to rest," she said. Her fingers trailed along his cheek as she slipped out from between his arms. He watched her cross to the door. She opened it, looked back him and smiled before she slipped through, closing the door behind her.

He could imagine a couple of things he'd like to do with two days extra rest.

He smiled to himself as he tested his feet on the floor. There, the numbness was gone. He could stand without falling over, always a good thing. Across the room on the desk, he saw a laptop and a bottle of water. He crossed to get some water; his mouth felt a little gummy. He twisted off the cap and drank some down. Room temperature, not his favorite. He preferred water cold from the fridge but he'd take what he could get. When he set the bottle down, he bumped the laptop. The screen sprang to life.

Not turned off, just sleeping.

He knew a lot of the In-Between used special forums to share information. He didn't bother with that. Instead he searched for newspapers from home. It made him feel a little closer to it although it also made him homesick. He wasn't sure if it was such a good idea, torturing himself this way, but he needed something, a reminder that there was a normal world out there.

He found several online papers and skimmed through, revelling in high school and college sports scores, weather reports, traffic accidents, supermarket openings and political punditry. He usually avoided the crime reports but found himself scrolling through a list. One item caught his eye: Motel fire kills ten guests and owners. Strange. Not even any indication of survivors. Hadn't anyone made it out alive? He clicked on it and read the whole article.

Small motel off the highway. Fire department suspected arson. No survivors. He felt an itch in his brain, the kind that always started when something wasn't right. Who would burn down an old motel with everyone inside? It wasn't for the insurance; the owners had perished as well so they wouldn't be able to collect. Besides, deaths like this would always be investigated more closely than an empty building.

Unless whoever did it didn't care about that.

The itch crept down his neck, hitching his shoulders up toward his ears. He didn't like the look of this. Not at all.

He checked the other sites for more details. They mostly regurgitated the same story except for one detail; a man had been found in the last room on the floor between the bed and the wall. His location had prevented the body from being burned too badly. Initial reports discussed trauma to his neck and a lack of blood.

His fingers froze on the keyboard. He stared unblinking at the screen until his eyes teared from lack of lubricant. As the screensaver switched on, he pushed himself away from the laptop.

Trauma to the neck and lack of blood.

It had to be a vampire, one who went on a rampage through the motel and tried to use the fire to cover his tracks.

Or *her* tracks.

It would have to be a fairly recent turn, he thought. The thought behind covering its tracks indicated less time under the influence of a clan head. Such a vampire would be quite independent and harder to catch.

It didn't mean anything, he thought. It could be any young vampire, turned less than ten years ago. They'd found any turned within that time span still maintained most of their independence and intellect. The older vampires were too dependent on the clan head and reverted to an almost primitive animalness. But there were lots of vampires under ten years. It didn't mean anything.

It didn't mean it was *her*.

But he knew it was.

Alexa.

His heart twinged. An old pain, at least it felt old, with an ache that seemed to settle into his soul. Thinking of her tugged him back into his old life, only a few short years ago, when he was a different person. A geeky, awkward college student instead of what he was now. And what exactly was that? A geeky, awkward In-Between, suspended between vampire and human by an aborted attempt by the vampire Bianca to turn him. If she'd been successful in it, in starting her own little clan, would he now be wandering lost like the others? If Constantine had been successful in tracking down the book by the first vampire, would Sebastian have been enslaved along with the others? Instead, he'd felt the call of the book, a link to Grellock, the first vampire, and slowly realized he could use the book to kill Constantine, just as Constantine hoped to use it. Spilling the vampire's blood on the book destroyed the clan heads, and yet even after, he'd heard it calling in his mind before Jessica torched it, breaking the link between him and the book.

Good thing she'd done it. He might have started a whole new mess. Although he'd been left with this whole new ability.

And after that, Alexa made her vow: *I'll make sure you pay dearly.*

Had the massacre at the motel been the first down payment? Or maybe it was just a warm up to the main course. He checked the location again. West Pennsylvania, almost into Ohio. She was making her way west. Making her way to Michigan.

Making her way to his family.

Forget Rome. They would have to deal with it without him. He'd already spent way too much time here, trying to help them clean up the mess when he should have been taking care of his family. He suspected she'd try to go after them and yet he let it slide because the In-Between needed him.

But enough was enough.

Time to go home.

He ran a quick search for flights heading back to the States, then he wiped the browser history and all the temporary files before turning the laptop off. He grabbed his jean jacket, which hung on the end of the bed, and shrugged it on. Heading to the door, he started thinking about money. He was going to need some to buy a plane ticket. He patted his pocket. He had maybe five pounds on him and his passport. He might not be able to buy a ticket but he could board the plane at least.

Time to get some money.

He opened the door and peered out into the hallway. Silence filled the upstairs of the safe house. Voices floated up from downstairs. He tried to but couldn't distinguish Jessica's voice from the general murmuring.

Either she was down there and not talking or she wasn't. If not, he had to find her. He couldn't leave without at least telling her.

With careful steps, he made it to the stairs without any creaking. He grabbed the handrail and headed down. He placed his feet gently onto each step before moving to the next. The voices grew louder in volume as he reached the bottom. Now he could distinguish them: Nigel, Hanson, a woman whose name he never remembered, and Joan.

Still no Jessica.

Damn, where was she? He didn't want to try to send out a psychic feeler for her, not with so many In-Between around. At least one of them would catch it; he knew Joan would for sure. She probably sensed him now anyway. She was the most sensitive In-Between he'd ever met.

"...need to hit hard and fast." Nigel's voice drifted out from the back toward the kitchen.

"My people are still trying to get accurate numbers," the unknown woman said.

"We send in a large enough group, they can handle it," Nigel said.

Typical of Nigel, Sebastian thought. Impatient and willing to risk people's lives. The only good thing was that at least he went in as well.

He turned away from the kitchen and took the narrow cream colored hallway toward the front of the house. At the doorway to the living room, he paused, peering around the corner. Empty. Just an overstuffed floral couch in pinks and yellows with a matching armchair. He shuddered. Now *that* was horrifying.

He made it all the way to front door before he heard the creak of the floorboard behind him.

"Going somewhere?" Joan's voice spoke quietly behind him.

He turned. She stood near the door to the living room, a tall, thin figure in grey pants and a plain green shirt who looked like she would be quite at home serving tea on that couch. Her grey hair had grown to brush the tops of her shoulders but he felt that same intensity in her hazel eyes.

"I was looking for Jessica," he said.

"She's running an errand," Joan said. "She should be back soon. Why don't you come into the kitchen? I'll make you some tea."

Dammit, he thought. He couldn't refuse her without some good excuse but he didn't want to go into the kitchen around the others. Even when Jessica returned he wouldn't be able to talk to her freely with them around.

Joan gave him a slight smile as if she knew the turmoil she'd caused. She stepped aside, gesturing back to the kitchen.

Dammit.

As he passed her, she squeezed his shoulder. Then she followed close behind.

He entered the kitchen. Hanson stood leaning against the counter, holding a teacup that looked dwarfed in his large hand. Nigel sat at the table. As usual, he stiffened at Sebastian's appearance. Even after he helped destroy the book, Nigel still didn't trust him. Opposite Hanson, a petite blond woman stood with arms crossed. She gave him a brief smile when he entered. He'd seen her before but he still couldn't remember her name. They all wore the same black pants and top from their raid the night before.

"How are you feeling, Sebastian?" Hanson said.

"Fine," Sebastian said. "I'm fine now. Just need a rest, is all."

"And some tea." Joan slipped past him, heading for the cupboard. She pulled out a cup and saucer and brought them back to the table. "Sit, sit."

He ended up across from Nigel, who didn't look any happier about it than he felt. Joan poured tea into the cup and then set a white porcelain bowl of sugar in front of him.

"I think we have honey if you prefer," she said.

"No, this is fine, thanks," he said. He didn't want to feel any more obligated than he already felt. As she returned the teapot to the cozy on the counter, he dropped in two teaspoons of sugar into his tea and stirred. At least that gave him something to do.

Across from him, Nigel stared into his own teacup, as if looking for inspiration. Silence stretched through the room as Sebastian lifted his cup to his lips. Obviously his presence had interrupted whatever discussion they were having. Why had Joan brought him back here? Had she wanted to stop the conversation? Mission accomplished, if that was the case.

"Why don't we ask Sebastian his opinion?" Joan piped up.

Nigel scowled openly into his teacup. Leaning against the counter, Hanson brought his cup to his mouth and sipped, efficiently avoiding the suggestion. But the woman looked interested.

"I think that's a good idea," she said. "I'd like more opinions."

"You mean you want an opinion that agrees with yours," Nigel said.

The woman frowned at him. "I think we need to think outside the box is all. Rushing in isn't the only answer."

"Oh and letting it fester is?"

"Let's hear what Sebastian has to say." Joan's voice cut through the comments that sounded like a rehash of an argument that had started before he walked in. Sebastian tried to give Joan a look that said 'don't put me in the middle,' but she wasn't looking at him. She gazed over at Hanson.

"What do you think, Joe?"

Hanson shrugged. "Don't matter to me."

A grin started to form on Nigel's face.

"Could use with more thoughts though."

The grin froze.

"Might as well tell 'em," Hanson finished.

Nigel's scowl reappeared.

"We got some intelligence that suggests a vampire group a short distance from here, about ten miles away, headquartering in an abandoned farmhouse," Joan said. "The thing is, it is behaving almost like a clan. We think one of the younger vampires has taken control and inserted himself into a leader position. We didn't think that was possible without the influence of the book. It's bad news if the younger vampires retain enough intelligence to reform into clans."

"We could see a rash of attacks," the other woman said. Shelly, he remembered her name now.

"They could start trolling for new members to fill their ranks."

"Which is why we need to stop them now," Nigel said.

"We need more intelligence about this," Shelly said. "We need to know if they're in contact with any other potential clan or if this is a one-off. Blundering in there in full force isn't going to achieve anything and we could lose the opportunity to find out what's going on."

Shelly nodded toward Sebastian. "What do you think?"

Nigel glared at him from above his teacup. Both Joan and Shelly held looks of expectation as if they were prepared for him to come down on their side. Hanson looked suitably neutral.

Sebastian fiddled with his teacup, playing for time. It was floral, like the couch, similar pink flowers blossoming over the sides. Why couldn't he have had just a plain white cup?

So which course of action did he approve of? Attack now or wait to gather more intelligence? Both stances had legitimate reasons and potential drawbacks. It all depended on the ultimate goal. Study the vampires or kill them?

He knew which he preferred.

"I think we should attack them outright," he said.

Shelly's eyes widened in surprise. Nigel's scowl curved into a grin.

"There's another vote for my plan," he said.

"How can you say that?" Shelly said.

"You make an interesting point," Sebastian said. "If I wanted to study them, I'd agree with you. But I don't. I just want them gone. All of them. I want to stop them from turning anyone else into vampires, or even into us. I want to stop them from murdering innocent bystanders just to send a message or for fun. I don't want there to be any chance of another person being cursed and destroyed this way. They have to die."

"But if we learn more about them, we'll have a better chance at stopping them for good."

"Why not stop them now?" he said.

Nigel sat back nodding in agreement. Even Hanson, leaning against the counter, gave a slight nod. Shelly frowned.

Nigel drained his teacup and set it on the table. He pushed his chair back and stood up.

"That's it then. It's settled. We head over there this afternoon to take care of the nest." He pointed a finger at Sebastian. "And you're coming with us."

CHAPTER 2

Sebastian straightened in his chair. "What?"

Nigel stepped around the table, heading for the front of the house. He patted Hanson's arm as he passed. "We'll head out in an hour, two at the most. Pass the word."

"Wait," Sebastian said but Nigel had already moved into the hallway. Hanson finished his tea and set the cup on the counter.

"I've got calls to make," he said and followed Nigel.

"I'd better tell my people," Shelly said. She left by the back door.

Joan picked up the teapot and carried it back to the table. She sat in the chair Nigel had vacated.

"Unintended consequences," she said. "We never know what they'll be. More tea?"

Sebastian pushed his cup away. "No thanks."

He fled back up the stairs to his room. He shut the door and leaned on it. What the hell had he done? He'd just given his opinion, said they should take out a nest and now they seemed to expect him to go along, like he was some expert. He could see it in the way they looked at him, at the way they deferred to him.

As if he knew what he was doing.

When the hell had that happened?

He had to get out of here. He had to get home but they'd never let him go now, at least not until after clearing out the nest. Then there would be the debrief, reviewing the fight, seeing if there was anything new they could learn about the vampires to take forward into the next fight. That always took at least a day or more to finish the full reconstruction of the battle. They'd make him stay for that. By then it would be time to head to Rome and they'd drag him off there.

He was never getting out of here.

Don't panic. His heart was already starting to pound in his chest. The way things were going it could be another eight months before he managed to get free of the In-Between. He couldn't wait that long.

Certainly Alexa wouldn't.

He had to go now. No more waiting. He had to go while everyone was gathering their forces. He could slip out before they realized it. Only when they were ready to go would they notice he wasn't there. If he went now he might be able to get an hour's head start.

And what about Jessica?

He'd have to leave her behind. But... how could he?

She'd understand. Especially when she talked to the others. At least he hoped she'd understand, but that didn't make it any easier. Even thinking about it made his heart ache. But his family, his parents, his brother Callum... They had no idea what was coming their way, no idea of how defend themselves. If he didn't go now, they'd die.

I'm sorry, Jessica. I'm so sorry.

He tried to send the thought out to her, tried to feel her somewhere but there was nothing. The blankness of the In-Between. He'd only ever managed to catch any feel of her when they were in physical contact, like when they made love. Other than that... nothing.

And he didn't think she'd hear it either.

One last shot before he left.

He crossed the room to the laptop and turned it on. It seemed to take forever to boot up. Finally he got into email and sent her an abbreviated message: "J, To GR, M. Fw? Lv S." He paused a moment, wishing he felt safe enough to send it to her in a chat program but he didn't know if they had surveillance on this machine. He wasn't even all that confident about the email but he couldn't find his cell phone so texting was out. Another moment longer with no reply and he couldn't wait. He had to log off.

He listened to the computer tick down as it turned off. No sound came from the door. He would have to risk it. He didn't want to try to climb out the window facing the front of the house.

Creeping to the top of the landing, he listened downstairs. Nothing. Maybe he could risk going down. With careful steps, he moved down the stairs, testing each before placing his full weight down. When he reached the bottom, he heard a sound from the back. Someone in the kitchen where he'd been aiming to go. Dammit! They were heading this way. He couldn't head back up the stairs without being obvious. He pressed himself against the wall.

Pass by, he thought, pass me by.

He focused with all his might and *pushed* the suggestion at her.

Through the railing, he saw Joan step through the kitchen door and head toward him, toward the stairs. His heart pounded. Surely she could hear that as it thundered in his ears. But she didn't give him a glance as she passed the end of the stairs and continued toward the front door. As she opened the door and stepped through, he realized she hadn't even glanced his way. Not even when she looked back to close the door.

She'd passed him right by.

He stepped away from the wall, staring at the door. Had he done that? He'd never Influenced an In-Between like that, not so thoroughly anyway. Maybe she just hadn't been paying attention. But it was Joan. She was always paying attention or she was always sensing things, sensing people.

But not this time. Not him.

Well, he could stand around here thinking about it or he could get the hell out.

He got.

The kitchen was empty as he stepped into it. He crossed to the back door and opened it. The small backyard of sparse grass extended barely twenty feet before it hit a worn wooden fence. Faded brown paint flaked off the wooden slats. Several slats near the right of the backyard listed to one side. At just over waist high, he knew he could climb the fence. Unfortunately anyone looking would be able to see him over top it but it was a chance he'd have to take.

He almost stepped outside, then stopped himself. What would he do about money? He needed enough for airfare. There certainly wasn't enough cash lying around here. If he stayed, the In-Between would pay his airfare. Eventually. But that could be another eight months from now. No, he'd have to figure out another way and he'd have to do it away from here.

The door clicked closed behind him. He rubbed his sweating palms on his pants and glanced around at the other backyards on either side of this small house. A breeze ruffled his hair and carried the scent of grass and moist earth, remnants of an overnight rainfall.

No one was out around lunch time. A few hurried steps carried him to the back fence. He climbed over and rushed across the facing backyard, a clear expanse of fresh green grass. When he reached the back of the red brick house, he paused. Now what? Head around the front? He needed transportation to make a clean break.

He angled around the side of the house and saw a blue sedan car in the driveway. He peered through the driver's side window. An automatic. He still wasn't great about the whole driving on the left side of the road but he could manage in an automatic.

As long as he could get the keys.

Telling himself he didn't have any other choice, he walked to the front door and rang the bell. After a moment, he heard footsteps and the warm scent of a woman wearing lavender before the door opened. Rich brown curls curved around her slim face. She wore a pastel green dress with matching heels. Her head tilted at him.

"Yes?"

He focused on her, matching his breath to hers. Her eyes defocused. Her hand drooped on the door frame.

"Give me your car keys," he said.

"Yes." She turned and moved back into the darkened foyer, leaving the inside door open. After a moment she returned with a yellow keychain hanging from her hand. The car key dangled from the bottom. She opened the door and held the key out to him. He took it from her hand.

"You will go lie down for a nap for two hours," he said. "You won't remember this when you wake up."

"Up," she said. Her mouth stayed open. A touch of drool appeared at the corner. Then she closed the door. He heard her footsteps move away, shuffling.

Sorry, he thought, and hurried back to the car. He unlocked it and got in, settling into the beige fabric seat to find his knees almost pressed up to his chest. He adjusted the seat well back, giving his gangly form room. Then he inserted the key and turned on the engine.

Now he'd see how well he'd drive here. Left hand side, he thought.

He'd have to keep remembering that.

He drove off.

He only forgot the whole left hand side thing twice. Fortunately it was within the first five minutes and he was still in the subdivision with no other cars around. By the time he reached the main road, he had it.

Even with the overcast day, he felt the light stabbing into his eyes as he drove and he didn't have sunglasses. More than an hour of this and the headache would be so bad he wouldn't be able to see. He had to stop somewhere for a hat and sunglasses. He should have asked the woman at the house but he hadn't thought of it. He'd been in too much of a hurry to get away.

Now he was suffering for that haste.

There had to be a shop around here somewhere. He kept glancing at each side while trying to keep his eyes on the road. There, up ahead he noticed a neighborhood shop. There had to be something there.

He found a parking spot just past it and pulled in. Turning off the car, he climbed out, stuffing the keys in his pocket. He checked his other pockets. His small wallet contained a one euro. His back pocket held his passport.

One euro would have to do.

The bell about the glass door tinkled as he opened the door and stepped into the shop. Candy lined the area beside the cashier, who glanced up as he entered then returned to reading his magazine. Over his head two televisions played. One showed a football match with the sound off. The other displayed the store in black and white. Sebastian saw his ghost image and resisted the urge to wave at himself.

He turned away from the cashier and headed down the nearest aisle. As he found the reading glasses and then the cheap sunglasses, he heard the tinkle of the bell from the front of the store. Another customer. He ignored it and dug around the sunglasses.

Pink was not his color. Didn't they have something in regular black?

He crouched to check the bottom shelf. There, a pair of plain, ordinary black sunglasses. Just what he wanted. Now he just needed to find a hat. Anything with a brim.

And not pink.

He stood up, listening to his knees crack. He headed across the back of the store, glancing down the aisles. No hats here, not here either. It looked like they were probably up front near the cash. He would have preferred to have both items in his hands before trying to Influence the cashier but he'd have to wing it.

He turned down the aisle farthest from the window and headed toward the front. As he approached, he heard voices murmuring. Probably the other customer asking a question. For smokes perhaps.

He turned the corner.

A man in jeans and a black hoodie with the hood pulled up around his face, pointed a gun at the cashier. The cashier stood back from the counter, both hands raised, the magazine lying open in front of him.

Sebastian's foot landed on something that crunched, the sound like a gunshot in the silence.

The gunman started. He spun toward Sebastian. The gun swung around.

Sebastian's hand spasmed, clenching the sunglasses. He sucked in a breath. The muzzle of the gun raised upward, aiming at him. He saw it in sharp relief, standing out against everything around it. Waiting to spit death at him.

NO!

His mind lashed out. He felt it as a surge of fear, masquerading as rage, rise up in him. The force of it made him stagger back a step. But the force surged out of him and blasted at the gunman. He almost saw it strike the man, sending him flying back against the magazine rack. His limbs and head flapped like a doll's. He slid down the rack to land on the floor, arms akimbo, legs out in front of him. A rain of magazines landed on his lap and across his face but not soon enough for Sebastian to catch a glimpse of brown eyes open wide in shock and death.

Pain exploded in Sebastian's head, stabbing into his temples as if someone had taken a sharp knife and jammed it into both sides of his head. Over the roaring of his blood, he heard laughter in a voice he recognized. No, it couldn't be... It couldn't possibly be...

Grellock.

The first vampire.

Out, he had to get out.

He staggered forward, past the cashier who was leaning over, staring at the man lying on the floor. As Sebastian passed him, the cashier spoke, "Did you see that?"

Sebastian grunted and pushed the door open.

"Hey, the sunglasses!" the cashier yelled.

The overcast light poured into Sebastian's eyes like burning gold. He shoved the sunglasses onto his face and hurried away. He staggered and stumbled toward the car. He couldn't possibly drive in this state, he could barely see and his body moved like he was underwater.

He reached the car and clung to the door, holding himself upright. Any minute now the police would be here. If they approached him he didn't know what would happen. A minute ago he would have thought the only problem he'd have was trying to Influence several people at once. Now he wondered if he'd be able to not blow them off their feet.

He had to get out of here. Without the car.

He pushed away from it and began to stagger toward the corner. With every step, his body became more coordinated. The underwater feeling diminished. Unfortunately, the headache didn't go with it. But at least by the time he turned the corner he no longer looked like he was drunk.

A siren wailed in the distance, coming closer. He sensed the police car just before it passed him. He turned away, toward the window of a furniture shop as the car sped past. Now he wouldn't even be able to retrieve his car.

Great.

Maybe they'd find the gunman unconscious but still alive. Maybe the cashier would be too traumatized to describe Sebastian.

And maybe he'd wake up tomorrow cured of being an In-Between.

The man was dead. He knew it. He'd caught a glimpse of his eyes, blank and empty as a marble. He knew that look, had come to know it intimately.

He shuddered as he remembered the laughter in his mind.

He forced his feet to move. People passed him by as dark blurs. He didn't even know what direction he was heading in, he just moved. His head pounded in time to his footsteps.

Was he losing his mind? Was that what was happening? The book was destroyed, he remembered Jessica burning it, even remembered feeling Grellock's dismay. He remembered that book, remembered the feel of it, the leathery feel of the pages made from human flesh, the ink from human blood. It had contained all the evil Grellock could pour into it. But the link was broken when the book was destroyed, destroying as well the power of the clan heads. So he should be free of it now.

Shouldn't he?

Then how had he thrown that man against the wall, killing him? How had he heard Grellock's laughter in his mind?

Was a part of it still in him?

Maybe that was why he was able to Influence the vampires the way he could. Did using that power make it stronger? Did it make it more of an Influence over *Sebastian himself*?

He shuddered as he walked. He didn't want to follow those thoughts where they led. It was a dark, terrifying road. He'd rather stay on this one.

Which was... where?

He stopped and looked around. He'd been walking for who knew how long. The shops had changed. No longer small convenience stores filled with trinkets, he was now standing on a street with quirky clothing shops.

Early afternoon sun blazed down on him, making him feel itchy. The air choked with the scent of people all around him, flooded with their perfumes and colognes. He needed somewhere quiet and dark to think. He caught a glimpse of a spire close by.

Now how was that for irony.

He angled off the main road into side streets, keeping an eye on the spire. Within a few blocks he found it, a small church of yellow brick. Wide concrete steps led up to a set of double oak doors. He climbed them and tugged on the handle. The door swung wide and he stepped inside.

Darkness. Quiet. His shoulders drooped. He moved to the last pew and sat down. The last time he'd been in a church was almost a year ago, running from vampires, looking for Stan only to have Stan betray him.

"That's something I never thought he'd do."

Sebastian jumped at the sound of the voice. His hands grabbed the back of the pew in front of him. He turned.

Charlie sat at the other end of the row. He wore the same faded blue jeans and black t-shirt. His blond hair had the same fashionably tousled look. A smile creased his face as he looked at Sebastian.

"Hey dude, long time no see!"

Sebastian closed his eyes. He really was losing his mind.

"You're not losing your mind, Sebastian."

He opened his eyes again. Charlie leaned back in the pew, arms stretched out along the wood. He hooked one leg up on the pew in front of him.

"How did you know..." Sebastian said.

"That you were thinking that?" Charlie said. "Hey man, we were roommates for almost three years. I know all your little neurotic thoughts." His head cocked to the side. "But you look a little different. A little less neurotic." He nodded. "Looks good on ya."

"You're not here," Sebastian said. "You're just stress."

Charlie swung his leg off the pew. His foot thumped to the floor. "Don't start that," he said. "Don't start with the whole 'figment of my imagina-tion' bullshit. I'm a ghost, okay? And you can see me."

"Why?" The word burst from Sebastian before he could stop it.

Charlie's eyes narrowed as he studied his friend. "I'm not sure. You're different than you were. You were even different when you first got bit." He chuckled. "Hell, you were *different* before that."

"What do you mean different?" Sebastian said.

"Hey, do I look like an expert? I'm just Charlie. I don't know any more than I did. All I know is you can finally see. About fucking time too."

"Finally?"

"Yeah, finally. I've been trying to get your attention for ages but you've been too busy doing all that vampire hunting shit. Didn't know you were so good with the knife, bro. And Jessica..." Charlie wagged his eyebrows, a smirk crossing his face.

"You didn't..."

"Sure I did. You see any ghost babes around here? I'm living vicariously, dude. Well, okay, maybe not living."

Sebastian barked out a laugh. It sounded off and felt even stranger coming out of him, as if he hadn't laughed in ages. He hadn't, he realized, not really laughed. Not laughed the way he used to when he was... normal. The laughter doubled him up, aching in his belly. He wiped at the tears in his eyes and glanced back over at the end of the pew. Charlie still sat there, his usual half smile on his face, looking exactly as he always had before...

Sebastian's laughter trickled off. "You are dead," he said. "Do you know...?"

"How?" Charlie said. "Oh yeah. I sort of remember. The transition is such a shock it's hard to get it all straight but I remember Alexa making a dive for me, yeah. Poor Alexa, I really thought we'd gotten to her in time." He shook his head. "It's not like the movies. The good guys don't always rescue the damsel in distress."

"I'm sorry," Sebastian said. "I should have realized it. I should have stopped her."

"Yeah sure, because you knew what you were doing, right? You were on top of it and all. Come on, Sebastian. We were all caught off guard. Not your fault."

Sebastian's chest tightened. "I've missed you, man."

Charlie chuckled. "Don't know how long you'll be saying that. You're probably gonna get sick of me."

Sebastian shook his head. "I don't care if you are just a figment of my imagination and it does mean I'm losing my mind. It's still good to see you. Hasn't been the same."

"Hmm, college classes. Vampire hunting. Yeah, I guess those are different."

"Can I help you, young man?" A voice spoke from the center aisle. Sebastian turned. A priest stood with his hands folded in front of him. He looked right at Sebastian.

"Can I help you?" he repeated.

"Ah, no thanks, father," Sebastian said.

The priest pursed his lips and began to turn away.

"Just a minute," Sebastian said. The priest turned back, eyebrows raised.

"Yes?"

"Is there anyone else sitting on this pew?" Sebastian said. He glanced over at the end. Charlie grinned at him.

"Anyone else?" the priest said. "No. Should there be?"

Charlie chuckled. The priest made no sign of hearing him.

Sweat trickled down Sebastian's sides.

"No," he said. "No, there isn't. Thanks, father."

The priest nodded and turned away. He walked back up the aisle, glancing back over his shoulder once at Sebastian before continuing on his way.

"You might not want to hang around here," Charlie said. "He's gonna call someone about you."

"Really?" Sebastian said.

Charlie nodded. "Oh yeah, you look a little odd. I mean, you are sitting here talking to a ghost. It looks like you're talking to yourself."

"He can't see you," Sebastian said.

"Of course not, he's not close enough to the veil or whatever the hell it is. You're an In-Between and you touched that freaky book. Besides, you're just a plain fricking weirdo anyway. Of course you see me but you're gonna be seeing the inside of a rubber room pretty soon if we don't get out of here."

Sebastian risked another glance to the front of the church. The priest was heading across to a door on the right. He was definitely looking over at Sebastian.

Time to go.

"Okay, I'm outta here." Sebastian pushed the sunglasses up his nose and crawled out of the pew. After the calm and darkness, he felt stronger. His legs carried him with purpose toward the back door. He noticed Charlie walking beside him. The sense of déjà vu made him stagger. How many hallways and rooms had they crossed together in just this fashion? Charlie on the left, Sebastian on the right. All he needed to complete the picture was Alexa walking on his other side.

His chest tightened again, remembering the sorrow he'd pushed away into a tiny corner of himself. Would it ever go away? Maybe in ten years. Maybe in twenty.

Sebastian pushed through the door, wincing as the sun struck him in the face. He took a covert look at Charlie. Out in full sunlight he looked a little... faded. It was the only way Sebastian could think of it. His friend didn't cast any shadow either. Was he a ghost of a hallucination? Sebastian couldn't tell and didn't have any idea of how to figure it out.

"There is one thing I want," Charlie said. "I know you're hell-bent on getting home but I want to see Stan first. Before we leave. I want to look that crumb in the face and find out why he betrayed me."

"He didn't betray you," Sebastian said. A woman pushing a stroller glanced over at him. Her pace increased.

"Watch it, Sebastian, you'll get more people calling the cops on you."

"How..." Sebastian stopped. He held his lips tight together and tried to talk. "How do I 'alk 'o you?"

"Just think as if you're saying it in your head," Charlie said. "And no I can't read your mind. Don't look at me that way. You have to purposely direct your thoughts at me or I can't hear it. Wouldn't be much to hear anyway, given that wide, vacuous..."

Fuck off, Sebastian thought.

"That's it," Charlie said. "You got it." He grinned.

I have to go home. I don't have time to take you to Stan, Sebastian thought.

"Find the time or I'll be haunting your ass the entire time. I'll drive you nuts too. Well, more nuts."

I don't even know where he is.

"Find out. It takes us a couple of days tops, then we head back to whatever, Michigan."

Michigan first.

"Stan first. I mean it, Sebastian. You owe me this."

Even with his faded form, Sebastian could see the serious expression on Charlie's face. It wasn't the mock serious one he'd sometimes put on but the genuine one. He wanted to see Stan.

"Email your brother, tell him to look out for vampires," Charlie said. "And you might want to look out for cops."

He pointed over Sebastian's shoulder. Sebastian glanced over. A police car was pulling up beside the church.

Sebastian pushed the sunglasses up his nose and ducked down the street, moving fast among the pedestrians. Within a few moments, he was gone.

CHAPTER 3

"Why?" the voice on the other end of the phone line asked again.

Sebastian tried to contain his exasperation. "I was there when he was caught," he said. "I think I deserve to know where you're keeping the man."

"Hang on." The phone clicked and Sebastian found himself listening to the vacuum of dead air. He hunched farther underneath the slight overhang outside the bank. More clouds had rolled in, taking the edge off the sunshine but even the hazy light pounded in his brain, made all the more annoying by the smells of the people around him and the sight of Charlie, leaning on a lamp post in front of him. Occasionally someone would pass too close to him and Charlie would reach out, passing an insubstantial hand through the person's body. Whenever he did it, the scent of the person's blood became even more acute to Sebastian, even more alluring. He clenched his teeth.

Stop it!

Charlie pouted and stuck out his tongue.

Do you want me to find out about Stan or not?

Charlie crossed his arms. When a woman walked by carrying a shopping bag Charlie just watched her go.

The cell phone in Sebastian's hand clicked. He focused back on it.

"I got an address," the voice said. "You got a pen? I'm not repeating it."

"Go." Sebastian held the phone in the crook of his neck and wrote down the address on a piece of paper.

"Better hurry if you want to see him," the voice said. "They're finishing up with him soon."

Finishing up. Sebastian knew what that meant. They'd been grilling Stan for the past eight months, trying to find the holes to patch and any other weakness Stan might be able to tell them about the vampires. Once the In-Between finished with their interrogations, Stan would probably disappear forever.

Sebastian had to get to him before that.

He managed half the address when the man finished and hung up. The cell phone buzzed in his ear, vibrating against his shoulder as he hurried to scribble the rest down.

There, he thought he had it. He thought he recognized it. An old safe house on the outskirts of London. Maybe an hour away.

"Can we go?" Charlie said.

"It's not that simple."

A couple standing in front of a magazine shop turned to look at him. Sebastian held the cell phone up to his ear. At least that gave him a good excuse to talk to himself. Maybe he should get one of those earphones. Then he could talk out loud to Charlie and no one would think he was crazy.

Or no one would *know* that he was crazy.

No one but him anyway.

Charlie shook his head. "You're not crazy. I'm real."

"Sure," Sebastian said. He shoved the paper in his pocket. "I'm getting one of those ear things."

Charlie shrugged. "Fine. Then can we go?"

"Yes. Wait here."

Charlie's lips thinned in annoyance but Sebastian turned away. He'd had just about enough of this nonsense. The blinding sun, burning in his eyes, giving him a horrible headache, and now Charlie turning up as a ghost.

All he wanted to do was get home.

How could it be so hard?

He found a small phone store half a block away. Even with his head pounding, Sebastian found it relatively easy to Influence the young man behind the counter. He got the same defocused look in his brown eyes, the same slack-jawed expression on his scruffy bearded face. He looked to be around Sebastian's age, early twenties. Maybe working here to earn enough money for school.

Sebastian could almost see himself doing that, standing behind a waist-high glass counter, displaying an assortment of mobiles and their accessories. He picked out a Bluetooth ear piece and the young man slid it over the counter without speaking.

Easy peasy.

Even if his head hurt just a little bit more from it.

He took another two steps toward the door and hesitated. He still needed money for the plane. He hated having to do it…

He had the young man empty the register into a paper bag and then erase the security video.

He wanted to apologize as he left but any unnecessary words could break the Influence. He had to settle for a frown.

Back on the street, he shoved the ear piece into his left ear, hooking it over the top. It felt a bit crooked. He adjusted it. Fine. Good enough.

At least now he could talk out loud and not look like an idiot.

He headed down the sidewalk. Charlie appeared beside him. He looked more substantial in the gloom created by the sunglasses.

Sebastian's gut twisted only a little. If only he hadn't let Charlie come along that night…

"Took the money, huh?" Charlie said.

"I had to. I have to be able to pay for a ticket home."

Charlie shrugged. "If you say so."

"How else am I going to get the money?" Sebastian said.

"I'm not judging, man. But if you can get that guy to give you money, why can't you get them to give you a seat on the plane?"

"It would take too much energy," Sebastian said. "I'd have to keep focused the whole flight so they wouldn't notice and ask me. I'm not like you. I can't just appear over there."

"Who said I can appear over there?" Charlie said. "Here I am with you. What does that tell you?"

"That you're annoying?"

Charlie shook his head. His blond hair shimmered and settled into a fashionable tossled look. "I'm tethered to you."

"What do you mean?"

Charlie shrugged. "I don't know. I just can't go too far from you. Maybe cuz you were there when I died. I don't know. I don't have all the answers. But I do know I want to see Stan so can we go?"

Sebastian sighed. Was Charlie holding something back? Did he really not know how he'd ended up here? He studied his dead friend. It sure looked like Charlie, everything was Charlie-shaped, every gesture, every cadence, every hrmph was all Charlie. Did he really not know anything? And why the insistence on seeing Stan? What would that accomplish?

Too many questions and no answers. Maybe if he took Charlie to see Stan something would come of it. Maybe he'd learn something.

He pushed the sunglasses up his nose.

"Let's find a car."

The safe house was a plain, yellow-brick, two story house. The hour long drive took Sebastian almost two hours as he tried to focus on staying on the left hand side, deal with his pounding headache, and ignore Charlie who kept flitting from the front seat to the back and then to the front again. Finally he had to threaten to pull over before Charlie would stop doing it.

Then Charlie settled into the front seat, arms crossed over his chest, pouting.

The sun glinted on the facing windows as Sebastian stepped out of the small Saab he'd stolen. Heavy curtains covered the windows, blocking any inside view. As he moved up the narrow cobblestone walkway, he couldn't hear anything from within and there was no scent.

None of the In-Between had any scent for him. A disadvantage since he couldn't tell how many there were inside.

But they couldn't smell him either.

Would they be able to see Charlie?

He glanced over at his friend. Charlie stood to the right of the wood door, in shadow. The deeper darkness from his sunglasses and the shade made Charlie look almost solid. For a moment, Sebastian could almost imagine him still alive.

If only…

Sebastian knocked on the door, using an In-Between code.

Then he waited.

A few minutes later, he heard the whisper of shoes on tile. The thin beat of a heart sounded from the other side of the door. But the door remained closed. He could almost picture someone standing on the other side, listening to him breathe, listening to his heart beat as he listened to theirs.

Stalemate.

He lifted his hand to knock again.

The door flew open.

A gun jabbed him in the nose.

Behind it, a woman with short red hair, wearing black pants and a khaki short sleeved top, scowled at him.

"Whadya you want, mate?"

No smell, just the hostility coming off her in waves, buffeting him.

"I need to see Stan," Sebastian said. "You've got him here, I understand."

"Don't know who you've been chattin' with, mate, but we got no one by that name 'ere," she said. "Best you be running along before I gets reason to use this."

She wagged the gun in his face.

Sebastian huffed out an annoyed breath. "I'm an In-Between like you," he said. "I helped catch Stan and I know he's here." He took a deep breath in. "I can smell him."

Her green eyes narrowed behind the barrel. "What's your name?"

"Sebastian."

Her mouth twitched. A flicker of recognition? He'd never met her before. How could she recognize him?

"You're the one who feels 'em, ain't ya?" she said. "You can Influence the vampires."

He could hear the capitalization of the word "Influence," the way her voice emphasized it. Her head cocked to the side.

"I'm not sure what I do," he said. "But that's me."

"Thought so." She lowered the gun and stepped back from the door. "Heard you destroyed that book. Killed a clan head." She gave him a nod. "Good job."

"Thanks," he said.

"You gonna stand on the step all day or are you comin' in, mate?"

"Oh right."

He stepped inside the foyer. She shut the door behind him. The lock engaged with a click. Would Charlie be able to follow? Oh what was he worried about, Charlie was a ghost.

Or the loose screw rolling around in his head.

"I'm Cath," the woman said. "Been In-Between for four years. Stationed here for two." In the shadows, he saw the frown turn her lips down. "Hoping to get stationed over in Europe soon. They keep promisin'."

Yeah, promises. He'd heard his share of those too.

In the darkness, they passed several small rooms. He took quick glances inside, caught glimpses of a beige couch here, a dining table with four wooden chairs there. Before they reached the kitchen at the back, she opened a door to stairs leading down.

She didn't bother with the light, just started down.

Sebastian followed.

The darkness deepened to pitch black as they descended. With each eye blink, he deepened his focus, called up his In-Between vision. Now he could make out the pale green carpeting on the wooden stairs. See the wooden railing affixed to the plaster wall on his right. They reached a landing and the stairs turned to the right, leading down. Another few steps, another landing. Odd, the plaster in front of him looked different. Then the stairs twisted down again.

And down.

This was no ordinary basement. Somehow they must have dug deeper. He could almost imagine them doing it over time, carrying out sacks or buckets of dirt as they dug, hauling tools and lumber up and down the stairs as they worked. Did the In-Between have other places like this? Other locations they'd adapted for some "use"?

There was so much he didn't know about them even though he was one of them.

More stairs down.

He lost count of the landings but it felt like they'd gone down about four floors worth. Finally, ahead of him, Cath reached level ground. She pulled out a flashlight, or torch as she would call it he knew, and switched it on. After the total darkness, the weak beam of light seemed almost blinding.

Sebastian blinked as tears flooded his eyes.

"Come on," she said.

She led the way down a dirt tunnel. He could feel the unfinishedness of it. The earth felt hard beneath his feet. The walls were packed down but some bits of grit still came away to his questing fingers. The tunnel gave him a scant few inches above his head and if he stretched his arms, he'd hit either side.

Good thing he wasn't claustrophobic, although the thought of the amount of earth above his head did make his heart pound a little.

Settle down.

In front of him, Cath glanced back and he caught sight of the amused smile on her face.

Of course she could hear his heart beat faster.

Dammit.

The last part of the tunnel had been finished with stone. He could almost feel the coolness radiating from them. A large wooden door sat closed at the end. Cath stepped in front of it, hiding the lock from view. Sebastian heard a click and the door scraped against the floor as Cath tugged it open.

The area beyond had been scooped out to create a larger room. The ceiling still pressed low, a few inches above Sebastian's head. The floor was still hard packed dirt but grey stone encircled the walls, giving it at least a feeling of strength, that the walls would hold up all that dirt.

To the left, a single cot sat against the wall. Opposite, a small card table butted against the other wall with a single folding chair. Two battery powered lanterns created dim glows. One sat on the table and the other on the dirt floor beside the cot. A few books sat piled on the table, casting a monumental shadow against the back stone wall.

Sitting up from the cot, Stan blinked and rubbed his eyes as he focused on the door. Sebastian stepped into the room. He nodded at Cath.

"Can I have a few minutes alone?" he said.

She shrugged. "Five. I'll be back."

She swung the door closed. The click of the lock echoed in the tiny room then Sebastian listened to her footsteps as she walked away.

Locked in.

With who knew how many pounds of earth above his head?

Time for answers.

If he didn't start screaming himself.

CHAPTER 4

Sebastian turned away from the door to study Stan sitting up on the cot. He sat with his feet flat on the ground, knees rising up above the cot with his thin body folded forward. He'd always been thin when Sebastian saw him before but now he looked skeletal, sharp bones and edges sticking out from elbows, shoulders, and knees. Stringy brown hair hung over his high forehead. It looked thinner now. Sebastian could almost see through patches of the brown hair to the man's scalp. The same granny glasses perched on his thin nose but the lenses were smudged and dirty, as if he couldn't be bothered to clean them anymore. He wore a shapeless grey t-shirt that hung on his frame and jeans. A belt around his waist looked like it had been hitched to the last hole.

"Stan," Sebastian said.

"Yeah," Stan said. "I don't know anything more. I tol' 'em everything."

He pressed his hands together. They shook on his knees. He bowed his head. His glasses slipped a fraction down his nose. He didn't push them up.

Sebastian wanted to step back, wanted to bang on the door to call Cath back. But five minutes, he'd asked and been granted five minutes in this hell hole.

What the hell was he doing?

"Let me talk to him."

Charlie's voice sounded from behind him. Sebastian turned his head a bit.

Charlie leaned against the wood door. In the dim light, he almost looked solid.

How?

"Relax and let me talk."

Sebastian shook his head. Crazy, this was crazy. But hadn't his whole life been crazy for the past few years? All because he'd been too stupid to watch where he was going during a late night walk home from a party, leading him to blunder into a patch of woods and get attacked by a vampire.

Crazy had become the norm of his life.

His shoulders sagged.

Okay. Go ahead and talk.

He saw Charlie straighten from the door and take a step forward. Another step and Charlie was within an inch of him. From this distance, the illusion of solidity shattered. Sebastian could see the door through Charlie's face. Then the image blurred even more as Charlie closed that thin gap.

Coldness prickled Sebastian's skin. His nerves tingled. He tasted a sourness, a heaviness, as if he'd taken in a mouthful of dirt. He wanted to spit it out but his mouth wouldn't move. His body wouldn't move. A coldness stole over him but his teeth couldn't even chatter, not under his command. But then his body moved. He could feel his foot sliding along the dirt floor, turning him back toward Stan.

But Sebastian wasn't doing it.

How?

Charlie!

He could feel Charlie inside, a cold presence overlaying him. His mouth opened, and it was Charlie who spoke.

"How's it going, Stan?"

Even to his own ears, Sebastian's voice sounded different. Stan started, staring at him.

"What?" he said.

"I was just wondering how it's going? Thanks for coming to my funeral, by the way. Nice of you. Even wore a suit but you couldn't bother with a tie?" Charlie shook Sebastian's head.

Stan leaned away from him. His hands gripped the edges of the cot. His shoulders hunched. A sour sweat smell wafted from him.

"Whadda you mean? Your funeral? What are you talking about?"

Sebastian felt his lips curl into a smile but it wasn't his smile. He knew what this one looked like, the lopsided, dopey grin.

Too bad he didn't have the shaggy blond hair to go with it.

"You know what I'm talking about, man, and you know *who* you're talking to."

Stan yanked his feet up onto the cot and scurried away until his back hit the stone wall behind him. He wrapped his arms around his legs. His entire body trembled.

Sebastian took a step forward.

"See? I knew you knew it was me, Stan."

Stan's head shook from side to side. "No, no, it can't be. Dead, you're dead!"

"Doesn't mean I can't drop in to say howdy once in a while. Howdy, Stan!"

Sebastian's hand lifted and waved in a crazed blur.

Stan yelped and buried his face down in his knees, lifting his arms to shield himself.

"Ah, don't be like that. Be sociable." Sebastian's hand reached out and grabbed Stan's hair. He yanked the man's head up.

"I want to talk to you, Stan."

"No, no!" Stan's wail echoed off the stone wall.

"I want you to explain to me why you betrayed me, Stan, why you betrayed my friends."

"I... I..." Stan shook his head. Tears leaked from his eyes. Drool frothed from his lips and sprayed in the air with every shake of his head.

"Explain to me, Stan!"

You're not getting anywhere. You're just scaring the shit out of him.

Inside, Sebastian felt Charlie's coldness deepen.

Serves him right.

Did it? Before he'd come down to this hole Sebastian would have been inclined to agree, especially since Stan had given the book to Constantine, but now seeing the state of the man... At what point did the means become even too horrible to justify the ends?

Stop being a pussy, Sebastian. You know what he did.

Yes, he knew what Stan had done. But did it justify tormenting him?

He's hiding something. I can tell. I can get it from him.

Beneath the sourness of Stan's sweat and the sickliness of his blood, Sebastian could smell how it all twisted and mixed into that stench of fear that he knew so well. And just at the edges, he recognized that odor of lying.

Stan was hiding something.

But was Charlie really the best one to find it out?

He was dead after all. Sebastian could feel how he'd lost the capacity to deal with any kind of subtly with the living.

Charlie'd become a hammer and was going to pound on everything.

He could pound Stan into dust before Stan could tell them anything.

Back off, Charlie. Let me do it.

No! He betrayed me!

You were already DEAD! He couldn't betray you anymore. Now back OFF!

He pushed at the coldness inside. It shuddered, trying to hold fast but then began to crumble. The edges twisted and frayed. It trembled then shattered. He felt it wash through him. A moment later it was gone.

He could feel his body again.

His fingers wiggled at his command.

He was alone with himself.

He saw Charlie standing at the edge of the cot. His face twisted with a frown, his jaw clenched. He glared at Sebastian. Sebastian felt the coldness of his anger steal across the air.

Let me do it my way.

Charlie's lips thinned.

Sebastian stepped forward and reached out for Stan. His hand settled on the man's shoulder. He felt the bones right through the thin fabric of his t-shirt, as if the t-shirt were the only skin he wore.

"Explain to me, Stan."

Stan flinched and looked up.

"It's you, not him."

"It's me now, Stan. But Charlie's still here and he wants to know. So do I."

Stan shook his head. "There's nothing else. Nothing else."

"Tell me, Stan. Just tell me."

Stan shook his head again.

Sebastian focused, preparing to Influence him, but the feeling shifted even as he pressed. His hand felt like it began to melt into Stan's shoulder, pressing through the fabric into his bones, his own skin shifting and changing. The dim lighting in the room darkened. Were the lanterns running out? He blinked, tried to look around.

The room was different.

Stone walls gone. Hard wood beneath his feet. Across the expanse of a twenty-foot-long dining room, he saw a bank of windows. Heavy burgundy curtains hung from the ceiling, dropping to within an inch of the polished, dark wood floor. Rich, cream wall paper covered the walls, almost glowing in the dim lighting from several candelabras set along a long oak dining table. Twelve carved chairs were set around the table, as if ready for a meal that would never come.

In the dim lighting, Sebastian could see the dust coating the table. He lifted a hand

(not his hand)

and touched the curtains. Grit and dirt coated the curtains. He saw smeared glass behind them before he let the curtains go. It fell back into place, a single puff of dust rising into the air and making his nose

(Stan's nose)

itch.

At the end of the room, a large, oak door creaked open. It scraped across the bottom of the floor then stopped three quarters of the way open.

Constantine stepped into the room.

Behind him, walked Alexa.

Sebastian felt his own heart start to pound. It felt like a distant thing, an echo somewhere. The image before him wavered. Constantine's form in black pants and a dark maroon shirt blurred.

He was losing the image!

Relax, he had to relax. He wasn't really here. It wasn't really him and this wasn't really happening. He wasn't quite sure what was happening but he had a suspicion.

Stan.

He'd been holding Stan's shoulder.

And now he was here.

No. Now *Stan* was here.

As he relaxed, the image before him solidified. Constantine stepped toward the table and pulled out the head chair. With some smooth move, he reclined into it, stretching his long legs in front of him. His hands folded on his chest. He looked down his long nose at Sebastian. An amused grin curled his lips.

Alexa leaned against the back of the chair, her hip almost brushing Constantine's shoulder. One arm draped over the curved back of the chair. Her hand almost touched Constantine's hair. She wiggled her fingers as if to play with his hair. Her head tilted the way Sebastian remembered whenever she'd been thinking about a difficult problem at school. Sometimes her tongue would poke out from between her lips. Her hair still had the same winsome pixie cut, tapered in gentle wisps around her face. Her glasses perched on her nose.

But Sebastian knew she didn't need them.

Vampires didn't need glasses.

"I understand you wish to negotiate," Constantine said. His voice boomed through the room.

"Yeah," Stan's voice said. "That's right."

"You have what we want," Constantine said.

"Sure I do," Stan's voice said.

The smile on Constantine's face grew. "What is to stop us from taking it from you?"

"It's not here. I don't have it on me."

Constantine laughed. "So what do you want, human?"

Sebastian turned toward the table and moved to a chair just down from Constantine. He pulled it out and sat down. The feel of Stan's body in the chair felt odd. Thinner, ganglier, elbows resting at a different spot from where Sebastian's would have been, feet stretching out at a different angle.

Weird.

But being inside someone else's memory was the essence of weird.

"I want to be like you," Stan said.

The smile faded from Constantine's face. He sat up, leaning forward. Even in the memory, Sebastian felt the power of that personality, the energy he pulsated at Stan. Even Stan, being only human and not as sensitive as an In-Between, seemed to feel it. He trembled in his chair.

"You want to be vampire," Constantine said. "Why?"

"I don't want to die."

The words blurted out of Stan.

Constantine tilted his head. Shadows carved across his face, accentuating the beard around his mouth. His black hair fell across his forehead but didn't impede the blackness of his eyes.

"Would I have to kill?" Stan said.

Constantine's lips curled upward. "Not necessarily. A vampire can survive on a pint of blood per night."

Sebastian felt Stan's body sag in relief.

"But you must give me a good reason to turn you," Constantine continued. "Tell me why you should join me. Where you will fit in my plan."

"Plan?"

Constantine leaned back in his chair, again folding his hands on his chest. "You think I want this book for decoration? Of course I have a plan for its use."

"What... what plan?"

Beside Constantine's chair, Alexa stirred. Her fingers tightened around the top end of the chair. Her hip moved away from Constantine's shoulder as she balanced on the balls of her feet. Her other hand curled into claws by her side. Her head lowered, mouth open, revealing the tips of her fangs. She looked ready to pounce.

Constantine held up a hand.

She settled back. Her hand uncurled. Her mouth closed.

But she still poised, ready.

"My plan," Constantine said. He glanced up at the ceiling. "I will select who I will turn, those who will be useful in the new world. Others I will enslave, tie to us. They will be bound to the clan, useful for any work in the daylight or for food."

"Not In-Between," Alexa said.

"No, of course not, not In-Between, but marked. With the power from the book, I can change how we take them. Make them compliant."

His gaze moved back from the ceiling, back to Stan.

"Tell me why I should not make you one of those."

Sebastian felt Stan's heartbeat speed up. Sweat trickled down his sides. His hands gripped the wooden arms of the chair. The wood felt slick under his palms.

"I can be useful," Stan said. "I'm a computer wiz. I can hack into anything, help with anything. You'll need a way to keep track of everything. I can help you do that."

"You really think I have need of your gadgets?" Constantine said.

Stan's mouth tasted dry and sour. He nodded in fast, jerking motions.

Constantine nodded. "Maybe I will. Yes, maybe I will. Never let it be said I don't keep up with the times. Right, my dear?"

He lifted his hand toward Alexa beside him. She smiled and slipped her fingers into his palm. His hand tightened around them and yanked her hand down to him. A gesture of control and dominance. Her body jerked forward. She stumbled, bumping her hip against the arm of the chair. Her knees wavered but she stayed upright.

"Yes, Constantine," she said.

He smiled, nodded and brought her wrist to his lips. His tongue licked the inside of it, then his lips fastened on. They curled back and Sebastian caught a glimpse of fang just before they sank into the flesh of Alexa's wrist.

He jerked away.

Grey stone walls. Dim lighting. He felt Stan's bony shoulder under his hand. He yanked his hand away, stepped back. His feet caught under each other, making him stumble. His arms pinwheeled, trying to stop his momentum, but he felt himself falling.

He landed on his rump. Pain flashed up his tailbone as he hit the hard dirt floor. He gasped at the force of it.

Stan stared at him.

"They had a plan," Sebastian said, "to turn people and enslave others as food. They were going to use the book to do it. To take over the whole world."

Stan's mouth dropped open. The muscles on his face slackened.

"How did you? How did you know that?"

"You just told me," Sebastian said. "You just remembered it."

Stan recoiled, pressing back against the stone wall. "How? You can't do that. How did you?"

He shook his head, pressing his hands to his mouth. Sebastian got up from the floor. His butt ached as he moved. His legs trembled a little. Good job. He managed to injure himself without any help from someone attacking him.

He took a step toward Stan but the man stiffened. A keening wail sounded from behind his hands. He pressed harder against the stone wall as if trying to melt into it. Sweat dripped down his forehead, dampening his stringy hair. His eyes widened until Sebastian could see the whites.

He wouldn't get anything else out of Stan now.

He moved to the heavy wood door and knocked. A few moments later he heard the click and it scraped against the dirt as Cath pulled it open.

"You've still got another minute," she said.

Sebastian shook his head. He looked back at Stan. The man was now rocking forward and back, still shaking his head.

"That's enough," Sebastian said. "I've used up enough time."

He stepped out of the cell and waited for Cath to slam the door shut behind him.

CHAPTER 5

"Is it just me or did old Stan not look his best?"

Charlie walked along beside him, once again looking solid in the fading sunlight. Finally sundown and with the setting sun, Sebastian knew he'd get relief from the pounding headache he'd felt since leaving the safe house. It wasn't his usual sun-induced headache, this was quite different, starting from the base of his skull and spreading around his head like a vice grip.

He was becoming quite the connoisseur of headaches.

Unfortunately.

"You didn't help matters," Sebastian said. He ducked his head so no one would see his lips moving.

"Yeah, okay. I got carried away there," Charlie said. "He pissed me off, man. I went to him for help and look what he did with it. I just wanted some answers."

"You happy with them?"

"Well, good to know, right? Good to know what the vamps were planning. All that world domination stuff, right?"

"It won't happen now," Sebastian said. "The book is destroyed. They won't be able to pull it off. They don't have the power or the organization left."

"Maybe not the old ones," Charlie said. "What about the new ones? Didn't your In-Betweenies say they were smarter?"

Sebastian looked over at him. "In-Betweenies?"

Charlie's lopsided grin spread across his face. "Suits you. You look like an In-Betweenie. Sort of a really pale one, though."

"Thanks a lot."

A woman in a pale yellow dress walked by, giving Sebastian an odd look. Her steps hurried up as she passed.

"Way to go," Charlie said. "Freaking out the little people."

Shut up!

Charlie's laugh echoed in his head.

Money was still a big hurdle. He needed at least a grand in US dollars to afford the flight home. As the sun sank behind the buildings, Sebastian hurried into various shops, Influencing the cashiers to hand over most of their cash. Charlie followed, tut-tutting the entire way.

As if Sebastian didn't feel badly enough about this, but he had to get home.

"Why don't you just contact your parents?" Charlie said. "Ask them for the money to get home."

Sebastian shook his head as they stood in an alley behind a fish and chip shop. He tried to ignore Charlie but his friend's ghost kept interrupting, messing up his count.

Start again... Ten, twenty...

"Why can't you call them?"

"It's not that simple," Sebastian said. "Will you shut up for a second?"

He started counting.

Again.

He couldn't just call his parents out of the blue. He knew them. They wouldn't just send the money without good reason, without asking a million questions, all of them he couldn't answer. Or he couldn't give answers that would satisfy them. If he tried, they'd be waiting at the airport with a white jacket with very long sleeves and two burly men waiting to load him into the back of a padded van.

Then he'd never be able to save them.

No. He had to get there on his own, the quieter the better. Any communication could possibly tip off Alexa and if she thought he was nearby... Well, he knew what a vampire would do.

He had to get to them fast.

And quiet.

Two hundred and forty-three pounds, would probably convert to around five hundred dollars, more or less. Almost half way there. He stashed the notes in a waist pouch he'd procured three shops ago. It was coming in handy.

Maybe it wouldn't be too long now.

Charlie was still giving him the disapproving look.

"Just a few more places," Sebastian said. "I'm not taking more than I need."

"You know if you went to the track it would be more legitimate. You could influence the horses or something."

"You see a track around here?"

"Well, true."

"Come on, let's hurry up. I want to be on a plane by morning."

He turned to head back up the alley toward the street. His shoes splashed in puddles left in the uneven asphalt. A dim bulb from the back of the building did little to illuminate the alley. Heavy shadows deepened into almost inky blackness but Sebastian didn't need much light to see by. One blink and his eyes adjusted, bringing the entire alley into sharp relief. He had a fine view of the pitted asphalt, the ragged brick on the walls of either side, the dented, grimy blue dumpster pushed against the right side and angled just so, the crumpled pages of the most recent tabloid waving in the breeze...

And the vampire hunched over a homeless man ten feet from the front of the alley.

Fuck.

It hadn't spotted him yet. It was too intent on its meal. It looked like a male, jeans and a dirty grey t-shirt over an almost emaciated body. Sebastian could smell the sourness of it from three quarters of the way down the alley. Almost as strong as the iron stench of blood from the homeless man who made a soft whimpering sound.

Back away. That's all he had to do. Just back away. He didn't have any weapons on him at all, nothing silver. No blade to decapitate the vampire, no holy water or garlic to drive it back.

Nothing.

So back away.

Why the hell weren't his feet listening to him?

Beside him, Charlie shook his head, blond hair flopping on his shoulders. "Well, doesn't that suck." He drove an elbow into Sebastian's side and it felt pretty damned real.

"Get it? It sucks!" Charlie laughed.

You're a fucking idiot.

"Oh yeah? What are you gonna do about it?"

Sebastian turned a withering glare to Charlie, but the ghost was pointing down the alley, toward the homeless man.

"What are you gonna do about it, Sebastian? Are you really sorry about me? About Alexa? Then how can you back away from this?"

The joking was gone from Charlie's face, leaving a depth of maturity that he'd never quite had while alive.

And he never would have it.

I don't have any weapons.

"Sure you do. You just whine like a girl about it afterward."

Influencing, that's what Charlie was talking about. But he'd never done it without backup, without someone to take out the vampire. He couldn't just stop it cold.

Could he?

Charlie folded his arms across his chest. He jerked his chin in the direction of the homeless man.

"Better do something quick."

Dammit!

Sebastian turned to stare at the vampire, the emaciated look of him. Couldn't be feeding on a regular basis if it looked that bad. Yet it looked like a young one, not even a full decade. Sebastian had thought all vampires under ten were still pretty smart but maybe this one was just stupid to begin with. Being an idiot in life wouldn't exactly improve after death, or er, vampireness.

Or whatever.

He focused on that, on a feeling of fullness, being satiated. Not another drop more. He'd explode if he drank more. Feeling quite bloated now, uncomfortable. Yuck. He heard the whisper of fabric sliding along the brick as the vampire released the man, dropping him to the alley floor.

Sluggish, tired. Just find some place to sleep.

Nothing to see in the alley.

Nothing at all.

Empty.

Sebastian felt the vampire turn to face him, but its gaze swept right by. Not seeing.

There was nothing to see.

Nothing at all.

Find a place to sleep. Sleep through the night. Sleep through the day. Enjoy the full belly.

Best place would be right on top of that building right there. Just climb the red brick, hand over hand. Fingers finding holes to grab onto. Toes finding perches. Pull upward, move upward. Nice and safe on the roof. Lie down and look at the lovely stars. All bright and beautiful. Vampire eyes could see more wavelengths of light, admire it longer.

Watch all night long.

Watch all day long.

Lie down now. Just lie down. Back reclining on the rough, gravelly surface of the roof. No clouds tonight, nothing to obstruct a perfect view of the stars. Light breeze rustling a grey t-shirt. No unusual smells, nothing to cause alarm.

Lie still.

Don't move.

Watch all night.

Lie still.

Watch.

Stay still.

Watch all day.

Stay…

The scrape of asphalt on his knees and palms brought Sebastian back to himself.

He'd fallen forward, his hands automatically going out to stop his fall. The sting of pain in his palms was nothing compared to the burning in his head.

Pain erupted through his temples and laced across his head, trailing down his neck to his shoulders. His jaw ached as if he'd been clenching it for weeks. His eyes felt like they'd been shoved back into the sockets. He tasted iron in the back of his throat, felt something wet on his lips.

Oh god, he hadn't taken a drink from that man, had he?

He lifted his head, wincing with every moment. Twenty feet away, the homeless man lay collapsed against the brick wall. His heartbeat sounded ragged, his breathing short and rapid, but he was alive.

Not dead. And from what Sebastian could tell from here, not an In-Between either.

He still had too much blood left in him.

Sebastian could tell that too.

He could smell the hot sweetness of it.

So if not that man's blood in his mouth, then whose?

His hand shook just a little as he lifted it to his face. Something wet on his lips. Blood. From his nose.

His own blood.

Oh, this couldn't be good.

"Don't look too good to me." Charlie crouched beside him. His blond hair flopped over his forehead. "But you did it, man. A hellva good show. That vampire climbed right up the wall to the roof."

Charlie pointed behind Sebastian. Sebastian turned to look but of course there wasn't anything to see now. No evidence a vampire had climbed the wall. But he knew it had.

Knew he'd made it do it.

And it was lying on the roof right now. Watching the stars. Waiting for day.

Not moving.

And it wouldn't move. Not even when the sun burned it to a crisp.

"Pretty fucking impressive," Charlie said. "I'm impressed anyway."

"I'll be impressed if I can stand up without my head falling off." The words mumbled from Sebastian's mouth as if he couldn't quite get it working right. Oh great. Had he given himself some kind of stroke or something?

His legs felt a little wobbly as he stood up, but they held well enough. The burning pain settled down to a severe throbbing ache. He tried a few slow breaths. Okay, that seemed okay.

Maybe a step now.

Moving caused a burst of pain that shot across his forehead. He clamped his mouth shut, trying not to scream. It seemed to reverberate in his throat.

Before it completely subsided, he tried another step. The pain flash wasn't quite so bad this time. Just enough to inspire weeping. He blinked rapidly to clear his eyes.

One more step.

This time the pain just throbbed a little. Got to keep moving, just get to the plane. Maybe he could negotiate with it. Offer it as many drinks as necessary on the flight. Just don't overwhelm him here.

Not in this alley.

He had to get home.

Please…

Another two steps and he could almost move normally. He just couldn't move his head much. If he wanted to look right or left, he would have to move his entire body. No head turning allowed.

He made to stand beside the homeless man. Soiled jeans and several shirts layered on top of each other, each one dirtier than the next. The stench of grime and sweat almost overpowered the smell of his blood.

Almost.

Sebastian put out a hand to the wall. The brick felt familiar...

(From the climb up the wall.)

Just brick like any other. He had to keep focusing on right now, right here, not let himself get pulled back to the vampire.

He didn't want to climb that wall himself.

But he couldn't get too close to this man lying on the ground before him.

The smell of blood was so sweet, so tempting.

He tilted his head to get a better look at the man's face. His eyes were still closed. Breathing more steadily now, his heart beat settling down.

From what Sebastian could tell, he'd stopped bleeding. The coagulants in the vampire's saliva had done their thing, he assumed.

He wasn't getting a better look to be sure.

No way.

"What are you doing there?"

Oh shit, police!

He was in no shape to run, not even in any shape to do any Influencing.

Not that he had much choice.

He turned toward the mouth of the alley.

Three figures clad in black fanned out, moving in swift, smooth motions to space themselves around him.

Oh shit, *not* the police.

Worse.

"He's not vampire," said a woman's voice. She was the one who'd come farthest into the alley, blocking retreat.

"Can't smell 'em," the man left at the alley mouth said. "In-Between."

"He was being attacked," Sebastian said. "I sent the vampire away. I'm just leaving now."

He pushed away from the wall and took a shuffling step toward the front of the alley. The three paced him.

"I just want to go," he said.

"Sorry we can't let you," the woman said. She tilted her head. Her dark hair was pulled back from her face, tied in a pony tail at the back.

Like Jessica.

He wasn't going to think about her.

"Nigel asked us to keep a look out for you," the woman said. "Sebastian."

Oh shit.

They took him with minimal fuss, not that he could give them much trouble, not in the state he was in. They even made a show of giving the homeless man a quick check, just to ensure he was resting comfortably. The man would wake up with a hell of a hangover and feel weak for days but he'd survive, and stay human.

Lucky man.

Luckier than Sebastian had been.

The three In-Between led Sebastian to a dark blue van and bundled him into the back, slamming the door. He heard the solid click of a lock and found himself in darkness. A moment later, he heard the three pile into the front. The engine started and the van began to move.

It took several blinks before Sebastian was able to get his eyes to adjust to the darkness. Hmm, that was interesting. Whatever he'd done had really affected him.

Not a comforting thought.

A candy wrapper in the far corner was the only thing inside the van. Stubby benches lined each side. Sebastian's legs were so long his knees almost bumped the bench in front of him. The window facing the front had been blocked off. Black rubber mats covered the floor.

Homey.

Charlie sat on the bench across from him, just to the right, avoiding Sebastian's knees.

"You couldn't help me here?" Sebastian said.

Charlie shrugged. "Sorry, not much I can do. They can't see me."

"Can't you push them or something?"

"Who do you think I am? Casper the friendly ghost? I don't have any connection to them, I can't influence them or touch them. I'm a flipping ghost, Sebastian. What part of incorporeal do you not understand?"

"That's an awfully big word for you, Charlie."

"Fuck off."

"Who are you talking to back there?" One of the men's voice drifted back, sounding muffled by the blocked window.

"No one," Sebastian said.

Charlie stuck out his tongue.

Sebastian tried to keep track of the turns and time of the ride but the gentle back and forth motion of the van soothed him. Charlie kept talking, almost trying to keep him awake but pain and fatigue wore Sebastian down.

He'd just close his eyes for a minute...

The click of a lock and scrape of a door opening jolted him. Sebastian blinked. What? Where? He glanced around. His head ached but it had settled into a dull throb at his temples and at the back of his head. Manageable.

Dim light filtered in through the open door, revealing the interior of the van.

Right, now he remembered.

The woman with the pony tail stood at the door. She gestured him forward.

"Come on, love. Don't give us trouble."

He sighed. If only.

He gave a glance to Charlie, who sat on the bench. Charlie shrugged. No help there.

Sebastian climbed out of the van, wincing as his feet hit the ground, sending a jolt through his body and reverberating through his head. Had he ever not had a headache? He wasn't sure he could remember that time. Maybe he should just cut it off and forget the whole thing.

His feet scraped on gravel. They were parked in a large circular driveway in front of a sprawling grey-bricked house. Turrets on either side reminded him of Corbin Remington's home. Not an In-Between himself, he'd been a scholar who had still helped the In-Between, and died for his trouble.

He'd also been the one who'd given Sebastian direction on where to find the book and the means to decipher it.

At this point, Sebastian wasn't sure if that was good or bad.

Okay, it was good that the book was gone, destroyed, and with it, the destruction of most of the vampire society, but Sebastian didn't much like the lingering effects exposure to the book had on him. Was it because he was closer to vampire than the other In-Betweens? He didn't know, but he didn't much appreciate being that special.

"Come on," the woman said. She took his arm and tugged. The other two In-Between flanked them on either side. Now they were carrying guns, Sebastian saw, pointed at him.

Great.

He glanced back toward the van and saw Charlie climb out to follow. He shrugged and gave a big smile to the pony-tailed woman. She, not seeing him, didn't respond. Charlie stuck his lower lip out in a pout.

Great. The only help Sebastian had here was a pouting ghost.

Just great.

They led him through the great oak doors and hurried him down some stairs to a basement.

"Can I get some food?" he managed to say before they slammed a steel door in his face. Even with his hearing, he couldn't hear anything from the other side of that door.

Soundproofed.

So here he was. Funny how closely this room resembled the room Stan was being kept in. A single cot against the far wall. Plain grey blanket and flat pillow. Porta-pottie in the corner. A single, hard-backed chair in the other corner. But no desk.

Someone had slapped beige paint over the concrete walls, not caring if they slopped on the concrete floor. He smelled dust from the door installation and from the small, inch wide vents near the ceiling.

Someone had finished this room recently.

Was he the intended occupant? Or had it originally been designed for someone else?

No windows, just those concrete walls and the steel door. Seemed a bit of overkill for an In-Between.

Why did he think that someone maybe thought of trapping a vampire in here?

Why the hell would anyone want to contain a vampire? Why not kill it?

He didn't like where his thoughts were leading him. It wasn't his problem anymore. He had a big enough problem worrying about Alexa.

Dammit, he had to get out of here!

Charlie faded through the door and stood half inside the room.

"Nice accommodations, great view of absolutely nothing."

Either get in or out. Don't stand halfway in the door. It's disturbing.

"What?" Charlie said. He glanced down and behind himself. "Oh sorry. Didn't realize I hadn't come all the way in." He stepped farther inside. "Better?"

It would be better if you could help me get out of here.

"And we just got here," Charlie said.

Remember Alexa? She's going after my family. I have to go help them.

"Yeah, yeah, okay. I gotcha. Let me take a look around. See what's going on. Then we can make plans."

Do those plans involving getting that door open?

"Patience, grasshopper. Let ol' Charlie do his magic."

He smiled and faded away.

Just like that.

The room felt weirdly empty after Charlie left, as if Sebastian wasn't even there either. His head ached, sending pain across his shoulders. His stomach felt hollow and he realized he couldn't remember when he'd eaten last. He was supposed to eat on a regular basis. That was one way to stay human, or at least as close to human as he was now. Not eating not only weakened his body but increased the blood lust.

No wonder that homeless man had smelled so good.

He'd asked for food. Hopefully they'd bring him some.

How long before Charlie came back? Before the other In-Between decided to check on him? Could be minutes or hours or even days.

He lay down on the cot. The mattress felt lumpy against his lower back. The right side dipped a half inch. The blanket felt scratchy against his upper arms.

Sleep claimed him as he lamented how his legs hung over the end.

The click of the door lock woke him. He sat up, blinking sleep from his eyes. As he swung his legs over the side of the cot and put his feet on the ground, pins and needles erupted across his feet and spread up his shins. Dammit, his feet had gone numb from hanging over the edge of the cot.

Being tall just never worked well for him.

The door creaked open. The hall beyond was dark and the person standing in the doorway stayed in shadow. An In-Between. He couldn't smell the person and he was still too tired to force his eyes to adjust.

"Coming in or staying out?" he said.

"Maybe I should ask you something similar."

She stepped forward and slammed the door shut behind her.

Jessica.

Thank god!

He forced himself to stand. His feet still felt like rubber and the pain burned in them, a distant echo of the throbbing in his head. At least that had settled down somewhat.

He smiled at her, then let the smile fade as he noticed she didn't exactly looked pleased to see him.

"Jessica?"

"What the hell were you doing?" She stepped toward him and stabbed a finger into his chest. "I go out and you take off. Without a word, without anything? What the hell were you thinking?"

"I found an article about murders near my home town. A whole motel full of people killed. There was trauma to the neck."

Her arms crossed over her chest. "We know there are vampires in the US. That doesn't mean it was…"

"It was, I know it was."

"So you just take off without a word, without anything." Her voice was flat. Her face blank.

"I tried to find you." His voice sounded weak, even to him.

"Right. You asked Joan where I was. Then you just left."

His body sagged at the disappointment in her voice. It was his family. Didn't she understand?

"But you don't go the airport, no. You go to the safe house where they're keeping Stan for a little chat." Her lips twisted into humorless smile at his surprised expression. "Didn't think we heard about that?"

Of course, Cath would have sent word out after he left. Hell, maybe even before, when he was still down in the cell with Stan.

"I had to see him," Sebastian said.

"Why? It was more important to you to see him than to go home to your family? I thought that's why you ran out on me."

"Charlie," he said. How could he explain to her? Would she really listen? With her crossed arms and then closed look on her face, she'd never believe him now.

"Charlie's gone, Sebastian. He's been dead for years now."

"Gee, he's been dead for years so let's forget all about him. He won't care. Let's forget about anyone who isn't in your little clique." Charlie appeared behind her, arms crossed, leaning against the door.

"Shut up," Sebastian said.

"What?" Jessica said.

"Not you."

"Not me," she said. "Then who?" She turned to look around the room, her arms spreading to take it all in. "There's no one else here."

Against the door, Charlie grinned.

Great, just great.

She couldn't see him either.

Sebastian sank down to sit on the cot. He put his head in his hands.

"Don't you have anything else to say?" she said. "Aren't you even going to try to justify yourself?"

He couldn't smell her but he could hear the hurt in her voice. And he'd caused it. She'd never done anything but try to help him and support him the entire time he'd known her. And what had he done for her? Disappointed her.

He had to make it up to her. But he couldn't just yet. He had to get home first. He had to make sure his family were okay.

He had to stop Alexa.

He looked up.

Charlie still stood behind her but Sebastian ignored the ghost. He pushed himself up off the cot. His legs still felt unsteady and he teetered a little.

"I'm sorry, Jessica, I really am. I want to explain everything to you because you deserve to know it all but I don't have time right now. I have to get home. I have to save my parents and my brother. You understand that, don't you?"

Did he detected a softening around her eyes and mouth?

"It doesn't matter what I understand," she said. "You deserted right before a mission. Nigel and the others will have something to say about that." She shook her head and turned back toward the door.

As she stepped toward it, Charlie slid to the right, out of the way.

"What do you mean they'll have something to say about it?" Sebastian said.

"They have to maintain discipline," she said. She didn't turn around. Her voice sounded muffled as she talked to the door. "It's important for the group to survive as a whole."

Discipline? Group survival? This wasn't the Jessica he knew. She sounded like she was spouting nonsense.

"Jessica..."

"You have to have loyalty somewhere or you won't survive," she said. "You have to know who you can trust."

And she couldn't trust him.

He could feel the unspoken words hanging in the air between them.

She banged on the door. A moment later it swung open and she stepped out.

Leaving him.

The door banged shut.

"Well," Charlie said. "That's a bitch."

"Shut up!" Sebastian said. "Won't you just shut up?"

"Hey, I didn't mean her. I just meant... Sorry, Sebastian." Charlie spread his hands. "You're in this mess because I pushed you to see Stan. Sorry. But I couldn't just let it go, do you understand? We were right here. If I let you just go back, I might never had gotten another chance."

Sebastian dropped back down to the cot. He spread his legs out in front of him, moving his feet to get the circulation working.

Why couldn't you just stay yourself and see him? Why did you need me to go?

Charlie moved to sit on the end of the cot. His shoulders shrugged. "I don't know. I don't really know the rules for this ghost thing. If there are rules."

Great, just great. He had a ghost "tethered" to him, his family was under threat from a vicious vampire who just happened to be the woman he used to love (and maybe still did, a little anyway), and Jessica would probably never talk to him or trust him again.

This day couldn't get worse.

Then they came to fetch him to see Nigel.

CHAPTER 6

The door opened and two In-Between men stepped inside the room. Sebastian didn't recognize them. They spread out on either side of him, as if they expected him to cause trouble. Looking at the muscles on both of them, he figured even with his height, he probably weighed about half of one of them.

Some trouble he could cause.

"Nigel wants to see you," said the one on the right. He wore the regular outfit of the In-Between, black pants with a black t-shirt stretching over his chest. Light brown hair bristled up an inch from his head, making it look flatter than necessary.

The other guy gestured Sebastian forward. He wore the same pants but a charcoal grey long sleeved top. His hairstyle matched guy number one except his bristles were blond.

Blond Bristles and Brown Bristles. He probably wasn't going to get names from either of them.

Sebastian got up from the cot and followed them out of the room.

They brought him upstairs, to a large room that reminded him of the ballroom where Stan had met with Constantine and Alexa. The resonance of it echoed through his mind as he walked in, images from Stan's memory (vision?) trying to reassert themselves over what he now saw. Heavy navy curtains darkened to burgundy then shifted back to navy. The white walls changed to beige wallpaper and then back. The plain oak table morphed into something more ornate, with curling legs and chairs with sloping arms before snapping back into clean, straight lines.

What the hell?

He shook his head.

Nigel sat at the head of the table. Several other lieutenants of the In-Between sat along the sides, leaving a couple of chairs empty at the end. He spotted Jessica sitting halfway down the table on the right. She sat between Joan and Hanson, the man from the kitchen.

She didn't look up.

Blond Bristles pointed at the empty chair at the end of the table.

Inquisition time.

Sebastian sat down. His feet and legs finally felt like the blood was moving through them again but a brief rest was welcome.

"Nice of you to join us, Sebastian." Nigel's voice boomed through the room, even without him trying to yell.

Impressive acoustics in the room. Whose house was this? An In-Between supporter or a vampire victim?

Too often they seemed to end up the same thing.

"We're here to decide what to do about you," Nigel said.

Sebastian shifted on the chair. The navy cushion was thinner than it appeared. The hard edges of the chair bit into him.

"What do you mean?" he said.

"You deserted," Nigel said, "and it isn't the first time. This seems a recurring pattern with you. You stick around for a while then take off when it's convenient for you. You don't even tell anyone."

His chin lifted in a nod. Sebastian didn't have to look to feel how Jessica stiffened at Nigel's words. From here, he could hear the sharp intake of her breath, how she let it out slowly.

Damn you, Nigel.

He slid his hands off the smooth surface of the table and curled then into fists on his lap.

"I have to go home," Sebastian said. "You know why and you know I have to go. I've told you many times over but you don't listen."

"Who is it that doesn't listen, Sebastian?" Nigel said. "I told you we had people in the US keeping an eye out. You knew we had vital missions going on that needed your expertise." He said the word as if he was spitting it out, hating the taste of it in his mouth.

"You knew things were changing with the vampires but instead of helping us, you leave. To go home, you say, but how do we know that? Do you think you'd be the first In-Between to hate yourself enough to want to turn all the way so you turn on us?"

"What?" Sebastian said. "Are you crazy?"

"That's it, isn't it?" Nigel's voice boomed down. He pounded a fist on the table. It gave a hollow thud that reverberated down the length. "You want to find the one who tried to change you and have her finish the job. You never fit in here."

Sebastian shook his head. He couldn't believe this. Did Nigel hate him that much that he could believe this garbage?

"That's a lie and you know it," he said. "I've done everything I could to help. I killed Constantine and burned that damned book. I've helped you on your raids. All I want is to go home and make sure my family is safe. You say you've got people watching out but that's not enough. She has to be stopped."

"Yeah, you burned that book," Nigel said. "Only when you were forced to. How do we know what you would have done if you'd been alone with it."

"This guy is a total prick."

Charlie's voice came from Sebastian's left.

Sebastian shifted his eyes without turning his head. He could just see Charlie out of the corner of his eye. Charlie shook his head, blond hair flopping on his shoulders. He crossed his arms again. He'd changed this time. He wore jeans ripped at the knees and a black t-shirt.

"You actually worked with this schmuck?" he said to Sebastian.

"Not voluntarily." Sebastian mumbled the words.

Across the room, Nigel frowned. His thin long face seemed to draw thinner. "What did you say?"

"He said you were a dick!" Charlie shouted.

Sebastian squeezed his lips shut to stop the laugh that threatened to spill out.

"You think this is funny?" Nigel said. "It's all a big joke to you, isn't it? You think you're so great just because you can Influence a few vampires."

"Made one climb up to a roof, you dick," Charlie said. "Gonna be a barbecue in the morning."

The smile that pressed against Sebastian's lips faded. He remembered the feeling of pushing that vampire, Influencing it so completely that it did what he wanted.

He had to tell them. If he could do it, maybe he could train some of the others. Maybe they had another way to fight the vampires.

But then they'd never let him leave.

He stayed silent.

"I think we should throw you down the sewer like we did that guy." Nigel waved his hand as if brushing dust from the table. "You could be neighbors at the end of that hole in the ground." Nigel's lips twisted down. "Unfortunately, a few of the others have pointed out that we still need you for the job in Rome."

"I have to go home," Sebastian said.

"You'll leave when we're good and ready for you to leave," Nigel said. "If it was up to me, I'd have kicked you out a long time ago."

His head tilted a little. Sebastian gaze followed this time. Jessica sat with her head bowed. Joan had a hand on her forearm.

"I bet I could pull his chair out from under him," Charlie said.

I thought you couldn't do anything.

"I'll have to concentrate really hard."

That'll never happen.

"Fuck off, Sebastian, or I'll leave you to deal with dickhead here yourself."

Sorry.

Charlie faded from beside him then reappeared behind Nigel's chair. As Sebastian watched, something shifted around Charlie. The air seemed to flicker and glow around him. His hands reached out for the back of the chair.

Around the table, the In-Between shifted and murmured. Even from the other end of the room, Sebastian could feel the shift in the air, like an electrical field pulsing. He could almost smell a tinge of ozone.

Joan turned to look over at Nigel. She sucked in a breath. Her eyes widened. She started to rise from her chair.

"There's..."

Charlie's hands tightened on the back of Nigel's chair. He yanked. The chair flew back. Nigel slammed forward against the table and fell to the floor.

Charlie's laugh echoed in the air. The chair clattered to the ground.

Sebastian couldn't help it.

He snickered.

Joan's head spun toward him. Her accusing glare froze the snicker in his throat.

"Who was that?" she said. "You know who it was."

Nigel crawled up from under the table. The two people beside him steadied him. A smear of blood showed under his nose.

"What the hell?" he said.

"It was a ghost," Joan said. "I saw it right before the chair flew back. The ghost did it." She pointed at Sebastian. "You know who it was, don't you?"

They all stared at him. He could feel the waves of anger and confusion buffeting him.

Great. Just great.

"Sorry, man. Didn't mean to jam you up worse. I thought it was funny."

Charlie reappeared beside him. He shrugged his shoulders.

I thought it was funny too.

"It's there, isn't it?" Joan said. "I can sense something."

"She's not bad," Charlie said, "for an older broad."

Shut up.

"Just tryin' to lighten the mood."

"You can see it, can't you?" Joan said. Her head tilted. "Are you talking to it?"

Now he felt fear as an undercurrent of that anger, like a sourness that prickled his skin.

"It's not an 'it,'" Sebastian said. "It's a him. It's my friend, Charlie."

Jessica gasped. She recoiled in her seat, pressing against the back.

Dammit.

After everything, she'd always been the one who didn't look at him like he was a freak but he saw that look now on her face. That look of revulsion.

He'd lost her.

He had to get out of here.

He pushed back from the table, the chair scraping against the floor, and stood up.

"I'm sorry," he said. "I have to go. I know you're trying to save the world and all but I just want to save my family. I'll come back and help, I promise. If you still want me."

He said it to the entire table but kept his gaze fixed on Jessica.

He started to back away.

She got up from the table and pushed past the three people to reach the corner.

"That's it?" she said. "You're just leaving? You won't even listen to what's going on?"

"I have to go," he said.

"What's happening in Rome, it could affect everyone," she said. "Won't you even wait to hear about it?"

His chest tightened. He wanted to reach out to her, wanted to stay and hear whatever she had to say. But an entire motel of people had died just a few days ago and he knew it was Alexa, knew she was heading for his family.

That motel had been her calling card. A little announcement just for him.

He couldn't wait any longer.

"I'm sorry," he said.

He turned away from her.

Blond Bristles and Brown Bristles blocked his path to the oak door.

Shit.

"Let me take care of these guys," Charlie said.

He vanished and reappeared behind them. This time, the glow happened much faster. Both men yelped as Charlie grabbed the back of their pants to administer the ultimate weggie.

Sebastian darted past them as they flailed.

He yanked the door open and was through before it even swung fully open. Maybe he should have shut it to block them from following him but he didn't have time. He raced across the wide front foyer, shoes slapping on the marble tile. The front oak door opened just as easily and he was outside, running down the gravel driveway.

The same van they'd brought him in was parked at the end of a line of cars. One good thing about having been with the In-Between for a while, they'd taught him how to wire a car. He yanked the driver's door open and jumped in. How thoughtful, they'd already pulled the wires out of the steering column. He twisted them together and the engine caught.

As he backed out, people began pouring through the front door, racing down the driveway toward the van. He pressed on the gas and the van shot onto the road.

He turned the wheel and drove away.

Charlie appeared in the passenger's seat. "Don't worry. I mucked up the car in front of the van. It'll take 'em a minute to get it out of the way."

"Thanks," Sebastian said.

"Hey, it's the least I can do. I didn't mean to mess things up in there. That guy was just such a dick. I couldn't help myself."

"Yeah," Sebastian said. "I know."

"What was that about Rome?"

Sebastian shook his head. "A job. Another nest of vampires to clear out. Same old thing."

Charlie frowned. "Didn't sound like the same old thing."

Sebastian glanced across at him. "Too late to worry about that now."

"Sure, buddy. Let's hit the airport."

Sebastian patted the bag at his waist. At least they hadn't taken the money from him.

It was going to have to be enough.

Already in the sky he could see the darkness lightening toward dawn. They'd kept him for hours. More time lost, and he'd lose at least another day in travel time before he made it all the way home.

Way too many losses. He just kept piling them up. It wasn't fair. How much more could he lose? Just when he thought there was nothing left, something else dropped away, stripping another layer off him, taking another piece of his soul.

Jessica...

He'd pushed too far. He saw it in her eyes.

Maybe after, maybe he could explain things. She'd lost her mother and her brother, had had to kill the vampire that came back to her with her brother's face. But that was a long time ago, and she didn't have any family left.

He might not be able to make her understand.

He almost turned the van back. As they came up to a stop light and he waited for the light to change, he noticed the road widened just up ahead. He could make a U turn.

He could still go back.

"Ah Sebastian?" Charlie said.

"What?"

The light turned green.

"Shouldn't you be driving on the left side of the road?"

"Fuck!"

He abandoned the van in the parking garage at the airport, surrounded by the smell of exhaust, drying road paint, and grime. Sebastian inhaled as much of it as he could on the walk to the airport, trying to overpower his sense of smell.

It might just help drown out the scent of blood around him.

As time passed, he got a little better at resisting the temptation but such a dense concentration of people still threatened to overpower his resolve. Sitting in an airplane, surrounded by that alluring smell was going to be hard enough, he had to get through the airport and the gate before he even got there.

And he still needed to get a ticket.

With only half of the cash he needed.

Easy, right?

He wished he was invisible like Charlie.

He joined the line at the order desk. Only three people in front of him. A quick check of the board above the desk told him the next flight to the

States was leaving in three hours. He had barely enough time to get a ticket and go through security.

He couldn't wait for three people.

He focused on the woman standing in front of him, in her navy business suit, skirt fashionably a half inch above her knee, black shoes a modest three inches high. She held a navy wheeled suitcase behind her. Her left hand clasped her passport and papers.

Bathroom, you have to go to the bathroom.

She shifted a little, left black shoe sliding on the speckled floor. She cleared her throat.

Bathroom…

Her right foot moved now, pressing against her left. She stood with her legs tight together. Her hand tightened on the passport.

Bathroom…

Her body wiggled. The toe of her right shoe tapped the floor. Abruptly, she spun, feet marching forward as she headed to the left. The suitcase wheeled behind her as she hurried away.

Sebastian moved up.

Only two more to go.

Each of the others was easier. He sent the man in the leather jacket and sneakers off for a coffee and bagel because of his imagined starvation. The other woman in jeans and flowing flower top, he sent to the bathroom as well.

Finally he was next.

The attendant behind the desk motioned him forward. He stepped up handing over his passport.

"I need to be on the next plane to the U.S.," he said. He pitched his voice low over the counter.

For a moment, he thought she hadn't heard him, hadn't heard the push in his voice.

Her head remain bowed, the fringe of dark brown hair around her face covering her forehead. Her mocha colored hands with perfectly manicured, pale pink nails trembled just a little. The cuffs of her dark blue flight attendant jacket shifted up her wrists. Her face lifted and he noticed the telltale vacant expression in her dark brown eyes.

"U.S.," she said.

"Yes, the next plane." He focused, feeling the dull pain in his head start to tighten around his temples. He just had to get her moving.

Her hands trembled a little more. Her fingernails scraped the tops of keyboard keys then settled onto them.

Press down, now he just had to get her to press down.

She began typing. At first her movements were hesitant, then they became smoother as she went along. Sebastian leaned against the counter, wishing he could rest his head against its cool surface. Pain radiated from his temples down into his jaw.

"Credit card please," the attendant said.

Oh shit, he'd thought he could pay by cash and Influence her into thinking it was enough.

He was going to have to improvise.

And oh, wasn't he so good at that.

"Um, use your own," he said. He closed his eyes and focused on her.

"Sure." Her voice sounded faint and distant. Her fingers sped over the keyboard. Each tap felt like a bludgeon against his temples. Finally she finished and printed off a boarding pass.

"Gate C78. Do you need to check any baggage, sir?"

"No," he said.

Amazing that he was able to keep his voice steady.

"Security is that way." She pointed to her right. "Next."

He grabbed the boarding pass from her hand and stumbled away, heading for security. Part way there, he realized he'd look suspicious with no baggage at all. He hunted through the various shops, finding a khaki bag he could us for carryon. He wandered through the stores, grabbing souvenir t-shirts, shorts, books, anything to fill the bag. He used up about half of his cash before he thought he had enough.

He could have Influenced people not to notice but the way his head was feeling now, he wanted to avoid it as much as possible. Besides, the In-Between might be able to follow his trail.

Not that he'd be that hard to follow.

Surprisingly, security passed him through with a cursory check. The squat, heavy-set woman, her light brown hair pulled back and styled in a fashionable bun at the base of her skull, waved the wand at him as he passed through the x-ray machine. She was nodding even before she finished.

His bag rolled down the conveyor belt without incident.

He grabbed it and headed for the gate.

Only another couple of hours and he'd be heading home.

That should give him plenty of time to come up with a plan to deal with Alexa but not nearly enough to figure out what the hell he was going to tell his parents and his brother.

CHAPTER 7

The worst thing about travel wasn't the security or the airports or the cramped seating or horrible, plastic-like texture to the food. It was the jet lag.

Sebastian stumbled off the airplane in Chicago, dragging the khaki bag with him. The stark, white light in O'Hare blinded him, pounding into his head. Everywhere was bright, the white tiles, the spackled walls, the gleaming metal gates he stumbled past. He desperately needed sunglasses.

Smells assaulted him from all sides. Stale, confined air seemed to swoosh out from the airplane behind him like an annoying dog he couldn't get rid of. Sour sweat from the people waiting at the gate mingled with the odors of sickly sweet perfume and cologne. The heavy, greasy smell of fried food seemed to crawl along the floor before coating the insides of his nostrils and sliding down to lodge in his throat.

And everywhere underneath these odors, he smelled blood.

The sweet, tantalizing temptation called to him. Over and over.

He sagged against the wall beside a coffee bar, letting the strong stench of burned coffee and sweet rolls waft over him. He could still smell the business man at the counter, could even hear the ticking of his watch. Expensive-looking polished metal (titanium? White platinum?) with some kind of jewelled setting. Too bad the ticking was off by a fraction of a second. Probably made the watch lose several minutes per year. From the coiffed hairstyle, the expensive, double-breasted, grey suit, and Italian-made leather shoes, Sebastian imagined the businessman would be pissed to learn that his ultra-expensive watch lost time like that. The man picked up his latte from the woman behind the counter and moved to the side, adding several packets of sweetener to it.

Shouldn't bother, he was already well on his way to getting diabetes.

Sebastian could smell it in his blood.

He turned away before the man finished pouring. There had to be some place with a few less people. Maybe with no people.

Just get him away from that smell.

The hours on the flight had left his resistance low. Too much open space in the airport. The large wide hall with the gates and food court spouting off on either side, filled with people. There was no getting away from the smell of people, the smell of blood. The air moved through the central hall like a wave, carrying the scent along and it called to him.

He could feel it.

Just one taste...

He forced himself into the washroom, surrounded by chrome. Shining paper towel holders and taps. Gleaming mirrors. Sparkling walls. Shining floor. It all burned his eyes, felt like it was frying the retinas at the back of his head, but he welcomed it, welcomed the pain of the harsh, bright light. At least it gave him some distraction from the sweet, seductive call.

Just one taste…

He splashed cold water on this face and used the industrial soap on his hands. The strong, detergent smell overpowered his nostrils, even driving out the scent of blood.

Finally.

"You don't look so good," Charlie said.

He stood by the chrome sink but Sebastian couldn't see Charlie's reflection in the mirror.

He hadn't realized ghosts wouldn't have reflections.

Of course, hallucinations wouldn't have reflections either.

"Tired," Sebastian said.

"Wish I could help you with that," Charlie said.

Sebastian nodded. "You did enough."

And he had. Charlie had sat in the seat next to Sebastian for the entire flight, forcing out the businessman who had booked the seat. The man had complained about the coldness and the weird feeling. At first the attendant hadn't believed him but then had felt it herself.

She arranged to move the man and hadn't disturbed Sebastian again, not even to offer soft drinks.

Sebastian didn't care. The flight had been hard enough.

"How long are we stuck here?" Charlie said.

"Four hour layover," Sebastian said. "Then an hour or so in the air."

"Not so bad," Charlie said. He smiled one of his classic Charlie grins as if they were still hanging out in their dorm room, talking about skipping class.

How many years ago had that been? It felt like centuries.

Sebastian splashed more water on his face. It helped a little, helped clear his head. He yanked a few paper towels from the dispenser beside the sink. The second towel tore in his hand leaving half hanging from the gleaming metal teeth.

Oh great. His hands still dripped. He dug his fingers underneath, trying to fish more out, feeling water dribble down his forearm, heading for his elbow. Just about to soak into his shirt. Terrific.

Was it good to know that no matter what happened to him he still managed to be an uncoordinated klutz?

Behind him, the door banged open and footsteps stumbled inside. Sebastian turned to look just as whoever it was disappeared around the corner. He caught the suggestion of jeans, maybe cowboy boots.

The solitude had been nice while it lasted.

Then he caught it, the slight hint of sourness…

Vampire?

No, it couldn't be. What the hell time was it? He glanced at his empty wrist. Right. He didn't have a watch, couldn't even remember what time he'd left London. What was the time difference? They were five hours ahead? He couldn't remember, couldn't concentrate enough on it because he'd spent the entire flight trying not to rip apart the people around him so he could soak in their blood.

What had he been…? Oh right, sourness.

He could still smell it, just a hint. Not a vampire, not strong enough to be a vampire. He should have realized that, of course, but he was tired. Someone who had been attacked? Another In-Between? No, that couldn't be right either. He wouldn't be able to smell another In-Between.

Who was this guy?

Better question: what was this guy?

"What's up?" Charlie said.

"Sour." Sebastian pointed. "In the stalls."

"So the guy has digestive issues. So what?"

"Not that kind, you idiot."

Charlie spread his hands. "Then what are you talking about?"

Sebastian reached the corner. He couldn't keep talking out loud to Charlie, not without the guy hearing him.

Vampire. He mouthed the word and pointed.

Charlie's mouth opened in an O.

Sebastian peered around the corner. The white tiles of the floor reflected off the brushed metal of the stall doors. They trailed away from him, lining each side of the aisle. Even without looking he knew most of those doors would be hanging just a little bit ajar, open and ready for the next person to use them. Only one stall was occupied.

By someone with a slight sour scent to them.

The only question was, could that person smell Sebastian?

He had to assume they could.

He clenched the strap of the khaki bag as he stepped into the center of the aisle. He didn't have any real weapon. There was no way to smuggle anything into an airport these days. He didn't even have a silver cross around his neck.

He wasn't much fond of silver for wearing. It made him itchy.

Just another reminder of how close to the edge he was. Sometimes he wondered if he'd ever slide over and not even realize it.

He moved with care, each foot lifting and setting down, quiet, the rubber soles not making a sound as he crept forward. With each step, he grew more certain this was someone he would have to deal with. The sourness grew in the air until he pinpointed it.

There. Second last stall on the left.

Damn, didn't he wish he had a knife or something. All he had was this bag.

He let the strap out, until the bag was almost brushing the floor. If he could swing it at the right height and angle, wrap it around the neck, pull it tight.

And manage not to smack himself in the head, it would all be good.

Another few steps. His left hand reached out for the door. If it was bolted, he might have to kick it in. Better to test it first. He pulled his right arm back, ready with the bag.

He shoved at the door.

The door swung inward.

A shriek sounded. The man cowered back. Pants still up. Toilet unused. He'd been hiding.

He slid down the wall to the floor and started scrambling under it into the next stall. Sebastian lunged forward and grabbed his leg. Faded jeans, just like Sebastian had thought. The man cried out again, kicking. Sure enough, cowboy boots. One scuffed heel just missed Sebastian's chin.

"Come on, Sebastian, get him." Charlie stood in the stall doorway.

"Help," Sebastian said.

Charlie shrugged. "Sorry. It would take me too long to concentrate to get solid enough. You'll be finished by the time I'm ready."

Typical.

Sebastian yanked, dragging the man back under the wall. As he slid, the man rolled over. He snarled and lunged forward, jaws snapping. Best defense, he probably figured. Sebastian brought the bag up and smashed the man across the face. He fell back, stunned for a moment. Blood trickled from the left corner of his mouth where his cheek had lacerated against his teeth. Normally this would mesmerize Sebastian but he could smell the sourness from here.

Infected.

The man had been bitten by a vampire, but not turned.

And he wasn't In-Between either.

What the hell was he?

Sebastian climbed to his feet then dragged the man up into a sitting position on the toilet. His head lolled then began to right itself. Awareness came back into his eyes, into his face. He glared at Sebastian. Blood dripped from his mouth and splattered on the front of his plaid shirt.

"Who are you?" Sebastian said.

"What are you?" the man said. "You have been tasted, I smell it on you, but you do not serve." His nose wrinkled. "What kind of thing are you?"

"Tasted?" Charlie said. "Sounds kinky."

"Shut up," Sebastian said, over his shoulder. He turned back to the man on the toilet. "Not you. You keep talking. What's your name? What happened to you?"

The man shook his head of shaggy brown hair. "I have no name. Only what She chooses to call me."

Sebastian could just about hear the capitalization of 'She' in the man's voice. Reverence. Deference. His stomach clenched in nausea.

"Who chooses for you?" he said.

For a moment, he didn't think the man would reply. His lips thinned. His shoulders hunched. His hands on his lap lifted up toward his mouth. He wiped at the side, smearing the blood across his lips, then he stared at his hand as if spellbound. He licked the blood away and closed his eyes, sighing.

When they opened, he looked right at Sebastian.

"You already know," the man said. "You've been tasted."

You've been tasted.

Sebastian's feet took a step back, pulling him away, as if his body already knew what the man was talking about, already knew because he recognized that particularly sourness above all others. He had only ever smelled it a small handful of times but he would never forget it, had, in fact, recognized it the moment he'd caught the scent in the bathroom.

But no, it couldn't be, wouldn't be. He couldn't let it be.

Her.

Bianca.

Remembrance flooded him. The crunch of leaves under his feet. The sick-sweet scent of moist vegetation, the remains of autumn's debris decaying underfoot and the tantalizing buds of the new life promised by spring on the trees. His feet stumbling on the uneven ground. The suggestion of movement between the trees. Then that smell...

That sour smell...

And the feel of her fangs tearing into his neck.

She'd been the start of this, the beginning of everything. Torn his old life away from him and left him with shards to try to build a new life, one that still cut and bled even as he tried to pull it together.

Bianca.

"Where is she?" he said.

The man shook his head. His blood-smeared lips twisted into a smile. "I'll not tell you anything, freak."

Freak, look who was talking but the word sank into him even though he didn't want it to. Freak. He was a freak even among the In-Between, had been so since Bianca had left him poised on the brink. Too far across to even be normal to the In-Betweens, it had just gotten worse and worse since he'd handled that book, that damned evil book written on pages of dried human flesh by the first vampire.

Now even this guy, this vampire servant or whatever he was, called him a freak too.

Maybe he'd better start living up to that reputation.

"Where is she?" Sebastian said.

He pitched his voice just so, a little low with a special lilt at the end. Just enough to present the question into the man's mind.

Enough to gain a foothold.

The man laughed again then his voice sputtered to a stop. His blood-smeared lips frowned.

Feel it now? Feel it? Feel me?

The man shook his head. Shoulders shuddered as if a shiver ran up his spine. Brent (yes, his name was Brent) bent over as pain pulsed at his temples. Fighting, he fought the feeling, the strangeness, wouldn't let go, wouldn't let it in, no... He couldn't.... No...

Sebastian closed his eyes. He took a deep breath then a moment later felt the echo in another body, in Brent's body. He felt his feet clad in black runners standing solidly on the speckled white floor tiles and at the same time, felt them encased in worn leather cowboy boots so old they had molded to his feet. His favorite boots, bought 'em almost ten years ago and he'd only had to resole them once. Best damn boots he ever bought, worth the five hundred even though his girlfriend, Amy, had yelled holy hell at him for it. He kept the boots and got rid of the girl. Another good decision, because now there wasn't any other space in his mind for anyone other than…

Her.

He'd just been a regular guy before Her, just a mechanic, second in line to Fat Louie who had lost over a hundred pounds but not the nickname. Living in a three story walkup on Bleeker Street, a stone's throw from the shop. Crappy neighborhood with cracked sidewalks and crackheads on the corners, begging for change or looking like they'd beat you for it, but they never bothered him. Not since he used these very same boots to kick one in the stomach as it made a lunge for him. Word got around. Don't mess with the man in the cowboy boots.

He'd been working late that night. Fat Louie'd left early for his grand daughter's first birthday party. Quite the formal occasion. Fat Louie was even going to wear his clean overalls. Brent stayed behind, working on the transmission of old lady Michaelson's Pontiac, a car he swore was almost as old as the lady herself. Normally he didn't like old ladies, they were snarky and complained a lot, but Mrs. Michaelson always baked cookies and brought them in, even went as far as to ask their favorite kinds.

He preferred chocolate chip. And he was looking forward to a plateful of homemade ones when *She* walked in.

He hadn't even heard her, she was just there at his elbow as he bent over the engine. He smelled the sourness over the heavy stench of grease and motor oil.

Her sourness cut through like nothing he'd ever smelled before.

He'd wrinkled his nose and started to straighten, feeling someone at his elbow. Just as he turned, he saw the curtain of dark hair, red lips pulling back from teeth that looked impossibly long. How could anyone have teeth like that? Then he was shoved hard against the grill of the car. Chrome edges dug into his back. Hands gripped his shoulders. He tried to break the grip. Strong, too strong. Then that sourness grew and grew until the exquisite bite in his neck.

He sank down and down...

Stop! Sebastian had to pull back. How easy would it be to sink into that memory, into that trap? He could feel the tendrils of her control woven through Brent's mind. That memory was the last one that was his alone, everything else came from *her*, *her* influence, *her* desire.

Sebastian had never felt this in a person who wasn't an In-Between or had been turned. Brent was still human but he'd been... tainted. Taken over. He was a puppet now. His mind a shell for what she wanted. Probably a steady supply of blood until she drained him dry, or a lure.

Or something else?

Had vampires been able to do this before and just not because of the structure they'd set up with the clans? Had the dissolution of their social order forced the vampires into new and different ways of trapping and manipulating humans?

Had *he* done this when he destroyed the book?

Was it *his* fault?

The vampires in Rome had been doing something new. Was it this kind of enslavement? Had he made a mistake leaving the In-Between?

But he'd had to, he had to get home. His family was in danger.

And hadn't he put them there?

No, he couldn't travel that road down to guilt. It wouldn't do him any good. Let his subconscious take the trip, he had other things to deal with.

Like this man, and Bianca.

Brent slumped against the back of the toilet, head down, brown hair stringy with sweat. His breathing sounded labored. His hands rested on his lap, giving the occasional twitch. That sour smell had a certain underlay of decay about it. Sebastian had to wonder how much of the man's mind was still his? How long before he fell into pieces for good?

Was there any way back from this for him?

Sebastian would like to think so, would like to think he could do something to help Brent get back to his regular life. It had felt like a pretty nice life with work he enjoyed and friends. The man deserved that life. Hell, Sebastian deserved that life, but if he couldn't have it, maybe he could still give it back to Brent.

Please let him be able to do that.

"Brent, can you hear me?" he said.

The man let out a soft moan. His head shifted to the right. It tried to lift then slouched back down, like a man trying to wake but being unable to break the spell of a dream.

"Listen to me, Brent," Sebastian said. "I can help you return to the garage, to Fat Louie, to fixing cars, to everything. Tell me where *she* is."

He pushed the emphasis on 'she', knowing Brent would hear it and understand. But was Bianca enough in his conscious mind to hear it as well? Could she listen and see through Brent like some of transmitter? Was that even possible?

Sebastian had no way of knowing. But he knew she had some kind of control over him. How Brent responded would tell him one way or the other, whether her control was live or conditioned.

"Brent, tell me where *she* is."

This time, the man's head lifted. Bloodshot eyes stared at Sebastian. Heavy lines pressed down along the sides of his mouth, dragging his lips down into a frown. Shoulders slack, he leaned forward a little. His lips trembled.

"Can't…"

Sweat popped out on his forehead. It trickled down the sides of his face. Hair stuck to his skin. His mouth kept moving a little, as if trying to form words.

"Can't…"

"Easy," Sebastian said. "Take it easy. Let's take it slow. Is she within ten miles of here?"

The stark lines around Brent's face eased. The tension in his neck lessened. He gave a slow nod.

"Okay, within five miles?" Sebastian said.

Another slow nod.

"Three miles?"

One more nod.

He narrowed it down to two miles. Damn close. What time was it? In the perpetual lighting of the airport, it always appeared to be daylight but Sebastian's time sense was screwed up from the flight. When had he landed? He couldn't even remember what time it would be in England now. Dousing fitfully on the plane had messed that up for him too.

Dammit.

Two miles…

He had the four hour layover. Certainly he could sneak out, deal with Bianca and be back in plenty of time to board his plane.

Couldn't he?

He couldn't just leave, knowing the one vampire who was the greatest threat to him, the one who could pull him across that narrow line between In-Between and vampire, was right here and he could finish with her once and for all.

He had four hours. What the hell else was he going to do?

"Brent, it's time you went back to *her*," Sebastian said.

CHAPTER 8

With the right pressure, the right Influence in his voice, Sebastian compelled Brent to stand. The man wavered a moment, then steadied. Sebastian backed out of the stall. Brent followed.

Sebastian kept backing away until he felt another stall door behind him. Brent turned to face the aisle, ignoring Sebastian. He began to move forward, gaining speed as he went.

"You're letting him go?" Charlie said. He stood beside Sebastian, against the stall door.

He'll lead me to Bianca.

Brent reached the door and headed out. Sebastian waited another moment and followed.

The bright lights of the airport hall stabbed at Sebastian as he slipped out of the bathroom. He winced at the pain flaring in his temples. Damn, he'd forgotten how bright it was in here. He really needed to get sunglasses but there was no time. Already he could see Brent halfway down the hall, heading for the main hub.

Dammit.

Sebastian dodged through the crowd, past men and women, some dressed in business suits and carrying various computers or smart phones, others dressed for vacations, carrying brochures and books. Why did they all seem to step in front of him as soon as he got close? Over the smell of sweat and cologne, he still smelled the sweet scent of their blood.

And it called, it always called…

That and the fucking light. His feet stumbled. He righted himself and pushed on but he wasn't fast enough. Brent reached the end of the hall and turned left. He disappeared around the corner.

Fuck.

Sebastian was too far away.

"Dude, you suck at this whole following people thing," Charlie said. "Let me show you how it's done."

He moved in front of Sebastian. For a moment, Charlie remained solid-looking, then the edges of his body and clothes became thin and wispy. He began to glide forward, still moving his legs, but he flowed at a speed impossible for the rate of his walking. As if by instinct, people moved out of the way without even looking, leaving a clear path for Sebastian.

Okay, that was cool.

No, it was cold.

As Sebastian followed the path cleared by Charlie, he felt the temperature drop in the air as if this section was being blasted by frigid air conditioning. He clenched his teeth together to stop them from chattering. His hands tightened into fists. He hurried as fast as he could, trying to get his muscles to create heat but the cold seemed to leach any warmth out of him.

Was this what those people were feeling?

They reached the end of the hall. Sebastian looked left. The short corridor led to the security exit out of the airport. If he left, he'd have to find a way to sneak back in. That would mean exerting enough Influence to bypass security. Did he have the strength right now?

Bianca…

He couldn't just leave her here. He had to finish it, finish her.

He nodded to Charlie. "Let's go."

Leaving the airport was as easy as walking out the door. Outside, Sebastian found the day was darkening toward twilight. Maybe another forty-five minutes to full dark, another forty-five minutes before Bianca was at her full strength. If he could find her before then, it would be easy.

He spotted Brent halfway through the parking lot on the right, a large concrete field of cars stretching out as if into the distance. The air felt heavy with the stench of exhaust but at least it smothered the smell of blood.

Sebastian stepped off the sidewalk and headed for the parking lot. He heard a hiss and click as multiple lights in the parking lot switched on. Must be on a timer. The sky was darkening but not yet that dark.

Please, not yet that dark.

Bianca wasn't the strongest vampire he'd faced, but she was the one who'd bitten him. She had a foothold in his mind, a connection she could exploit. That made her more dangerous than another vampire. He didn't want to face her at night.

He would if he had to.

But he could really use a weapon.

He started looking for anything, even a piece of rebar but only gravel and dirt covered the surface of the parking lot. He threaded his way among the cars, passing Fords and Toyotas, Escalades and Mazdas. How many cars like this had Brent worked on at his garage? Would he ever be able to work on them again? If Sebastian killed Bianca

(no, *when*)

would Brent be freed to return to his life? Was enough of him left to do that?

What would happen to him if there wasn't?

Sebastian pushed the thought away. He couldn't think about that. Bianca had enslaved the man. He deserved his freedom, no matter what that meant.

Ahead of him, Brent reached the end of the parking lot and continued to the right, heading across a green area. Farther in the distance,

Sebastian spotted a row of trees, already becoming indistinct against the darkening sky.

No, dammit.

He sped up until he was almost running. He scraped against the cars, almost bouncing off several before he kept going.

His legs would be a mass of bruises after this.

He reached the green area and started to hurry across. Brent was halfway to the trees now. Spongy grass yielded under Sebastian's feet. Away from the parking lot, he caught the fresh scent of the grass and an undercurrent of water. Of course, the lake, just nearby. It smelled different than the ocean, not as tangy.

No salt water here.

Brent reached the tree line. Sebastian sprinted forward, feet pounding on the ground. His heart thudded in his chest. The khaki bag bumped against his back as it swung from his shoulder. He reached the tree line a minute after Brent disappeared.

He couldn't see any sign of the man.

He stopped, sucking in air, resting his hands on his knees. In front of him, a row of trees, with thick veined leaves dipping low, spread out in both directions. He smelled the heady scent of them, the fresh new buds, the wet, dank scent of decaying vegetation on the ground.

It reminded him of another set of trees, just a few years ago, and a night that changed his life forever.

If only he'd never left that party...

"So, are we just going to admire the view?" Charlie stood beside him, hands shoved into the pockets of his jeans. In the darkening light, he looked more solid again and he'd lost the frigidaire effect.

"No," Sebastian said. "We're going in."

He stepped forward among the trees.

"I died surrounded by trees, didn't I?" Charlie said behind him. Sebastian glanced back. Charlie was following but didn't make any noise. His feet didn't disturb any vegetation on the ground. As he watched, one of the Charlie's feet passed through a large outcropping of rock.

"Yeah, there were trees," Sebastian said.

"Thought so," Charlie said. "I remember that."

"Why are you here, Charlie?" Sebastian said. "Do you know?"

"Getting tired of me already, huh," Charlie said. "Better be nice to me. You're burning your bridges faster than you can build 'em. Think Jessica'll ever talk to you again?"

"Shut up."

"Ooooh touchy. You really suck at the whole relationship with women thing. I thought you were just a pussy with Alexa but it turns out you can't sustain it with any woman."

Sebastian spun around. "Oh yeah? And you were such the expert. Tell me, great expert, what am I doing wrong?"

"You don't listen," Charlie said. "You don't talk to them. Women like to talk and they like to be listened to. That's the secret to my success. I listened. Give a nod in the right place, a sympathetic noise, and they love you. Maybe if you listened to Jessica, told her what you were doing, what was really going on with you, she'd trust you."

Sebastian turned away. "Shut up."

"Sure," Charlie said. "Run off. That's what got you into this mess in the first place. You couldn't stay and talk to Alexa. You ran."

The air around Sebastian seemed to vanish. He felt his lungs collapse inward, his shoulders hunch. Hiding his height, always hiding his height, hiding himself. He shuffled forward. Running. Yes, he was always running and it had been the thing that got him into this mess, gotten all of them into this mess: him, Alexa, Charlie, even his own family.

His eyes burned with tears. The rough, black bark of the trunk in front of him blurred. He blinked to try to clear his vision. He'd done his best, was trying to make things right, even the things he knew could never be right again. So many ripples cascaded out from that one stupid night, so many people caught up in whirlpools of destruction, even Stan. How could Sebastian ever fix it for them when he couldn't even fix it for himself?

"I'm trying," he said. His voice sounded thready and weak even to his own ears. "What am I supposed to do?"

"Maybe stop trying to do everything yourself," Charlie said. "Maybe ask for help sometime."

"Can you help me, Charlie?" Sebastian said. "Or are you just going to keep criticizing?"

"Buddy, I am helping you."

"This is helping? It's almost dark. How am I supposed to kill Bianca before nightfall now?"

"Maybe you aren't supposed to kill her before nightfall," Charlie said. "Maybe you aren't supposed to kill her at all."

Sebastian stared at him. "What the hell are you talking about?"

Charlie shrugged. Through his shoulders, Sebastian caught a shifting of leaves. Darker now.

Almost night.

Enough of this. He had to go.

He inhaled deeply, catching a subtle whiff of sourness lingering in the air. Brent. He'd gone this way. Sebastian headed off.

He didn't turn to see if Charlie followed.

The uneven ground slowed his progress, tripping him with upraised roots and slippery congealed leaves and grass. He pushed on, even as the shadows darkened around him. He couldn't see through the branches and thick foliage above his head but he could feel the encroaching night, feel as it hummed in his veins.

Bianca would be waking very soon.

He had to find her before then.

The sour smell intensified, thickening until he could almost taste it. He slowed, pressing against the rough bark of an old tree that bent sideways at an angle. Large, heavy bushes grew on the other side of this tree. Sebastian followed the curve of the trunk, pushing several of the thin branches aside. Sharp thorns pricked at his fingers, scratched at his forearm as he cleared a small space.

He peered out.

A small clearing glowed on the other side of the bushes, golden in the final dying rays of daylight. He spotted Brent crossing to the other side. He disappeared between another set of trees. Sebastian hurried after him, then stopped. Brent stood just on the other side of the tree, facing away. At his feet was a large wooden trunk. Old fashioned, with brown, aged leather straps arching over the curved top. A huge padlock hung open.

Brent reached down and pulled off the padlock. It fell from his loose fingers, bouncing once on the ground before rolling to a stop.

Brent paused, still leaning over the trunk, like he was a windup toy that had reached the end of its track. He needed another good wind before he would move again.

Sebastian knew exactly when that would be. As soon as the sun finished setting.

Less than fifteen minutes now.

"Sebastian, wait." Charlie's voice came from behind him.

No, he'd already waited too long. If he waited any longer, she would be awake and he knew he wouldn't be able to resist her. His Influence on vampires would backlash on him when it came to Bianca. She was the one who'd infected him. Any attempt to Influence her would only strengthen her hold on him. Then she'd be able to finish the job.

And he didn't want that. No, he didn't.

Although deep inside a tiny part of him feared that maybe, just maybe he did.

NO!

He pushed through the bushes, feeling the branches and thorns grabbing at his shirt and pants, as if trying to hold him back. He wouldn't let them, wouldn't let anyone stop him.

He pushed through.

Brent didn't move. He stood poised over the trunk. God, he did really look like a giant doll.

Bianca had made him that way, stripped away his life, his dreams, everything. Turned him into a doll that she could feed off of and kill at her leisure.

Not anymore.

Sebastian pushed Brent out of the way. The man stumbled. His left leg collapsed underneath him and he fell to the ground. He lay unmoving.

As if he didn't even realize what had happened.

Sebastian grabbed the edges of the trunk. They bit into his palms as he clenched them but he didn't care, didn't give a fuck at all.

He yanked, feeling the weight of the lid drag down. God, it was heavy. The muscles across his back and shoulders strained, his arms grew taunt. It shouldn't be this heavy.

Bianca was trying to hold the trunk shut, trying to stop him from opening it before sundown. All she had to do was hold on for a few more minutes.

His heart hammered in his chest, sending adrenaline shooting through his system. He couldn't let her hold on, couldn't face her again in the full night.

Couldn't risk saying yes to her, couldn't risk that deepest fear.

That maybe he really *did* want to say yes.

His hand tightened. He gave a final wrench.

The lid flew up.

She shrieked from inside the trunk. Legs folded to the side, she curled in the bottom of the trunk. A wave of decay and sourness wafted out. The heady strength of it made him stumble back. Her hand reached up to the lid.

He kicked out as hard as he could, using every ounce of In-Between strength he had. The lid snapped back, the hinge breaking. It flopped on the ground. Bianca gave another wail. She shook her head from side to side, the dark curtain of her hair obscuring her face. Her hands came up, hooked into claws, shielding her face. In the dying sunlight, her skin was almost translucent, so white, so pale.

Sebastian grabbed her wrists and yanked her arms up. Her upper body came out of the trunk even as she struggled against him. She wore a sleeveless dark red top. Black pants covered her legs. She twisted and turned her body, her arms. He felt the effort in her wrists as they slid in his hands. But she wasn't at full strength. Not enough to break his grip on her.

Only a few minutes now...

He backed away, dragging her by the arms. Her body rose out of the trunk. Her legs flopped over the side. They kicked out but she didn't yet have the coordination to stand. Whimpers and moans came from her throat.

The clearing was only a few steps away. Just a few steps and he could throw her into the last golden glow of the sunlight.

He prayed it would be enough to kill her.

Thorny branches and leaves scraped at his back and arms as he dragged her forward. His feet crunched over twigs and dried vegetation. He felt every crevice in the earth, every root that tried to trip him up but it wouldn't work this time. Not this time.

Her arms twisted in his hands. Her skin felt slick with sweat, or something close to sweat. Did vampires actually sweat? He didn't know, but something on her skin made her arms slippery. He tightened his grip, felt his fingernails dig into her flesh.

His shoulders ached from dragging her, from fighting her. Even in this uncoordinated state, her strength taxed him. All he had to do was hang on, just another minute, just another few steps...

He felt the crunch of grass beneath his feet. The weak heat of the last of the sun warmed his face. He gave another yank and backpedaled as fast as he could, dragging her the extra few inches into the center of the clearing.

Bianca's screams rose in volume. She thrashed in his grip. Her legs flailed, her arms jerked. Heat emanated from her skin, almost burning his hands. Her head whipped back and forth, sending her hair flying, obscuring her face but he caught glimpses between the flying hair.

Her skin darkened, appearing to wrinkle and shrivel at the same time. Her lips, usually full and red, seemed almost translucent and thin as they pulled back from her teeth. Her gums looked bloodless. Her fangs stood out even more prominent as she opened her mouth to cry out.

The shrieks lessened, becoming higher pitched as if her vocal cords were shriveling as well. Her movements became jerkier, more spastic, her legs kicking out. The fabric of her clothing slid over her body as if the muscles were shrinking.

The temperature in her arms rose so high he couldn't hold onto her wrists any more. He dropped them but stood ready to grab her again if she made a dash for the trees and darkness, but she fell back against the grass. Her hands and feet flailed and grabbed as she tried to rise up but she didn't have the coordination to do it. The skin on her arms darkened. The bones became more prominent. He watched as the fingers on one of her hands snapped back as she hit the ground. A moment later, the forearm of the other arm cracked against the earth, the jagged edge breaking through her now paper-thin flesh. Brackish blood oozed out.

Her smell, always sour, became fetid, a stench that made him gag. It coated the air around him, leaching into his nostrils even as he tried to hold his breath. It mixed with the rot of the decaying vegetation, making him think that this was the final result of vampirism, the very essence of it, a mingling of rot, decay and degradation so sour it seemed to poison the air and ground around it.

Her struggles weakened. The flesh on her face molded to her bones and had the color of burned leather. Smoke curled up from her cheeks, carrying with it the acrid stench of burning flesh. It began to rise from every part of her body, snaking out from under her clothing. The smell of it, of her, grew in strength until the sourness of it burned his eyes. He blinked, tears streamed down his face. After a moment, she gave a few more final spasms, legs and arms twitching, before her body sank down. A final gasp issued from her gaping mouth and she stopped moving.

Shadows from the trees reached across the clearing, finally covering her and Sebastian in the soothing darkness of night but it was too late for Bianca. The death process was too far along. Even a few moments before, she might have been able to recover but not now. He watched as the skin continued to decay at a faster and faster rate. Her body settled into the ground. Gentle clicks sounded as the bones cracked and crumbled. Her clothing deflated. Her skull turned away from him, the hair sprayed out against the ground before it began to shrivel and crumble into the grass.

The heavy scent of decay began to dissipate. The subtle scent of leaves and growing buds began to reassert themselves, reclaiming the air.

Another minute and all that was left of her was the clothing, flat and full of dust.

He'd never watched it happen all the way before, not a daylight death. Relief made him sag into himself. Bianca dead! The one vampire who could have turned him, gone. The realization left him trembling. He took a step back, wiping the tears from his face. The stench of her death still lingering in his nostrils, strong enough that he wondered if he'd ever smell anything else ever again, or would he just continue to smell her death, over and over.

Maybe he'd never be rid of her.

But at least Brent would be. And she'd never infect anyone else again.

That had to count for something.

He stepped around the flattened clothing, wondering for a moment if he should do something with them but then he decided no, leave it.

It didn't matter. Let some animal or something come along and scatter them, scatter the dust remains of *her*. After everything she'd done, she didn't deserve any other kind of rest.

Maybe that was a bit self-righteous of him but so be it. She'd stolen his life. He was glad he could finally return the favor.

He pushed through a set of bushes, feeling their spindly branches scrape at his arms. They burned on his skin, just adding another layer of mild pain to the ache that spread through his muscles. Dragging her had been harder than he would have thought possible. Did it have something to do with the link they'd shared? Did his reaction have to do with her death?

It didn't really matter. He would never have that reaction again. No vampire would have that kind of hold on him.

The shadows deepened into darkness but his In-Between vision let him see easily. He spotted Brent lying on his side, just a few feet from the trunk. Dazed maybe, shocked by Bianca's death. Sebastian hoped there was enough of the man left to be able to reclaim his life.

At least he would have a life to reclaim.

Sebastian felt a twinge of envy even as he reached down toward Brent. At least he didn't have to live the rest of his life as an In-Between. At least he didn't have to contend with being a freak even among freaks. Maybe he could even have a semblance of a normal life after this. Sebastian would do whatever it took to help make that happen.

After he took care of his family, of course.

"Brent, it's over," Sebastian said. He grabbed hold of the man's shoulder. "Wake up."

Even before he flopped over onto his back, Sebastian knew the man was dead. In the darkness, the blood coating his nose and mouth looked brackish. It gave off a vaguely sour stench. Lifeless eyes stared out, distended, the veins inside burst, filling the whites with blood. His mouth was open in silent agony. His arms and legs curled up, his hands twisted into claws.

Sebastian touched his neck, feeling for the pulse he knew wasn't there. The skin beneath his fingers felt cool to the touch. Rigor mortis already setting in.

Why? Why had Brent died?

"I hate to say I toldja."

Charlie's voice sounded from behind him.

CHAPTER 9

Sebastian turned. Charlie looked almost insubstantial but there was enough of him for Sebastian to see he wore a different pair of jeans and a dark green t-shirt with a white hoodie over top. Hands shoved into the back pockets of his jeans, Charlie gave a shrug. His blond hair shifted over his shoulders.

"What the hell are you talking about?" Sebastian said. He stood up. The muscles in his legs protested. He could feel them bunching.

"I told you maybe you shouldn't kill her," Charlie said. "What do you think happened to him?" He pointed at Brent's body at Sebastian's feet.

"How should I know?" Sebastian said. "Maybe she took too much from him and he couldn't survive it."

"He couldn't survive her death you mean," Charlie said.

Sebastian shook his head. "You don't know what you're talking about. Her death should have freed him."

"He doesn't look all that free, unless you consider death the ultimate freedom. I'm not going to argue the point."

"Something was wrong."

"Yeah, that something is you killed Bianca."

"What the hell was I supposed to do?" Sebastian's voice rose to a yell. He could hear the hysterical edge to it but he didn't care, didn't care if anyone else heard him but he doubted anyone was around.

"Maybe I should have asked her politely," he said. "'Oh Bianca, would you release Brent? And while you're at it, just kill yourself when you're done because you're a bad, bad vampire.' You mean something like that? Yeah, that woulda worked."

"I don't know, Sebastian," Charlie said. "I just think maybe there were other options."

"Like what?"

Charlie shrugged again. "I don't know. I'm just a ghost. You're the half-vampire expert guy and if you don't know, maybe you should be asking for help."

"Enough. I've had enough of this."

Sebastian stepped past Charlie. Through the trees, he could see the glow of the airport. If he was lucky, he could Influence his way back inside and still make his flight.

"Are you going to leave him here?" Charlie said.

Sebastian stopped and looked back. Brent's body lay on its back, legs still curled underneath him. The toes of his cowboy boots poked out from under his thighs. His hands huddled on his chest.

What could he do for the man? He wasn't even sure if he was from Chicago. The memories he'd touched in Brent's head hadn't been specific enough. It could have been any town nearby.

"I'll call the police from the airport," he said. "They'll come and take care of him. Do you have any other ideas?"

Charlie shook his head. "I guess not."

Sebastian turned away and trudged back through the underbrush. In the soothing darkness, everything was heightened. The cool breeze that brushed across his arms, the light scent of vegetation mixed with the heavy scent of jet fuel and car exhaust. The leaves gleaming silver-green in the dim light. And through it all, he could still smell the overlying warmth of blood.

It still called to him, even after Bianca's death. He'd killed her and it changed nothing. He wasn't free, any more than Brent was but at least Brent didn't have to suffer anymore.

He still got to experience the joy and wonder of being an In-Between, and being a freakish one at that.

Oh what fun.

The lights of the parking lot glinted yellow between a pair of trees. Sebastian aimed for that. Car engines mingled with the rumble of airplanes. He could almost feel it vibrating in his torso.

Something slammed into his back, sending him flying forward. He barely managed to get his hands out before he smashed into the ground. Dirt and grass mashed against his face. Pain flared in his mouth where his teeth had split his cheek. He tasted his own blood.

Hands closed on his arms and flipped him over onto his back. A figure straggled him. A man, grey hair, pale skin, wiry body but with the strength to hold Sebastian down. The man's mouth opened and Sebastian caught a whiff of sourness.

Vampire!

He bucked, trying to dislodge the man, but the man clamped his leg tight against Sebastian's sides. He snarled and darted forward, aiming for Sebastian's neck. The searing pain in his neck eclipsed the pain in his mouth.

Sebastian screamed.

The vampire reared back. He released his hold on Sebastian's arms and scrambled away. He gagged and spit, retching until dribbles of reddish saliva trailed from his mouth. Finally, he glared back at Sebastian.

"In-Between. Useless."

He wiped his mouth with the back of his hand, smearing Sebastian's blood across his lips and cheek. His hands tightened into fists. Muscles bunched.

Telegraphing movements. He wasn't even trying to be subtle.

When he lunged, Sebastian rolled to his right. Knees bending, he managed to regain his footing and spun to meet the vampire. Off balance, the vampire stumbled, falling to one knee. Sebastian brought his fist down on the vampire's shoulder, aiming for clavicle. He felt it snap as he slammed the vampire down. The vampire screamed.

Sebastian jumped on its back, shoving it face first into the ground. The vampire's left hand flopped, useless, but the right hand tried to scramble at the ground. Sebastian grabbed the vampire's arms and pinned them with his knees.

"Talk," he said. "What are you doing here? Were you with Bianca?"

Face in the dirt, the vampire snarled. Even wounded as he was, he was stronger than Sebastian. Sebastian had only a few moments before it gathered its strength to toss him off.

Better make the most of them.

He focused on the back of his grey hair and *pushed*. He hadn't pushed like this since the vampire in the alley, since sending it up to the roof.

(*Since the nose bleed and who knew how many brain cells he'd killed?*)

But he needed to do it now, needed to know who this vampire was, what it was doing here and what it knew.

Any information might help him when he had to face Alexa.

So…

Just relax, lie on the ground, feel the earth press against him. Just relax. No need to struggle, no need to fight.

Relax…

Beneath him, Sebastian felt the vampire's body sag whereas a moment before it had been tensing for battle.

Good… good… stay relaxed.

Think about why you're here…

Sebastian let his eyes close and his head drop forward until his chin touched his chest. After a moment, he couldn't feel the cool night air on his scalp or the breeze rustle his shirt. Instead, he felt the press of ground against his body. Something heavy on his back… but that didn't matter. It was unimportant. He just had to relax…

And think about what he was doing here…

Returning to Bianca. She was as close as a clan head as he, Thomas, knew. She'd turned him just recently and taught him to tether a food source to him. Thomas wasn't so good at it just yet, he tended to get greedy, the blood lust too powerful for him to resist and he ended up draining every one he tried to tether, drank every last delicious drop of blood, the warmth flowing down his throat, staining his lips, dribbling down his chin to drip-drip onto his shirt, so messy, so wasteful as Bianca said, but he couldn't help it, always had to be drinking drinking drinking, smelling that warm, delicious odor that called to him over and over, even now as he relaxed on the ground, he could hear it calling calling calling from just through the trees, a whole large building full of warm blood sources that he could just go and drink forever, fill his mouth, his belly, tasting and smelling and swallowing and feeding…

Sebastian reared back, gasping in shock. The unrelenting blood thirst filled him with loathing and desire. He understood it in a way he so wished he didn't. How easy would it be to just swallow a few mouthfuls, then all his worries would be over. He just needed to stop fighting his true nature…

NO!

He pushed himself back, scrambling off the vampire and stumbling away until his back hit a tree. He leaned against it, shaking.

From the ground, the vampire raised itself up on its good arm. The left arm still hung useless at its side but already it was starting to flex the fingers.

"See how fast we heal? Minutes instead of days. You're so close to us. Just a little taste. Cross on over. You wouldn't be a freak anymore, not like you are among them. Among us, you would be a king, the beginning of the new order. You have touched the book and the book has touched you. You feel it awakening power within you. All you have to do is claim it. You will be the new god."

The vampire lunged.

Sebastian… *PUSHED!*

The force of the thought lashed out, surging forward like it had at that gunman in the shop just a few days before. It stopped the vampire's lunge. It's body and clothes rippled as if in a strong breeze, then fluttered back. The vampire landed on its back, arms stretched out. Its head lolled then stopped, eyes staring upward.

The strong, insistent telegraphed desire for blood that pressed against Sebastian's mind just…

stopped.

Sebastian fell to his knees as his legs buckled. The pain in his head washed over him, almost as strong as the fatigue that swept through his body. He tried to lift his head, tried to open his eyes because that vampire was going to get up again, any minute now.

But his eyes refused to open.
He fell forward onto the grass.
And relaxed.

<hr>

Sunlight warmed his face. He turned his head away from it, felt something rough against his cheek. The taste of dirt lingered in his mouth. He spat, smelled grass and vegetation.

His eyes cracked open.

Sunlight (too bright) poured in, forcing him to squint against it. His head pounded from it. God, he needed to remember to carry sunglasses all the time now.

His hands pushed against the ground, lifting him up, and it suddenly occurred to him to wonder what was he doing sleeping on the ground? Why was he lying here in the middle of the day?

Where the hell was here?

Then even through his squint he saw the pile of ash and clothes in front of him.

And the memories flooded back.

Even after Sebastian had fallen unconscious, Thomas hadn't attacked him. He had just lain there until the morning sunlight killed him.

(If that was what killed him.)

No, of course it had, what else killed a vampire that way? Certainly nothing else, certainly nothing that he could do.

Nothing like just a thought.

But it had been nighttime, just a short while after sundown. How could it be sunny now?

"You've been out of it for a while."

Charlie's voice came from his left. Sebastian looked over. Charlie leaned against a tree. He looked a little more faded now, Sebastian could see the trunk through his blond hair. He was back to wearing a black t-shirt and low slung jeans with a wide brown belt.

Sebastian pushed against the ground until he sat up. The dirt taste lingered in his mouth. He spit it out. His face felt flattened where it had rested on the ground. He hadn't stirred for hours. He rubbed his face and felt something crinkle above his lip. He pulled his fingers away to look.

Flaking redness.

Dried blood.

From a nose bleed.

Maybe it wasn't just the sun causing his head to ache.

He climbed to his feet, grabbing hold of the tree trunk behind him as a wave of dizziness swept over him. The image of the trees around him dimmed. His fingers tightened on the trunk. He focused on the rough bark that dug into his palms, scraped his skin. He felt himself waver, as if he was on water instead of land.

Steady, steady.

After a moment, the wavering motion faded. The brightness of the day returned, making him wince. Okay, at least he could stand now.

"What time is it?" he said.

"Do I look like I have a watch?" Charlie said. "I dunno, it's early."

"My flight," Sebastian said.

"I'd say you missed it. Unless you had a hell of a layover here."

"You're so helpful," Sebastian said. He pushed off from the tree and aimed for the direction of the airport. His feet dragged on the ground. He missed the pile of ash by an inch. He flinched and stumbled away from it.

"Something wrong?" Charlie said. "You killed him. Aren't you happy about that?"

"What's the matter with you?" Sebastian said.

"Funny. I'm asking you the same thing."

Sebastian shook his head. Oh, bad idea. The dizziness came again. He stopped and closed his eyes. He could feel his body wavering on his feet as if he were being buffeted by a strong wind. After a moment, the dizziness passed.

He opened his eyes.

"How can you say I killed him?" Sebastian said. "The sun burned him up."

"The sun burned his remains but he was already dead. You killed him with that mind thing you did."

"No way," Sebastian said. "I couldn't possibly."

Charlie crossed his arms over the black t-shirt. The tree trunk looked a little less distinct.

"Oh really? You were the one reading vampires in London, then you sent that one up to the roof and blasted that other guy in the shop. Seems whatever you got in your head is getting stronger, Sebastian." He shrugged. "Taking a toll as well, it seems."

"Don't be ridiculous." Sebastian started moving again, heading for the airport. There had to be another plane leaving soon. If not, he could take the train or rent a car. It was only a five hour drive home from here. He could do that.

What he couldn't do was think about what Charlie was saying.

Instead, he could think about what he'd learned from Thomas.

So Bianca had tried to set herself up as a clan head. That made sense, it was what she wanted all along. But this tethering, that was new. He didn't think vampires could do that.

Could they?

Obviously they could. Maybe they just hadn't bothered before but now with their social structure in tatters, a steady food supply would be very attractive. Also, without the clan heads to enforce their order, vampires could do whatever they wanted.

But why wouldn't clan heads want vampires to tether food sources to themselves?

He kicked at the asphalt as he reached the parking lot. Like last night, the lot was full with cars in neat rows. A heavy tinge of exhaust hung in the air, making him wrinkle his nose. Sunlight came at him from all sides, reflecting off windshields, chrome bumpers, polished painted fenders, side mirrors, and windows.

He put his hand up, trying to shield his eyes even as he closed them to slits. Didn't help much. Pain like lava poured into his eyes. His skull tightened. His shoulders hunched.

Only halfway through the parking lot. He had to keep going, aiming for the large white building to his right. Keep going.

Ignore the sun. Think of something else.

Vampires.

Why tether now? Why not before? Wouldn't a ready food source make the most sense? Hadn't the clan heads been planning to use the first vampire's book to convert massive numbers to vampires? Why wouldn't they want to ensure they could be fed?

The airport lay just ahead. The air shimmered in front of him. A low hum started then grew in intensity, finally sounding like an engine. Above the airport, he caught sight of a plane soaring into the brilliant blue sky. Going where? Somewhere south? Vacation maybe? People with no real cares in the world escaping like in all the ads he'd ever seen for island vacations. Sitting on beaches, drinking umbrella drinks.

Ads…

Discovery!

He stopped moving.

That was it. The vampires hadn't wanted to risk discovery, not until they were ready. So nothing to make regular humans suspicious. No tethering because that would cause people to act like Brent, kind of spacey, leaving his home for no reason. Maybe it could work occasionally, with people who were alone, but if it got too widespread, if too many people started disappearing, started acting strangely.

It would raise too many questions.

But now the vampires didn't have their social structure to guide them. Free for all.

Now they didn't necessarily think long term. Now it was about survival.

And when you backed a predator into a corner, fighting for its survival, it would lash out with everything it had.

Things like tethering humans and who knew what else?

Maybe stuff like what was going on in Rome and other places.

Had he been selfish to leave?

No, he had to look after his family, his parents, his little brother. But once he took care of Alexa, once he made sure they were safe, he'd return to Europe and help the In-Between.

He'd make it up to Jessica. Somehow.

If she ever spoke to him again.

But this tethering, this was new behavior and he should tell her about it, about his theory about how vampires were now fighting for survival and willing to do anything.

It wasn't just an excuse to call her. He owed her. He owed the In-Between.

He dug in his pockets. No cell phone. Where had he left it? In that ugly khaki bag he'd bought, along with the sweat shirt and whatever else he'd found in the airport to stuff into it to make it look like he at least had carry on baggage.

Wait a minute, where was the khaki bag?

He remembered having it in the airport, in the washroom, even when he followed Brent through the parking lot into the wooded area. Then?

Had he dropped it after fighting with Bianca?

Dammit, he had to go back.

He turned, wincing at the sunlight. It seemed to beat even worse than before. He remembered the first few days after being bitten. The confusion, the pain. He'd been sensitive ever since, even more than the other In-Between, but it was getting worse now.

He was getting worse.

What exactly was he getting?

Shut up, just shut up and get the damned phone.

Sweat trickled down his sides as he hurried back across the parking lot, ducking his head to avoid the worst of the glaring light. He was sweating because he was hot.

Not nervous.

Not scared.

Dammit.

Being under the trees brought a welcome shade that allowed him to open his eyes a little wider. He pushed through the underbrush, moving branches and leaves out of his way. It was just through here…

And he came face to face with the muzzle of a gun.

CHAPTER 10

A glove covered hand held up the strap of Sebastian's khaki bag. "Looking for this, mate?"

A dark, not unamused face, framed with a short graying afro gazed at him. The In-Between man wore a black pullover top and black jeans tucked in black ankle boots. He looked familiar but Sebastian couldn't remember his name.

"Friend of yours?" Charlie spoke from behind him.

Sebastian ignored him.

"That is my bag," he said to the man. "Are you going to use that?" He gestured to the pistol in the man's hands.

The man glanced at the gun as if surprised to see it in his hand. "Just making sure who you were," he said. "Can't be too careful these days. Not with the latest tricks the vampires are pulling."

He slipped the gun into the holster at his side and tugged his top down to cover it. Then he extended the strap toward Sebastian.

Sebastian took the bag and slipped it across his chest, onto his shoulder. He patted it, feeling the soft cushion of clothes and at the bottom, the hard, squareness of his cell phone.

"Looks like you've had a busy night, Sebastian," the man said. "I can see why you haven't made it to Grand Rapids yet."

"How do you know? Who are you?" Sebastian said. "You look familiar."

"We only worked together once," the man said. "I'm Gareth."

Now Sebastian remembered. Some little town in northern France. Gareth had been the lead In-Between for the mission. Even Nigel had deferred to him, although he'd grumbled about it.

And one other thing Sebastian remembered: Jessica had known Gareth well.

"Remembering, I see." Gareth nodded. "You pick up quick enough, despite what Nigel thinks. But that's Nigel for ya. That's his problem, trying to keep everything contained. That's his way of dealing with it."

"Dealing with it?" Sebastian said.

"With being In-Between. We all have our ways of dealing with it. Nigel tries to keep everything neat and organized. You go off on your own, doing your thing."

"How do you deal with it?"

A smile spread across Gareth's face. "Oh me? I research, try to learn everything I can. That's why she asked me to come along. She thinks you're losing it but I think you're gaining it. What it is, I don't know yet but I don't think you know either, do you?"

A chill tightened the muscles up and down Sebastian's back. He became acutely aware of how close Gareth stood, how his hand hung so casually by his gun. The man was at full strength while Sebastian was tired, head pounding from the sunlight, weakened by his *efforts*. Would he even get five steps away from the man?

Then he felt his brain click onto one of the other words Gareth had said: *she*.

Could that be...

Jessica?

After everything, after he'd run out, was she still trying to reach him? To help him? He was afraid to hope.

But Gareth said she thought Sebastian was losing it.

She was probably right.

"Research," Sebastian said. "Did you know about the book?"

Gareth nodded. "I never saw it but I knew Grellock had written something. There are origin legends about the vampires, how he made a pact with the Devil for eternal life in exchange for blood sacrifices."

"Yes. Yes, that's right," Sebastian said. His fingers tingled. He remembered holding the book. He remembered scratching across the pages, his hands not his own, learning the secrets of what Grellock had done.

"Still affects you, doesn't it?" Gareth said.

Sebastian shuddered. "No. I'm fine."

Gareth chuckled. "Right. As fine as an In-Between ever gets."

No judgment, not like Nigel who picked apart everything Sebastian did. Not like Jessica who worried. Gareth just looked amused.

"Well," Sebastian said. "Maybe not fine." He glanced over his shoulder. Charlie still stood there, arms crossed, a quizzical look on his face. He cocked his head.

"So?" Charlie said. "You gonna ask or just keep being a dick?"

"Fuck off," Sebastian said.

"Pardon?" Gareth said.

"Not you." Sebastian turned back. "Him." He cocked his thumb over his shoulder. "My old college roommate, Charlie. He's dead and a ghost."

Now the man would really think he was nuts. But the amused look returned to Gareth's lined face. He nodded.

"Ghost, right," he said. "Joan mentioned something about that. You talking to them now?"

This wasn't quite the reaction he was expecting. Where was the incredulity? Where was the denial? Then again, they were both In-Between, they both knew vampires were real. Were ghosts that big a leap?

"Just the one," Sebastian said.

"Tell him to come along then," Gareth said. "We got to head off. Don't want to keep her waiting. It's already taken me this long to catch up to you."

His feet rustled the grass as he stepped forward Sebastian. One hand lifted to grasp Sebastian's arm, turning him back toward the airport.

"Her?" Sebastian said.

That was as close as he could get to asking, as close as he'd let himself get. His chest tightened. His heart thudded. It felt almost painful, this horrible thing called hope.

"Jessica," Gareth said. "Who else?"

Gareth had a small Ford with blacked out windows. Sebastian got into the passenger's seat. The dim lighting eased the vice grip around his head. Gareth reached into the glove compartment and pulled out two pairs of sunglasses. He dumped one pair on Sebastian's lap before slipping the second pair onto his own face.

"Always be prepared," the man said. He grinned. "Tell your ghost friend I'm sorry about the cramped back seat. I didn't expect it'd be more than us."

Sebastian glanced into the back. Half of the back seat was taken up with packed boxes. Charlie sat with his legs stretched through them. He gave Sebastian a thumbs up.

"He's fine," Sebastian said.

"Then let's go."

Gareth swung the car out of the airport parking lot. A few more turns and they hit the highway, speeding northeast.

"Grand Rapids, right?" Gareth said. "That's where your folks are?"

"Yes," Sebastian said. "I was heading there."

"And got sidetracked," Gareth said. "Only way I caught up to you. Jessica took another route. We figured one of us would find you."

Sebastian wanted to ask but he couldn't. He hardly knew this man, he couldn't ask him about Jessica.

He turned his face to the black window and stared at the dull reflection of his face. With the sunglasses, he looked like an alien with huge bulbous eyes.

Maybe he was more alien than he liked to think.

He stared at that alien face, wondering how he was going to explain any of this to his parents until the hum of the car engine and the gentle rocking of movement lulled him to sleep.

"Hey! Wake up!"

Charlie's voice yelled in his ear. Dammit, was he late for class? How could Charlie be up before him? That wasn't possible. Didn't that defy some law of the universe? Charlie stayed up to all hours and Sebastian was the one with the early morning classes. That was the natural order of things. He had an eight-thirty economics class, one he never missed because he got to see Alexa. Alexa with brown hair in a pixie cut that framed her impish eyes and stylish glasses. And that soft, perfect mouth with pale peach lips so beautiful when she smiled…

and revealed her fangs.

Sebastian jolted up.

"'Bout time you woke up, man." Charlie hung his arm over the armrest of the car. "I've been yelling in your ear for practically ever."

Sebastian blinked sleep from his eyes. Dark. Everything looked so dark. Then he realized he still had sunglasses on his face. He yanked them off. They clattered from his hands, bouncing off the gear shifter before falling to the floor at his feet. Sebastian ducked down to grab them. His foot shifted, knocked the glasses. They disappeared under the seat.

Oh great.

"Will you forget the glasses?" Charlie said. "I can't believe you're still so uncoordinated." He shook his head. His blond hair shifted along his shoulders.

But Sebastian could still see the back seat through his head.

Charlie's dead ghost head.

No more college. No more Alexa. Not the Alexa he knew anyway. Sebastian turned back to face the front of the car. He brushed his hand over his forehead, wiping the sweat from his brow and pushing his black hair back over his head. Jesus, after a few years you'd think he'd get used to waking up to this nightmare.

Guess not.

The driver's seat sat empty. They were parked in a parking lot behind what looked like a strip mall. The sound of traffic filtered in through the window. Not too far from the highway then.

"Where's Gareth?" Sebastian said.

"I think he went to take a leak," Charlie said.

Sebastian stared out the window. Something about this stop looked familiar. The angle of the grey building, coated with dust from the highway. The buzz of traffic as it whipped along, curving toward the right just ahead. He could tell from the way the sunlight angled that the sun was just starting to go down.

They must have been driving for hours.

That's why he knew this rest stop. It was just outside Grand Rapids.

He spun toward the driver's side, groping along the steering column. Dammit, no keys! Where the hell was Gareth? They had to go, had to go *now!*

"Sebastian?" Charlie said. "What's up?"

"Where is he?" Sebastian said. "We have to go."

"I told you, I think he went... hey, where are you going?"

Sebastian shoved the passenger's door open and jumped out. The sunlight pounded at his head, making him wince. He shut the door and headed across the expanse of parking lot toward the rest stop building. In front, two sets of gas pumps sat empty. The parking lot held about twenty cars, not quite halfway full. Gravel skidded along under his feet as he walked. He took a deep breath, smelling the exhaust from the traffic and... something else. He paused, scenting the air. Was it? Yes, it was, water. The river and possibly the lake.

They must be closer to home even than he thought.

Dammit, where was Gareth?

"Dude, we should wait in the car," Charlie said. He appeared beside Sebastian. Now he wore his usual black t-shirt untucked over his ripped jeans.

"I'll find him," Sebastian said. He headed off again.

"Dude!"

Sebastian reached the set of glass double doors and yanked the right one open. He moved past a set of vending machines, including one of those square ones with the claw.

"Hey man, remember that one time at the fair?" Charlie said.

Sebastian did remember. The time the three of them went to the Ridgewater Fair and spent the evening on the midway, playing stupid games of chance, losing way too much money and eating way too many corn dogs. At the end of the night, Sebastian had tried in vain to grab a plush dog for Alexa from one of those vending machines but he couldn't get the claw to work fast enough. The grinding of the motor filled his memory punctuated by the sounds of Alexa laughing at his efforts. He could still hear it.

No, it was the set of kids standing at the machine to his left. A boy and girl, faces pressed up to the glass, pointing and laughing at the contents.

Gareth, he had to find Gareth. Don't get sidetracked. He had to get home.

He passed the kids and stepped into the food court area. It seemed like everyone from those twenty cars sat at those plastic tables with those plastic seats attached to them. Had every one of those twenty cars been filled to capacity? The room was filled with adults and kids of all ages, wearing all sorts of clothes in all colors. Reds and blues and browns and greens assaulted his eyes. The steady hum of conversation even drowned out the incessant buzz of the traffic outside.

The air seemed filled with the overriding stench of greasy food. He spotted French fries and hamburgers at most tables. If he took a deep enough breath he knew he'd smell the sourness of relish and the sharp tang of ketchup and mustard.

But all of it paled against the warm, inviting scent of blood.

He stopped in the doorway, feeling the air currents move around him. The chug of a ventilation shaft sounded about his head. He felt the movement of air rustle his hair across his forehead. It carried to him the smell of blood from all through the food court.

There in the corner, he could smell the sweetness of the blood of that little girl sitting with her mother. Not yet full of junk food, her blood would carry the sweet innocence of her, just like the way she tucked one ankle behind the other as she swung her legs while sitting in that plastic seat.

And there, against the window, that older couple had a tinge of bitterness in their blood, a product of too much smoking, Sebastian had ascertained over time. Still their blood would taste good. He could almost feel it on his tongue.

That one there, the young man sitting by himself, back to the counter as he stared intently at the worn book propped open on the table in front of him. Was he a student? He had that student look. Shabby jeans, plain t-shirt, hoodie with frayed cuffs. Despite his disheveled appearance,

Sebastian could tell from the smell of his blood that the young man had never gone hungry. In fact, probably only ate organic the majority of the time except for the occasional indulgence.

Like today.

Sebastian felt a temptation to indulge himself.

His foot slid along the grey tile floor, leading him into the food court area.

As he cleared the doorway, the left wall fell away, revealing more diners sitting at more plastic tables. The scent of their blood wafted forth. Sebastian breathed it in, turned his head to the left to survey them.

Against the far wall, he saw a family of three. Two parents and a boy. The mother with long dark hair sat with her back to the wall, facing Sebastian as she bent over the table, picking up a French fry. The father sat on her left, wearing a beige spring jacket, unzipped. He lifted a hamburger to his mouth. A drop of ketchup squeezed out of the end and dropped, splat, down onto the napkin on the man's lap.

Across from him, sat the boy. Maybe twelve or a little older, shaggy black hair that needed a trim, the boy stirred a French fry in a puddle of ketchup on the wax paper in front of him. Picking at his food. Long gangly arms and legs tucked around the table and chair as if the boy wasn't quite sure how to make his limbs fit in properly, as if he'd grown fast and he wasn't yet used to them. Sebastian remembered that feeling. Callum was just starting to get like that too. Last time he'd seen the boy, Callum had grown over an inch in the space of a few months.

Callum...

What the hell was he doing?

Sebastian spun away from the food court. The stench of greasy food flooded his nostrils, making him want to gag. He clutched the doorway and stumbled forward. Just ten feet across the entrance hallway, past the vending machines and he could be outside in the air. Away from the greasy stench.

Away from the call of blood.

A hand tightened on his elbow.

"What are you doing?" Gareth's voice hissed in his ear.

"I..." Sebastian shook his head. What the hell had he been doing? He couldn't remember, he just knew he had to get out. Had to.

"Come on." Gareth's grip steered him forward. Sebastian's feet fumbled along the floor, as if they'd forgotten how to walk. He staggered but Gareth's steady hand kept him upright. They moved past the vending machines, past the one with the claw. Sebastian caught a glimpse of two kids standing in front of the glass. They no longer looked at the trapped toys, they looked at him, staring as if he was a crazy person.

Closer to the truth than they knew.

Through the door now. The rush of air, filled with dust and car exhaust, brushed away the lingering stench of grease and blood. Sebastian inhaled, drawing it deep into his lungs. It washed away the overriding urge, leaving him sagging against a concrete barrier in front of the rest stop.

Gareth released him. He shoved a white bag in front of Sebastian's face.

"When was the last time you ate?" he said. "You know better than that. Eat this."

Sebastian took the bag and opened it. The paper crinkled in his fingers. The greasy food smell wafted out. A cheese burger and fries. His stomach tightened.

"Eat it," Gareth said. "Or I'll stuff it down your throat."

He stood in front of Sebastian with arms crossed against his chest. His top rode up a little on his waist, revealing a hint of the gun holstered there. Sebastian didn't feel any menace from the man but he did feel the determination.

Besides, he knew Gareth was right; he hadn't eaten any regular food in days. He'd left himself vulnerable to the call of blood.

His own damn fault.

How was he going to take care of Callum and his parents when he couldn't even take care of himself?

He pulled out the cheeseburger and took a bite. It felt like cardboard in his mouth. Bland, tasteless cardboard. His stomach clenched. He felt bile rising in his throat. His tongue wanted to push the food out of his mouth.

He forced himself to finish every last bite. Including all the French fries.

As he wadded up the bag and tossed it at the orange plastic garbage receptacle by the door, tension drained out of Gareth. He nodded at Sebastian.

"Good job. It's good to see you've got some sense when forced into it. We're almost there."

"I know," Sebastian said. "I recognize this area." He tilted his head at the man. "You stopped here to make sure I ate something."

"The way she said you took off I knew you probably hadn't eaten anything. I know how it gets when you skip for any length of time. I figured you didn't want to see your family like that."

"You figured right," Sebastian said. "Thanks."

Gareth nodded. "I've been at this a while. Lot longer than two years. Let's go."

He led the way back to the car. Sebastian followed. Each step brought coordination and strength. He could almost feel the food working in him. He'd forgotten how it helped.

He wouldn't forget again.

They climbed back into the car. Gareth backed out and headed back onto the highway. As they settled in with the traffic, Sebastian turned to him.

"How long have you been In-Between?" he said. "If you don't mind talking about it."

A flicker of a smile crossed Gareth's lips but he kept his gaze fixed on the road ahead. "A while. I was about fifteen when I was bit. My own stupid fault. Hanging out in the wrong area of town with the wrong kinda kids. Cutting through an alley to get home before my momma found out I'd been out 'til all hours. This vampire slid up behind me and before I knew it, chomp. I think he was probably trying for a full feeding but something interrupted him. All I knew is I woke up in the middle of that alley in the morning, feeling like hell, weak as a kitten with my head pounding from the sunlight. I thought my momma's anger was the worst thing I faced that day." He shook his head. "Didn't realize that would be the best thing I faced for a long time."

"How did you find out what happened to you?" Sebastian said. "How did you cope?"

"A couple days after, another In-Between found me. We can't smell each other, right? That's how you know someone's an In-Between. This older guy, early twenties. At first I thought he was a pervert or something but then he started telling me about my symptoms. He knew everything about what was going on, the sunlight sensitivity, the food problems. He explained it. Told me my life would never be the same. But he gave me a choice."

"A choice?"

"He said I didn't seem too bad. I might be able to adjust to it, maybe have a regular life of sorts. Or I could join him and help fight the vampires. Nobody had ever asked me to help with anything before in my life. I was just a punk kid. I couldn't see much future except for working night security somewhere, making minimum wage. I decided I wanted to do something better, something that was important. What's more important than stopping vampires?"

He glanced over at Sebastian. Sebastian shrugged.

"The In-Between took me to London and I ended up living with Corbin Remington. He got me into research. I'd never had much use for books and such in school, too busy causing trouble, but when I had a purpose, it made all the difference and I realized I was good at it. I could remember and cross reference things faster even than Corbin. Losing him was such a waste."

"That's how you knew about the book," Sebastian said.

Gareth nodded. "I'd heard of it, researched about it but never saw it. We knew Frank had information about it, heard it had been out on the west coast but I spent most of my time in England except for a few years in central Europe. That's where I was when the book showed up and everything went down."

He glanced back at Sebastian again just as he turned the wheel to the left.

Sebastian realized they were driving down a suburban street. When had they entered the city? How had he not noticed? He'd been so focused on Gareth's story. Now he stared out the windows at the houses passing. The last rays of sunlight splashed across the pale blue sky, darkening to night. He watched well manicured lawns with straight driveways leading to double car garages perched in front of large, two story houses, or ending in single car ports attached to single story bungalows. His family lived in an older subdivision, not filled with cookie cutter houses but with a range of different houses.

Sebastian had always liked that about the neighborhood. It felt more homey, more natural, than the same house repeated endlessly.

But something seemed wrong here.

He couldn't tell what it was. The houses looked the same, a few with newly painted walls or new siding. Lawns looked well cared for. A few gardens had different plants in them. Nothing that would cause this anxiety.

He was just anxious to be home. That was all. He was so close and in a few minutes, he'd be there. How would he explain himself to his parents? He hadn't even thought about it, had only been focused on getting to them, on protecting them.

Any possible explanation had dropped out of his head.

It didn't matter. He'd deal with it, as long as Charlie kept his mouth shut.

Sebastian glanced over his shoulder into the back seat. Charlie looked back, mostly solid in the fading light. Charlie's lips pressed tight together. He gave Sebastian a nod.

Okay, that wasn't the reaction Sebastian had been expecting. He thought Charlie might give him a rude gesture or something. But maybe death had mellowed his friend.

Yeah, he'd been so mellow so far.

Gareth reached the end of the street. A right turn here onto Meadow Vale Boulevard and just down the street a few blocks. Sebastian's hands tightened into fists in his lap. He was just nervous. That was all.

That was what he told himself.

He spotted the police caution tape before they were halfway down the block.

His hand grabbed the door handle and yanked up. The door buzzed but the lock stayed engaged.

"Sebastian, what are you doing?" Gareth said.

"My house," Sebastian said.

"Just wait, we're almost there."

Sebastian's hand kept tugging at the door handle. He stared down at it. It was like he couldn't control it. His hand had a mind of its own. It wanted the door open and was going to keep tugging until it did. How strange. Why did it want the door open so badly?

Gareth angled the car to the right, pulling up behind a dark minivan that had parked two houses down from Sebastian's parents' place. Minivans were pretty common in this neighborhood but not black ones with blacked out windows. As Gareth stopped the car, the back of the minivan swung open.

Jessica jumped out.

Sebastian tugged on the door.

She hurried to the passenger's side of the car. He watched how her ponytail swung from side to side along her back. Did it look longer than before? The last rays of the sun gave an almost golden highlight to her hair. How he longed to touch it, run his fingers through her hair. Bury his face in it and never look up again. Never look at that yellow tape…

His hand released the handle just as Jessica wrenched the door open.

"Sebastian," she said.

He folded himself out of the car. After hours on the highway and at the rest stop, the rush of air smelled sweet and clean. He could pick out the roses three houses down and the daisies across the street. The heady scent of fresh cut grass hung in the air, making him think of summer days and sitting in the backyard eating watermelon. His mother always made them sit outside because he and his brother ended up spitting the seeds at each other.

When was the last time he'd done that with Callum?

Years.

(Now maybe never again.)

What was that? Where had that come from? Bullshit, that was bullshit.

"Sebastian," Jessica said again.

The breeze rose up, bringing a stronger scent of roses, brushing several stray strands of Jessica's hair across her forehead. The yellow tape behind her snapped and rustled, almost as if calling for his attention. As if he didn't notice.

As if he didn't see it stretching across the front lawn of his parents' house.

The house floated forward. Or he was moving. He couldn't tell. He blinked and he was at the front door. A hand grabbed his arm, tugged at him.

"Sebastian, don't go in there."

Jessica's voice, right in his ear. He started to turn toward her. He had so much he wanted to say to her, to apologize, to ask for her help.

He stood in the living room.

Beige carpet. His mother's choice, although she hated how often she had to vacuum it. She complained whenever she had to do it but then enjoyed the smooth look of it afterward. The way it complimented the navy plush couch and arms chairs set in front of the bay window.

Dad's photos hung on the back wall, his portraits of autumn leaves and rusted tools. He'd always been able to take regular objects and make them beautiful, just by changing the angle or the light. They hung behind frameless glass on the white walls.

Both mom and dad would be upset about all that red...

Paint. It had to be paint. Vandals must have broken in. Splashed paint around. Dull reddish brown paint.

That smelled the same as dried blood.

Puddles on the beige carpet. His mother would be furious. He'd better get some cleaner, scrub it out before she got home. She'd think he did it.

She'd blame him.

His fault. All his fault.

A hand on his arm tightened, pulling him away.

"Sebastian, come on."

Jessica's voice. He turned to her. Worry on her face, crinkling around her eyes and mouth, creating lines that aged her. Lines that shouldn't be there. Worried for him.

His fault.

"Let's get out of here," she said.

But his parents. Callum.

The front lawn. Warm, familiar scent of cut grass filled his nostril, driving out the scent of paint

(blood)

that he'd breathed in in the house.

Where were his parents, his brother?

Jessica's hand on his arm tightened. "Sebastian."

"My parents," he said.

She shook her head.

They must not have been home, not there when the vandals broke in to splash the paint

(blood)

around the living room.

"They're gone," she said. "Do you hear me? Sebastian, they're dead."

No, that was ridiculous. He shook his head. She was wrong, they weren't dead. They hadn't been home when it had been vandalized. That was obvious. His parents would never have let that happen, never let vandals splash red paint

(blood)

around. They must have been out somewhere. Visiting someone, or shopping. They hadn't been home. They *hadn't*.

"Callum," he said.

Now Jessica shook her head. "I don't know. We didn't find anything. None of that... It wasn't him. We couldn't find any trace."

Callum hadn't been home. If Callum hadn't been home, neither had his parents. They wouldn't let him go out without them. Well, maybe to a friend's house... but no, they hadn't been there. They hadn't. It was paint.

It was *paint!*

All he had to do was find Callum, visit his friends, find him and Callum would know were their parents were. Easy. It would all be fixed easy. Then there wouldn't be any blame.

No fault.

It wouldn't be his fault.

"I'm sorry," he said.

He didn't know who he was talking to, it just seemed like it would be the right thing to say. The only thing he could ever say. The only thing he'd ever say again.

I'm sorry.

Sorry to Jessica, to his parents, to Charlie, to Alexa, to everyone, but most of all to Callum.

Callum.

Where are you, Callum?

Part Two: Soul

CHAPTER 11

The boy lay curled on his side on the dirty concrete floor. Alexa had wondered about the dirt when they first got here. Was it clay? Top soil? While the boy whimpered and curled himself into a ball, she sniffed at the dirt and rolled specks of it around in her fingers. Just garden variety dirt, she decided.

Should have been graveyard dirt. That would have been more fitting.

A crypt would have been even more fitting, or some decrepit, rotting mansion, but she had to settle for this abandoned factory in the south end of town. Some old furniture place, she could tell from the faint hint of furniture polish and sawdust that still seemed to linger about the place. She really thought she'd be out of town sooner but it had taken her longer to find the house and then once she was there... well, she just couldn't stop herself from indulging. She'd wanted to wait until Sebastian got there but it had been too tempting.

She had to give in.

Constantine had told her about waiting for the opportune moment, had promised to teach her about holding back her baser instincts, prolonging the joy.

But he was gone now. Everything was gone.

All that was left was retribution.

All that was left was the boy.

And oh, he'd tasted sweet.

She could still smell him from here, where she crouched against the wall beneath the stairs leading from the main floor to this basement. She'd locked and blocked the door so no one could wander down here. The boy didn't actually need to be down here. She hadn't turned him just yet. Wasn't even sure if she was going to.

She hadn't really thought that far ahead. Originally, she was going to kill them all. As her nails sliced open the woman's jugular, spraying blood across the living room wall and splashing across those bland, boring photographs on the wall, Alexa had really just thought of killing all of them, drinking herself sick and getting out. Even when the man jumped at her, howling and swinging a hammer toward her head, she snapped his neck with one twist of her hands, letting his body jerk and spasm before dumping it on the floor. She still planned to drink from him; his blood would still be delicious even if he was just dead.

Then she spotted the boy in the doorway.

The familiar shock of black hair swept across his forehead, sticking out from the back of his head. Similar wide blue eyes. The angle of his face almost the same, just a touch different, just a touch rounder, looking more like the mother than the father. Thin, like *he* was, but shorter, definitely shorter. Not fully grown to his height yet.

He never would if Alexa had anything to say about it.

And he smelled delicious.

Fear seeped from his pores. The sharp stench of urine pierced the air as he pissed himself. The flood of pheromones signaling shock and anxiety. As she dropped the man from her hands, letting the body flop to the floor, the boy shrieked. His voice echoed high off the ceiling, sharp and keening. Oh, how she wanted to kill him, wanted to swipe her hand across his face, slice open his neck with her claws and drink from the wellspring of blood that gushed out.

But he looked so much like *him*.

So much like Sebastian.

And she got a better idea.

Now he curled up in the dirt on the concrete floor in the basement. Whimpering. She could hear his whimpering in the darkness.

Just like he'd whimpered when she bit his neck for a first drink.

She took just a few swallows, just enough to allow his taste to permeate her, so she could call him from wherever she was. Not enough to turn him, not even enough to draw him to that horrid twilight in-between state. Just enough to bind him to her.

Enough to claim him.

And suddenly that seemed a more fitting retribution. Death was too quick. Too simple. She regretted killing his father so fast. But the mother... That still had possibilities even as her blood soaked into the carpet. Her body had still jerked a little as her heart pumped.

Alexa sent the boy to wait in the hall while she finished with the mother.

By then, it was only an hour or so til dawn. Not enough time to get out of town. Just enough time to find a hiding place for the day.

So here they were, in an abandoned furniture depot. She could hear rats scurrying in the walls. Smell their little ratty bodies. She'd eaten her share when there wasn't a human around. But now she had the boy.

She'd have to be careful though. He was still young, still small. It would be too easy to get carried away and drain him completely. That wouldn't do at all.

Not with what she had planned.

Oh, this might turn out to be better than she could have ever hoped.

The boy whimpered again. The plaintive sound echoed in the darkness, making her smile.

Oh yes, this was going to turn just about perfect.

She smiled as she breathed in the scent of the boy's blood.

Maybe just one more taste. She wasn't really hungry but she wanted to be sure he was bound to her.

After all, it suited her plans nicely.

When her hand closed around his upper arm, the boy cried out and started to cry. Poor thing. Too bad his brother had ruined everything for her.

Payback was a bitch, and so was she.

She sank her fangs into the boy's arm and drank until his cries diminished into whimpers.

Ah yes, nothing like fresh blood.

She could get used to this.

CHAPTER 12

Sebastian stood at the back of the black van, standing in the shade from a large tree at the end of the gas station parking lot. He didn't quite remember driving here. Hands had pushed him into the van. Her hands. Jessica holding onto his arm as they drove away even as he tried to reach for the door to get out.

Callum, he had to find Callum.

"We'll find him," Jessica said. She kept saying it, as if answering him.

Had he actually spoken out loud?

The heady scent of gasoline brought him back to the gas station. The white and red brick convenience store sat off to his left, behind the set of four gas pumps. The pumps cast long shadows across the grey asphalt, as if reaching for the store. Already mid afternoon. How long had they been at the house? It felt like moments. It felt like years.

Gareth and one of the other In-Between, a man Sebastian didn't know, had gone into the convenience store a few moments ago.

Jessica stood a few feet away, arms folded across her chest. A light breeze teased at the loose strands of hair and fluttered them across her forehead. He wanted to brush them back into her pony tail. But he didn't move.

He didn't have the right to touch her anymore.

His fault.

Everything was his fault.

And it would stay that way until he did something. He had to do *something*.

He pushed away from the van. His legs shook. He weaved as if he were drunk. But all he had to do was start moving, just get moving.

He took a step, then another.

"Sebastian, where are you going?"

Jessica hurried over. Her hand on his arm stopped him short. He didn't have the strength to pull away.

"I have to," he said. "I have to go. I have to do something."

"Do what?" she said. "You can't just run off with no idea. Dammit, Sebastian, for once let me help you."

Angry, of course she was angry. He deserved her anger. Deserved whatever she dealt out to him.

But Callum couldn't wait.

"Callum," he said.

"I know," she said. "We're already looking for him. Joan is tracking down his friends. We're checking the hospitals and the morgue. Give us a little time."

He blinked at her. They had already started doing that?

"When?" he said.

"As soon as we found your house in that state," she said. Her hand tightened on his arm. "It's not the first time an In-Between's family has been targeted."

Targeted. That's what Alexa had done. Targeted his family. If only he'd gotten here sooner.

"You couldn't have stopped this, Sebastian," Jessica said.

He shook his head. "How do you know?"

Her lips thinned. "She would have just waited until you were gone, or until you let your guard down. Once a vampire decides to do this, the only way to stop it is to kill them."

"I would have," he said. "I will."

"Sebastian, I'm so sorry," she said.

She was sorry? What did she have to be sorry about? She'd done everything for him, always been supportive and he'd disappointed her. He shook his head.

Her hand touched his face. Her skin felt smooth and cool against his cheek. He wished he could smell her but all he could smell was a trace of soap and the overriding stench of gasoline.

She released his arm and pulled him closer, wrapping her arms around him. He brought his hands up to her back but hesitated to touch her. It still felt wrong, like he didn't deserve it, didn't deserve her, not when he'd screwed everything up.

Everything.

"Stop being an idiot." Charlie's voice sounded from behind him. "Hug the girl back."

He wanted to. His hands moved of their own volition, pressing against the muscles of her back, familiar contours smoothed and curved under his fingers.

He missed this more than he wanted to admit.

She pulled back, keeping her hands on his shoulders. "We'll find him, Sebastian. I promise."

"Go on, kiss her," Charlie said. He stood just over Jessica's shoulder, making shooing motions with his hands. His blond hair looked thin and anemic in the sun.

"Shut up," Sebastian said.

"What?" Jessica said.

"Not you," he said. "Ah." He glanced back over her shoulder. Jessica turned her head, following his gaze.

"What?" she said.

"Nothing. It's nothing."

She turned back to him. "It's not nothing. It's something and that something is Charlie, right?"

She let go of his shoulders. She got that challenging look in her eye, the one that said he'd better tell her the truth if he knew what was good for him.

He'd ignored that look before. He wouldn't do that again.

He didn't want to.

Truth.

"Yeah, it's Charlie," he said.

Her brows grew together in uncertainty. She glanced back over her shoulder again. "What did he say?"

Charlie grinned. "Tell her. I dare ya."

"Will you shut up?" Sebastian said. "It's not important."

"Not important? You have a ghost talking to you. I'd say that's important," she said.

"See?" Charlie said. "She thinks I'm important."

Sebastian pursed his lips. *That's because she doesn't know you that well.*

"What is he saying?" Jessica said.

"It really isn't that important," Sebastian said.

She folded her arms across her chest. "Let me be the judge of that. Now spill it."

"Spill it," Charlie said. He nodded enthusiastically. A grin spread across his face.

Sebastian sighed. "Fine. He said I should kiss you."

Her mouth dropped open. "What?"

"I told you it wasn't important."

"You don't think I'm important?"

"I didn't say that," Sebastian said. Over her shoulder, he saw Charlie start shaking his head, one hand to his forehead.

"I just didn't think you would want me to," Sebastian said.

"Oh? Maybe because you don't talk to me? You don't tell me when a ghost appears or when something starts going wrong? Maybe if I was all that important you'd actually talk to me," she said.

One of her feet moved back, angling her body toward the store.

Away from him.

Dammit. He'd screwed up again. Or was in the process of it. He had to stop it.

"You've been through so much," he said. "I didn't want to drag you through more."

"So you didn't even ask?"

"It seemed crazy," he said. "And there was no time. I had to get home." His head turned toward the road, back the way they'd driven to get here. "But I was too late. I'm always too late."

"Maybe if you didn't try to do everything yourself," she said. "And Charlie was right about one thing. You should have kissed me."

Approaching voices made her turn her head. Gareth and the other man, Brian, were returning, carrying plastic bags. Gareth held a cell phone to his ear.

"Right, give me the address," he said into the phone. "We'll be there right away."

He lowered the phone and slipped it into his pocket.

"Joan," he said to Jessica. "She's at the morgue."

Sebastian felt all his breath leave his body. His stomach concaved inward. He hunched over.

"Your brother's not there," Gareth said. "Sorry, I didn't mean to imply he was. But Joan got records of the attack. I thought we should check it out. Might be some clues there."

Jessica nodded. "Good idea. Let's go." She turned to him. "Sebastian?"

"Yeah, let's go."

He straightened, aware that even though her hand had reached out to him, she hadn't in fact touched him again.

"Man, you are hopeless," Charlie said. "It's a wonder you ever got laid."

Shut up!

Brian steered the van down the narrow alley to the back of the morgue. A squat two story red brick building, it hunched over a narrow sidewalk in front with the alley leading around to the back parking lot.

Shadows thickened as the afternoon waned. Sebastian noticed them overlap each other, like thin slices of darkness, gradually building up to full dark. His parents had always told him there was nothing in the dark that wasn't there in the light.

They'd been wrong on so many levels.

Brian pulled into a parking spot a ways from the door. As the engine ticked off, the back door opened and Joan appeared. She wore a grey business suit, slim pencil skirt falling just below her knees. Black pumps on her feet. Her single button jacket buttoned over a white shirt.

She looked like someone who might work there.

Was that how they did it? Certainly Joan would be better at Influencing than the others, maybe even better than him.

But then again, thinking of Thomas the vampire, maybe not.

Of course, she probably hadn't killed anyone with her Influencing.

She gave a sharp wave of her hand. They opened the doors and piled out. They all wore some variation of dark pants and black shirt, just different enough that they didn't look completely in uniform but close enough. As he followed Brian up the stairs to the door, Sebastian noticed the man wore cowboy boots.

Like Brent.

God.

Another ghost, this one haunting him in his head.

He followed them into the building.

Joan faced them in a beige corridor. Black and white tiles trailed off in both directions. Dingy industrial paint covered the walls. In the distance, Sebastian heard people moving, talking, not loud enough to understand but loud enough for him to realize they were quite some distance away.

His weird In-Between senses again.

Would he ever get used to it?

"I found your parents," Joan said to him. "They're still in the main autopsy room but are scheduled to be released to the funeral home tomorrow. I am so sorry, Sebastian. It isn't fair."

None of it was fair. Nothing would ever be fair again.

He nodded at her. "Thanks."

"I thought you would like a chance to say goodbye."

"But, what about the funeral?" he said.

He could feel something ripple through them. Quick glances flittered back and forth. Joan took a breath.

"It probably isn't a good idea for you to go to the funeral," she said. "There's still an investigation going on. The police will want to question you, delay you. Any delay could be critical for your brother."

He nodded. Of course. He didn't have time to grieve for the dead. He had to worry about the living, about Callum. His grief wouldn't do anything for his parents anyway. It was useless, worse than useless. He could feel himself wanting to cave in, curl up into a ball on the floor.

Useless.

Think of Callum.

His parents would want him to take care of his little brother. The thought steadied him, slowed the pounding of his heart. He took a breath in, felt it rush down his throat.

"Right, okay," he said. "I'll say goodbye now."

Maybe later he could visit their graves.

Later.

Another lifetime.

Joan stepped back and turned to lead him down the hall. Her black pumps made clicking noises on the tile as she walked. He followed, feeling the others fall into place behind him. Jessica, Gareth, Brian. They moved like shadows down the hall. He could hear the soft hiss of their shoes on the floor, but no scent. Not like the other people in the building.

Nor the subtle scent of decay that grew as they approached the morgue.

Joan led them into a windowless office with beige walls and pale grey carpeting. A desk faced the door, a computer screen angled toward the empty chair. Papers spread across the desk blotter. A half finished cup of coffee sat on a warmer to the left of the screen. The chair turned just to the right, as if someone had just turned it to get up and walk out of the office.

Sebastian looked at Joan. She smiled.

Impressive. He'd only been able to Influence anyone within eye line. Joan was obviously even better than him at it.

She stepped across the room to the closed door at the other end. She beckoned Sebastian forward. He moved, feeling the thin carpet under his feet. As he passed the desk, he caught a faint hint of perfume and the warmth still emanating from the chair. He could imagine the woman sitting at the desk just a few moments ago, bent over her papers, over her keyboard, maybe taking a sip of coffee before something compelled her to get up from behind her chair and leave the office. Good thing. He didn't know what he would do if someone with warm, fresh blood stood in front of him.

Joan touched his arm as he drew up beside her. Her other hand closed on the door knob.

"You'll only have a couple of minutes," she said, her voice pitched low for his ears only. "I'm sorry it couldn't be longer but I can't hold them all away for long."

He nodded, not trusting his voice. There didn't seem to be anything to say anyway. She gave him a brief smile and opened the door.

He stepped into the main autopsy room. Steel seemed to gleam at him from every surface, the doors lining one wall in three rows, the three gurneys that sat in a line down the center of the room, the metal trays filled with instruments. Everything steel and shining. The glare pounding at his head almost as bad as sunlight.

But it wasn't the pain of sunlight that made his head ache.

He closed the door behind him and moved into the room. The sour scent of decay hung like a fog in the room. He could feel it cling to his clothes and his skin, coating the insides of his nostrils. His stomach clenched. He pressed his nostrils shut but that forced him to breathe through his mouth.

Did he really want that taste in his mouth?

Out. He wanted out of this room of death. But… his parents were here. David and Sarah Lockhart, parents of Sebastian and Callum. When had he last seen them?

Christmas break, just a few short months before it happened, before he went from being a normal college student to being an In-Between. He remembered his mother fussing over his old winter coat, complaining it was losing its down and wouldn't keep him warm. His father sitting in the armchair in the family room, snapping his paper the way he did whenever his mother was annoying, before reminding her about the stuffing, which sent her careening into the kitchen.

Other memories: his father sitting at the kitchen table with Callum, helping him with his math homework. His mother standing in the front hall, sorting the mail. She wore heels even in the house. Had always looked polished and lovely. His father would sometimes steal up behind her and kiss the back of her neck when she wasn't looking. It always made her jump, then her laughter would trickle out. He remembered hearing that all over the house.

The shining steel blurred in front of him. He blinked back tears.

Goodbye. He had to say goodbye.

He didn't even know which drawer they were in. The thought of opening them all up and having to look horrified him. He couldn't do it.

His feet carried him forward across the tile to the first set of doors. Then he noticed small cards tucked into the front with names written on in pen. Oh thank god. He wouldn't have to guess.

He found them four sets over, side by side in the middle row. It seemed fitting they should be beside each other. His hand tightened on the handle of his father's drawer but he didn't pull. Did he really want to see him? Did he really want this image of his father to be the last thing he remembered? But to not look felt almost like a betrayal. He hadn't even warned them. He'd been too worried of how to tell them, of what to say. He thought he'd make it in time. His own stupid arrogance.

The least he could do was say a proper goodbye.

He yanked on the drawer.

It resisted a moment then slid forward, gaining momentum until it was almost halfway out before it slowed to a stop. The body lay on the metal base, a plain white sheet draped over him. Eyes closed as if asleep. A slight stubble of beard dotting his cheeks. Black hair, liberally laced with grey, lay across his forehead. For a moment, Sebastian held his breath, waiting to see the rise and fall of the sheet across his father's chest.

But there was nothing.

Of course there wasn't. He was dead.

Standing on his father's right, Sebastian saw the way his father's neck bulged to one side. *She'd* done this, snapped his neck. Had she stopped for a taste?

He pushed the thought out of his mind. No, he couldn't face that. Wouldn't let it take root and fester in him.

Just say goodbye.

He laid a hand on his father's forehead. The skin felt cool, almost waxy. The hint of decay teased at his nostrils. Not even a hint of his father's aftershave, mingled with the scent of his father's skin. It was as if death had seeped away all vestiges of his life, leaving a fake dummy behind. A husk in the shape of his father but the spark, the life, the energy that was him was gone.

"I'm so sorry, dad." Sebastian's voice even in a whisper seemed to boom through the room. He leaned closer to speak only to his father.

"I should have warned you. I should have told you what was going on but I didn't want it to touch you. I didn't want you to worry. I didn't want you to know about this horror show. This is my fault but I promise I'll find Callum and take care of him. He'll be okay. I promise."

His father's image blurred. He didn't bother to swipe at the tears. They dribbled down his face and fell, soaking into his father's sheet.

"I love you, dad. I'm sorry."

He leaned over and kissed his father on the cheek.

The drawer rumbled as he pushed it back into place. The door clicked shut.

Now his mother.

God.

His shoulders hitched up toward his ears as he turned to the next drawer. "Lockhart, Sarah" read the tag on the door. His hand shook a little as he reached for the handle.

Fast. Just do it fast. Get it over with and get the hell out.

They would have understood.

He still had to find Callum.

So get it done.

He took a deep breath and pulled on the drawer.

It slid out like the first one, the metal wheels grinding loud in the silence of the room. It stopped with a shudder that shifted her body on the drawer. Sebastian shivered.

His mother lay on the slab, another plain white sheet covering her body. Did they get them at a volume discount here? Cut to a certain size to fit in the drawers? He felt a crazed giggle try to rise in his throat. He pushed it down.

He wasn't going to go there.

He'd never stop and that laughter would turn to screaming.

Say goodbye.

Her skin looked a little less sallow than his father's, more pale than grey. Her chocolate brown hair, coming more from a bottle these days, tumbled around her shoulders. She normally wore it pulled back from her face, clipped up on her head or at the back of her neck. He'd only ever seen it loose like this in the mornings, after she first got up to make them breakfast. She'd wear her worn, pink, flannel bathrobe, matching slippers on her feet making a shushing sound as she shuffled around the kitchen. Her loose, brown hair would flop across her forehead and bob around her shoulders.

And every time she put something down in front of them, a plate, a napkin, a glass of juice, she'd plant a kiss on top of their heads, and Sebastian always felt the soft brush of her hair against his cheek as she turned away.

Seeing her hair loose like this made it seem even more like she was asleep. Even more so than his father. Any minute now she'd open her eyes and yawn.

If only.

But she wasn't asleep. She was dead. She'd never open her eyes again. She'd never smile at him again or nag him to wash his face or finish his dinner. This was just a husk, like his father. Nothing alive here. Nothing...

But the movement of the sheet, up and down.

No, it was just a trick of the light. Just his imagination. He shook his head. He hadn't seen it move. She was dead. He could smell the decay. That sour, fetid odor.

Sour...

No, it wasn't.

He reached up to touch her face. His right hand was shaking. Why was it shaking? Why would it do that? He stared at it, trying to reason with it, tell it to stop shaking. There was nothing to shake about. Just touch her face, cup her chin and turn her head.

Turn her head so he could see…

His hand still shook even as he touched the cool smoothness of her chin, moving her head toward him. He bent over to peer around her head. Her hair, loose and tumbling, shifted, created shadows.

He would have to push it aside.

Even his left hand trembled as he lifted it.

Why?

A sudden burst of sourness made him gag. He coughed, hunching over. Noticed her face. Her eyes.

Her open eyes.

He jumped back as his mother snapped at him, lunging half off the slab. His feet slipped on the smooth tile, sending him crashing to the floor. Pain erupted from his palms where his hands slapped the hard surface. His feet dug for purchase, trying to push him backwards as on the slab, his mother sat up.

The white sheet pooled in her lap, leaving her bare-chested. She shifted her body toward him and he caught sight of the puckered Y incision that cut across her chest and down to her abdomen. Her thin lips pulled back, revealing the over-developed incisors of a vampire.

She growled.

He shook his head. No, this couldn't be happening. It couldn't be real. Wasn't his life enough of a nightmare?

No, please, not her.

Her eyes narrowed at him. Her hand gripped the edge of the slab as she swung her legs over the side. She dropped to the floor, wrapping the sheet around herself like a toga.

"Sebastian," she said. Her voice hissed out of her as if she wasn't used to talking with larger teeth in her mouth.

His back hit the wall. His bruised palms pressed against it, helped him scrabble up to his feet. He leaned against the wall, uncertain if his shaking legs would hold him.

"Mom," he said.

She turned her head to survey the room. Her blinks were slow.

"Your father? Where's David?"

Tear blurred Sebastian's vision. He blinked them away. Dammit, he couldn't cry now. Not with a vampire in front of him. She was a vampire. He had to remember that.

Not think about who she was.

"He's dead," he said. "Like you're supposed to be."

Her face turned back to him. "I'm not dead."

"You're undead," he said. "You're a vampire. You know that, don't you?"

Her mouth tried to smile but it came out a grimace. "Don't be ridiculous. I'm not dead." She spread her arms toward him.

Her grimace widened. The sickly sour smell thickened.

Oh god.

She darted forward, faster than he could have thought. He dodged, but her hand caught his arm, hand tightening in a lethal grip. She wrenched him back. His head hit the wall. Then her other hand came up, grabbing his head, turning it to the side.

Exposing his neck.

"No! Mom, no!"

Her dark hair moved like a curtain. Her sourness enveloped him as she stepped closer. He felt her moist, fetid breath on his skin. He struggled but her grip was tight and he was pinned to the wall.

Pain lanced through his neck.

He screamed.

She gagged and pushed away. Her body spiraled across the room until she grabbed hold of the slab.

Sebastian fell to his knees, holding his neck, feeling the blood pulse through his fingers and run down his t-shirt.

His blood smeared the bottom of her chin. She swiped at it with the back of her hand and spit.

"Poison. You're poison."

"I'm In-Between," he said.

She snarled. She started to back away toward the door.

"There's more of us out there," he said. "You aren't going anywhere."

He could feel the blood at his neck thickening, the trickle slowing. He pushed himself back up to his feet.

"I'm sorry, Mom. I couldn't stop this from happening to you but you aren't leaving this room as a vampire."

Her hands tightened into fists.

"You can't stop me," she said.

"Yes," he said. "Yes, I can."

She spun away, heading for the door.

No, he couldn't let her leave, couldn't let her out into the world like this. Not like this.

He *pushed*.

She stopped a foot from the door. Her body shuddered, rippling, trying to reach. He could feel her leaning toward the door, focusing on escape. No, come back. Step back.

Her foot moved. Slid. Backward.

One step. Then another.

Stay in the room, lie down on the slab.

He focused, hard, drawing her back. He felt her fight him all the way, with every sliding step. Once, she almost broke free, managed to reach her hand out to the door knob before he pulled her back.

Pain laced up his head and down his neck. The iron stench of blood filled his nose and he knew his nose was bleeding again. All he had to do was relax but he couldn't, couldn't let her go.

Stay, mother.

At the word, her face turned toward him. Her hair shifted on her forehead, revealing her eyes.

Her eyes.

She was still in there! He could feel the spark of her deep inside, buried under the oozing weight of darkness, shriveling against the horror of being a vampire. Inside, a part of her that was still *her,* still *Sarah Lockhart,* existed inside.

And he could almost touch it.

"Mom?"

Was that his voice? He sounded like a little kid again. Her lips twisted. Her eyes crinkled at the corners the way they always did when she smiled.

And he felt that spark of her even stronger. Calling out to him.

Begging him.

Free me!

And beneath that, another message calling out to him, piercing his soul.

Save Callum!

The emotional longing buffeted him. He staggered back, bumping against the wall. His head throbbed, pain arcing down his shoulders. The vampire in front of him hissed, tried to take another step toward the door.

But it was a vampire. *Not* his mother. It just wore her face.

And the small part of her left inside wanted to be free.

His vision blurred as tears formed and ran down his cheeks.

I'll free you, Mom. I'll free you and save Callum. I promise.

There was only one way to do it.

He *PUSHED.*

The vampire shrieked as his thought lashed out at her. Searing pain roared through him, drowning out the spark of his mother. He cried out, grasping for her, but the wave was too strong, too powerful. She disappeared beneath it. It crashed through the vampire and rebounded on him.

Falling. The room spun. Tile, walls, shining steel, whirled in front of his face. Shrieking filled his ears. Pain screamed in the nerve endings up and down his body. He felt his limbs jerk on the floor. Iron smell filled his nostrils. Red cloaked his vision. Red, all red.

All blood.

Until, finally, darkness.

CHAPTER 13

oldness on his cheek. Wetness on his lips. Fuzzy light with shifting shadows that slowly solidified into faces peering down at him. The stipple ceiling tiles glinted above them, making him wince.

"Sebastian, can you hear me?" Jessica said. Her pony tail flopped over her shoulder, the edges of it hung only a few inches from his cheek. If he lifted his head, he would feel the softness against his skin.

He didn't know if he would be able to move his head ever again.

"Can you sit up, mate?" Gareth appeared on his left. He felt hands grab his shoulders and start to lift him.

Pain erupted in his forehead and poured down his neck. He hissed at the suddenness of it. His whole body seemed to vibrate with it. He clenched his teeth, trying to breathe through it. Just breathe.

After a moment, it subsided to a searing pain that pierced his temples and spread across his shoulders. Funny how something he would have considered agony before was now mild.

Hands steadied him. He was standing now. He winced at the gleaming steel around him. Still in the autopsy room then. As he blinked his vision cleared. Gareth stood on his left with Jessica on his right. He couldn't see Brian and didn't want to turn his head to try.

"What happened?" Jessica said. "That woman. Is she…?"

Her voice trailed off. She turned her head to the right, moving back a few inches so he could see.

His mother's body lay on the floor, her legs tangled in the sheet, arms outstretched. Her mouth gaped open. Her eyes stared sightless up at the ceiling.

Dead.

"She was a vampire," he said.

"Vampire," Gareth said. He frowned. "But she's dead."

Shoes hissed against the tiles and Brian crossed out from behind them. He approached the body slowly, holding a wooden stake at the ready. He crouched beside her and searched for a pulse. Finally he pressed his head to her chest. After a moment, he looked back them and shook his head.

"Nothing. She's dead."

"She couldn't be a vampire," Gareth said. "I know you've been under a lot of stress, Sebastian…"

"Was she?" Jessica said. "Was she really?"

Sebastian nodded, then winced as the pain sharpened. "Yes, she was."

He had to stop doing that.

Jessica's lips thinned. "Did you… did you do this?"

His head wanted to nod again but he stopped it. He could feel Brian staring at him, brows drawn down in disbelief. Behind Jessica, Gareth frowned.

So should he deny it? Push her away for good? Would she even believe him?

He had to take the chance.

He had to try to ask for help.

"I did it," he said. "I don't know how. But sometimes I just seem to be able to *push* them."

Gareth shook his head. Brian gave a disbelieving grunt as he stood up.

Jessica nodded. The lines in her face deepened as she frowned.

"I believe him."

"Are you kidding?" Brian said. "You can't kill a vampire with your mind."

"*You* can't," she said. "I've seen him do things and he had that book. Grellock's book. It affected him. We don't know what that would do to any of us but it affected him. Sebastian's always been farther along than us. Who knows what that means?"

Uncertainty crossed Brian's face. He opened his mouth to respond but the click of the door behind them interrupted him.

"Time to go." Joan's voice called.

He couldn't walk very well so Gareth supported him down the hall and the door. As the door swung open, Sebastian noticed the darkness of twilight's end.

That was why the vampire could wake up.

Night.

Alexa would be waking.

With Callum.

Where are you?

He had to find them. He'd promised her.

How the hell was he going to do that?

As they hurried across the parking lot to the black van, every step on the asphalt caused shooting pain that reverberated to the top of his head. Gareth still had a steadying hand on his arm. How was Sebastian supposed to find his brother when he could barely walk?

He remembered Charlie's frown and crossed arms as he admonished Sebastian for not asking for help.

Before it was just him, and his stupidity only affected himself, but now he had to think about Callum. He couldn't be stupid now.

Jessica stood in front of him, her hand wrapped around the handle of the van's back door. He heard the click as she unlocked it and tugged the door open. The overhead light winked on, yellowish light illuminating the back. Grey industrial carpeting on the floor. Benches along either side. Weapons racks lined the sides, filled with guns, knives, swords, and polished, wooden stakes.

Everything the well equipped vampire hunter needed.

Except for one thing.

"I have to find Callum," he said. "Will you help me, Jessica? Please?"

She turned to stare at him. Her eyes widened. She blinked. He thought he saw tears in her eyes.

"Of course I'll help you, Sebastian."

She held out her hand to him.

He reached out to take it.

They huddled in the back of the van. With the door closed, Sebastian saw the crosses carved into the doors and along the sides of the van. He threw a questioning look to Jessica. He thought crosses didn't work. She shrugged.

Any little bit, he guessed.

Gareth spread out a paper map across his knees. He sat across from Jessica, with Brian on his right. Sebastian sat across from Brian. Joan huddled beside Jessica, her knees pressed together as the skirt rode halfway up her thigh. She looked like she should be attending some boardroom meeting somewhere, not huddling in the back of the van with the rest of them. She glanced up at Sebastian and winked at him, as if she knew what he was thinking.

She probably did.

"Your father's car is missing," Gareth said. "We have to assume Alexa took it. From what we can gather from the police reports, the attack happened close to midnight. Looks like she spent some time there so assume she had four to five hours lead time to get away. If it was just her she'd be long gone but she had your brother with her. Controlling a human always takes more time and energy for a vampire. Slows them down considerably. That gives us a better chance of finding them."

He nodded to Brian. Brian lifted his hand, tracing a thick index finger in a rough circle in the map.

"We figure this is the perimeter of our search. Obviously we don't have to worry about the river itself but I think the area along the river might be a good place to start. Especially the industrial area."

Gareth nodded. "I agree. She needs a place to stay for the day, some place she won't be disturbed. Industrial locations, warehouses are standard choices for vampires."

"If she burrowed in deep enough, no one would find her," Jessica said.

"We can't ignore other possibilities," Joan said. "She probably knows we'll be looking for her or at least that Sebastian will be. She could have found some other place to hide. We need to split up to cover more ground."

Gareth's lips thinned. Even Brian didn't look happy with the suggestion.

Beside Sebastian, Jessica sighed. "She's right. We'll cover more ground in two groups."

"Brian and I will hit the industrial district, moving in a sweep this way," Joan said. Her hand passed over the map. "You three look here." She traced a semi circle over the lines of streets. "Sebastian, you know your brother. You should be able to pick up his scent. The rest of us can scent for vampire. It's not the best way to search but it is the fastest. We check in on the hour every hour with progress reports. I've got my mobile and Gareth has his."

He nodded. His hand dug into his pants and he fished out his keys. He passed them to Joan.

"Take my car. We'll take the van."

"Let's get started," Joan said.

Gareth folded the map as Joan opened the door. Cool night air drifted in, carrying the smell of cut grass and moist humid air. Sebastian felt instantly homesick. He knew all the smells of this city, the tang of the river, the muskiness of the trees, the sharp stench of the cars. It all brought up so many memories but he didn't have time for them.

This city wasn't home any more for him, it was just another place infested with vampires. Another place he had to hunt them.

Stop thinking of it as home. It would make it easier.

He climbed out of the back. The overhead lamps in the parking lot cast yellowish light across the lot, giving everyone an odd tinge to their skin. Funny, the only one it wouldn't affect would be Charlie.

Wait a minute, where was Charlie?

Sebastian looked around. The ghost wasn't anywhere. Now that he thought about it, he hadn't seen Charlie for a while, not since he'd gone into the morgue. Was he gone? Had he done what he had to do?

But what was that?

It couldn't have been talking to Stan, Charlie had still hung around after that.

But he'd been disappearing, Sebastian realized. This wasn't the first time. The other times were only for a moment, maybe a few minutes.

This was the first time it had been this long.

Why did it bother him? Would he rather be haunted?

When he turned back, he noticed Joan watching him.

"Is something wrong?" she said.

He hesitated. All of them turned to look at him. He could feel the weight of their gazes. Jessica cocked her head. Her hair shifted on her shoulder.

He'd asked for help. Was he going to back away from that?

"Charlie's not here," he said.

"Your ghost friend?" Gareth said.

Jessica stiffened. Her lips thinned as she pressed them together. Even under the yellowish tinge of light, Sebastian could see the color drain from her cheeks.

"Where did he go?" Joan said.

"I don't know," Sebastian said. "He was at the house and the gas station but he wasn't at the morgue." He nodded to Joan. "Can you sense him?"

She closed her eyes. He could almost feel her questing. He felt something like a tickle in his mind then it moved on. A frown grew on her face. She opened her eyes.

"I don't feel him. Nothing at all."

"Isn't that a good thing?" Jessica said. "I'm not sure how fond I am of having a ghost around."

"But there's a reason he's here," Joan said. "And that reason has to be fulfilled. Ghosts don't just come to hang around. There's always a purpose to their visit. Did Charlie tell you why he was here?"

Sebastian shook his head. "He didn't know."

"Maybe he was lying," Jessica said.

Joan's mouth twisted. "Doubtful. If he was lying he would be acting much more maliciously. He hasn't been, has he?"

"No," Sebastian said. "Well, he wasn't pleased with Stan. And he didn't like Nigel too much."

"Any other hint as to what he was doing here?" Joan said.

"He was just… Charlie. Like he was before." Sebastian shrugged. "I don't know."

"I don't like it," Joan said. "A ghost vanishing for no discernable reason is a bad omen. It goes along with…" She stopped. A muscle along her jaw jumped.

"We should head out. Brian, let's go." She turned away, clutching the keys to Gareth's car in her hand. "I have to remember to drive on the right hand side."

"Wait a minute." Sebastian hurried forward and grabbed her arm. "What does that go along with?"

Joan shook her head and pulled her arm out of his grasp. "Never mind."

"Tell me."

"Well, maybe if you hadn't just taken off, you might know what's going on."

"Joan!" Jessica's voice lashed out from behind him.

"I'm sorry, Jessica, I can't coddle him anymore. I know how you feel about him but he needs to know." Joan turned back to him. Her shoulders tensed. "I've always liked you, Sebastian, but you're too impulsive, without any thought for the group. Rome was a debacle. We could have used your expertise to help us but you ran away. Nigel and the others went in anyway and were routed."

"What do you mean routed?" he said.

"Slaughtered." Charlie's voice sounded from behind him. "She means slaughtered. Huge gooey mess. Wanna see?"

Sebastian turned. Charlie reached out toward his head, thick, almost translucent fingers stretched toward Sebastian's forehead. He felt freezing cold on his skin, spread across his skull.

Then the yellow parking lights winked out.

Blaring traffic noise flooded his senses but he couldn't smell anything. Narrow streets. Old brick buildings glistening in a misty rain that blurred the edges of everything. People hunched under umbrellas as they hurried along. Only a few stayed outside in the darkness, in the night.

The image blurred, shifted to an alleyway, like so many he'd been in the last few years. He hated fighting in alleys but it was better to try to minimize the damage, keep the vampires contained.

Shuffling, hurrying footsteps. Worn boots kicking past debris on the cracked pavement. Still no smell, even with the refuse dotting the alley. He spotted several In-Between huddled along the walls, black on black. Only faces exposed as they peered up the alley toward the end. He saw Nigel at the front, gripping a pistol in one hand and a long sword in the other. His thin face set and determined.

He never liked Nigel but if there was one thing he could say for the man, he did always do his part in a fight.

Movement at the end of the alley. It was hard to spot in the shadows. Sebastian caught a glimpse of broken lights up on the wall near the back. Another movement, a shadow stepping out from the shadows, coalescing into a figure.

A woman.

She took several steps toward Nigel's position. Her flat shoes slid along the pavement as she barely lifted them to step. Her expression was slack, eyes unfocussed. Her mouth moved as if she was trying to speak but no words came out.

Sebastian could almost feel the confusion in the In-Between. Who was this woman? She wasn't a vampire.

More movement in the shadows. Now a boy stepped out, dragging his feet as well. He stumbled and fell to his knees. He stared at the ground in front of him and then began to crawl. He didn't even bother to lift his head.

Sebastian heard shuffling behind them. He turned. More people at the mouth of the alley. Again the same shuffling steps, the same unfocussed look. Hands reaching.

Hand signal from Nigel. Sebastian could feel the In-Between tense, get ready. Could almost feel himself tense. Even in their confusion, the In-Between had to be ready for anything.

Blinding light. Snarls coming from in front and behind. Beyond the human shields, other movement. Fast. Shapes, shadows flashing in front of spotlights. Someone cried out. The gooey sound of ripped flesh. Blood sprayed across the alley. Splashed across the brick walls. Dripping down, running down the crevices. Soaking into the mortar. Screams echoed in the air. Gunshots exploded, deafening him, drowning out the screams. Now his vision got used to the light and he could see figures surrounding the In-Between. Ripping, tearing. In-Between struggling, mouths open in silent screams.

Nigel at the front, fired at an advancing vampire. The bullets knocked it back but a hand appeared from the side, slicing down. Claws ripped through Nigel's forearm. He staggered. The gun dropped to pavement, skittered along to stop against a pile of paper. Nigel dropped to his knees, reached for it.

Claws slashed again. His throat opened. Blood poured out, soaking his top. He tried to swing with the sword but could barely lift his arm. Laughter sounded. The vampire kicked out. The sword went flying, clattered against the brick wall opposite and dropped to disappear behind a dumpster.

Nigel grabbed his throat as if trying to stem the blood flow but it poured over his fingers. His thin face grew even paler. Mouth opened, trying to speak, trying to give orders. Maybe even trying to call for a retreat.

Too late.

Another slash ripped across the back of his neck this time, cutting through his spinal cord.

His head rolled away as his body dropped to the ground.

He didn't even twitch.

The vision turned to take in the entire alley. Perhaps twenty vampires rampaged through, ripping the In-Between to shreds. While around the perimeter, in a ragged circle, bodies slack, heads lolling on necks, the human shields waited for the vampires to finish their battle.

How could this happen? The clans were broken. Vampires had been living like little more than animals for years, the older ones too chained to the clan heads for complete autonomy, the younger ones too inexperienced to survive well. What had changed?

"They adapted." Charlie's voice filled his ears, his head. "The last couple years, you guys took out all the slow ones, the stupid ones. Paved the way for the smarter ones to come in. I think they've got a few new tricks up their sleeves."

Tricks like human shields. Tricks like the bond Bianca had unleashed on Brent. The signs had been there all along. Even without Grellock's book, the vampires were starting a major offensive.

The In-Between had tried to tell him. Nigel, the others. Would it have made a difference if he'd gone to Rome? Would he have been able to tip the balance? Confuse the vampires enough to stop the slaughter?

But he had to come home. He had to save his family.

And how's that working out?

Screwed up. He'd screwed up. Worse than screwed up. He was responsible for those deaths. Maybe some of them would have died if he'd been there but maybe not. Maybe he could have made a difference.

But he'd been too concerned with his own agenda to find out.

At least Jessica hadn't been there.

Had she?

"Not that I could tell, not directly."

Charlie's voice again, sounding in his head, as if he were standing just off Sebastian's right shoulder.

Charlie, what's going on? How are you doing this?

"You needed to see this, pal. I'm stuck with you but I can take some short trips. Little hops before I boomerang back. Saw this on my travels and thought you needed to see it."

Charlie, why are you here in the first place?

He almost felt his friend's shrug. "I don't know. But I'm not much enjoying the show. Feels like we're getting farther away from it. I think you should have gone to Rome, Sebastian. Big things are brewing. There are going to be more Romes before it's done. You need to deal with it."

Why me? What about my brother?

"Why you? How should I know? You're the one with the weird shit goin' on in your head. Have you told your friends about that?"

Sebastian didn't respond.

"Didn't think so. They might get more insistent about you getting back to work."

I will. Once Callum is safe. Can you at least help with that?

Nothing. No response.

The image of the alley before him shimmered and dimmed, like a badly tuned television set. Darkness swallowed him. Silence filled the spaces. He couldn't even feel his body anymore.

Then the yellow parking lot lights stabbed his eyes.

"Sebastian!" Jessica's voice. He felt hands on his arms. Something hard on his back. Asphalt.

He blinked, his eyes watering.

He was lying on the ground. Jessica hovered over him, grabbing his arm and shoulder, tugging at him to sit up.

"What happened?" he said. His mouth felt like it was full of cotton. He put his palm on the pavement and pushed himself up.

"You just fell over in a dead faint," Jessica said.

"Are you okay, Sebastian?" Joan knelt beside him. She put a hand on his forehead. Her skin felt cool and smooth.

She looked at him with concern but when he met her gaze, she looked away.

She knew.

"Charlie came back," he said. "He showed me what happened in Rome."

They all froze.

CHAPTER 14

“Were you going to tell me?” he said. He turned to look at Jessica.

Now he really didn't like the lines he saw on her face. They outlined the shape of her frown and made her look far older than she was. She carried too much, too many worries, too many stresses. And too much of it was because of him.

He'd been so selfish.

“There isn't any point to it now,” she said. “Your brother isn't going to wait. We can have this discussion after we've found him.”

Her grip tightened on his arm. He stood up.

“Let's go,” he said.

Joan and Brian took Gareth's car, leaving Gareth, Jessica and Sebastian with the van. By the time they headed out to their search area, full dark had taken over the city. Sebastian stared out the back window of the van, watching the houses blur by as Gareth drove. Was Alexa moving farther away even now? Taking his brother to somewhere unknown?

How could they possibly find them in this city? And if Alexa managed to get out, how would he ever catch her trail again?

If she wanted revenge, retribution for what he'd done to Constantine and the other clan heads, she sure had it.

Beside him, Jessica gave him a weak smile and squeezed his hand.

They settled into a routine quick enough. Sebastian would step out from the back of the van, letting the night air surround him as he breathed it in deep. Around him, the neighborhood slumbered, houses in darkness, vague suggestions against the shadows. He could hear the buzz of televisions, the hum of computers and throbbing bass of music. The air brought him tales of its own: exhaust, damp grass, earthy sod of the people who had replaced old lawns, stale garbage hinting at what the families had eaten in the last week.

But no sour smell of a vampire.

No scent of his brother.

No Callum.

Five minutes was all it took for him to tell if there was any trace within a few blocks radius.

The answer was always no.

He turned to Gareth and Jessica and shook his head.

"Next," Gareth said.

And they piled back in the van.

Every hour on the hour, Joan called. The phone rang shrill and hollow inside the van. Jessica plucked it out of Gareth's hand, letting him drive. Even without listening hard, Sebastian could hear the negative response from Joan filtered through the tiny speaker.

Nothing so far.

Was it already too late? Should he have skipped the morgue and gone right after Callum? That would have meant leaving his mother as a vampire. He shivered against the thought. She would have woken in that drawer, escaped and killed people.

No, he couldn't have faced that. He'd never forgive himself for letting that happen to her, for letting her *become* that.

Oh, Alexa was taking her revenge on so many levels.

The van swung down another street. Sebastian recognized this neighborhood. Friends from elementary school lived here, in that house there. The split level with the grey siding and the black shingles. Twin boys, Brian and Ben. Their mother always made apple pie with so much cinnamon their house would smell of it for days. He used to love visiting them, until they moved away during middle school.

But there was nothing else. Only his memories.

Just a whole lot of nothing.

He kicked at a discarded soda can in frustration. Had they made a big mistake thinking Alexa had stayed in the city? Couldn't she have done what Constantine and the other clan heads had done, escaped in some private transportation? Wouldn't it have been smarter to get out?

And miss this? Miss his agony? If there was one thing vampires enjoyed as much as blood, it was tormenting their victims, as if somehow they fed on the anguish as much as they did on the blood.

No, Alexa wouldn't have left. She would have stayed so she could enjoy tormenting him.

And if that was the case, she'd make herself easy for him to find.

He'd been thinking about this all wrong. He'd assumed she was trying to hide from him but what if she wasn't? What if she just wanted to find the perfect spot to finish him off?

Where would that be?

Not here, he realized. Not in this city. They had no history together here. This was his place, from his time before her. She'd pick a spot where they'd been together.

Where they'd shared a life.

The scrape of Jessica's heel on the sidewalk behind him caught his attention. He turned, seeing the tension in her face. Her hands were fists in her pockets.

"Anything?" she said.

He nodded. "I know where she's going," he said. "We won't find her here."

"Where is she going?"

"Home," he said. "Where it all started. It's time I went back to college."

Gareth frowned when Sebastian told him.

They stood in the shadow of the van, parked on a side street across from a convenience store. Sebastian could smell the sticky sweet stench of the syrup from an icy machine under the heavy smell of stale tobacco.

"You can't know that for sure," the man said. "We're just as likely to find her here. I told you how hard it is for vampires to control humans that way."

"You assume that," Sebastian said. "That was with the clans and their hierarchy. We don't know what kind of influence the higher vampires had on the lower ones, what restrictions they imposed to keep order. Maybe it's easier than we like to think. But I do know we aren't going to find her here."

Gareth scratched at his beard, his lips still thin with displeasure.

"Are you sure he's not thick or something?" Charlie said. He'd followed Sebastian around as he walked the neighborhoods but this was the first time he'd spoken in hours.

Shut up. Sebastian pursed his lips in Charlie's direction. Attitude from a ghost was the last thing he needed. It sure wasn't going to help his case.

"Jessie girl, what you think?" Gareth said.

Sebastian blinked. He'd never heard anyone refer to Jessica that way. He'd never consider it himself, not and risk a punch to the face. He glanced over at her quickly. Was she going to let loose on Gareth? She stood just beyond the van's shadow. Her hair caught a glint of light, casting gold highlights against the dark brown. Her hands hooked into the pockets of her black pants, hips cocked, her head tilted to one side.

The tilt of her head and the shadows crisscrossing her face reminded him of the drive so long ago when she'd told him about Timmy, her own brother lost to the vampires. After a disastrous camping trip, he'd come back but she'd already been contacted by Frank and another In-Between. Wait, he remembered now. Gareth, it must have been Gareth.

Had she been Jessie before the vampire attack? A different name for a different life. A light, fluffy name full of fun and energy maybe reflecting the girl she'd been before the darkness killed her family and swallowed her life whole. Who would she have been as Jessie? He couldn't picture it. That girl with the carefree name was long gone.

Now she was Jessica. And Jessica got down to business.

She shrugged. "From anybody else I'd say he was nuts, but he knew Alexa."

"The vampire isn't the same as the human," Gareth said. "You know that."

"Yes, I know that but this is personal to her. Sebastian killed Constantine, her sire, her leader, right in front of her. I don't think she's going to hide her revenge from him."

Gareth gave a slow nod. "Good points. Are you sure you want to stop looking here?"

He addressed the last question to Sebastian.

Was he sure? It was a huge risk leaving to head back to Ridgewater City. If Alexa stayed here... He glanced toward the front of the van. Charlie stood by the front bumper. He was back to wearing his ripped jeans and black t-shirt. In the dim light, he almost looked solid. He cocked his head at Sebastian.

What do you think, Charlie?

Charlie shrugged, his blond hair shifting over his shoulders. "Your call, man. I follow where you lead."

Why?

"Don't know. Wish I did. I'd kick your ass to do it if I knew."

Was that right? Did Charlie really not know why he was here or was he just stringing Sebastian along. Looking at the ghost, Sebastian couldn't tell. Could he even be sure it was Charlie? He'd just accepted it and never really questioned.

But he'd felt Charlie inside when he'd spoken to Stan. That feeling, that *aura* couldn't be faked.

Could it?

He just didn't know and the only person he could think to ask was scouring the industrial district with Brian. But would even Joan know for sure? She was the closest thing he had to an expert.

Even setting aside the question of Charlie's (or whoever he was) motives, Sebastian still had to decide. Stay and keep searching, or go?

He glanced again at Charlie, at the ghost standing by the front of the car.

One look at that open, near grin on his face... yes, it was Charlie, it had to be. Only Charlie could be so annoying and so amiable at the same time.

Stay or go?

Why was it so hard to decide?

Because he already knew what he had to do and he was afraid of it. Afraid of what it would do to him. Afraid of what he would become in the doing, of what could happen to Callum.

But he'd promised her. He'd promised mom before she died.

He couldn't back down now, not just because he was scared.

His shoulders hunched as he turned back to Jessica and Gareth.

"Yes, I'm sure," he said. "We go."

"Okay." Gareth pushed away from the back of the van, wiping his hands together. "I'll call Joan and we'll go meet them."

He ducked back into the van. Jessica moved forward until she was right beside Sebastian.

"Are you sure?"

Her voice pitched low although of course Gareth would hear it. He'd been polite enough to slip into the back of the van to give them privacy. Sebastian knew full well the man had his cell phone in his pocket.

"Yeah," he said to Jessica. "I am. Thank you by the way."

A trace of a smile turned the corners of her lips up. "I know how it is with brothers."

Of course she did. Was that the only reason she was helping him? Out of some loyalty to her dead brother?

Then her hand slipped around his upper arm. He felt the warmth of her palm against his skin. He closed his fingers over hers.

Not the only reason.

His other hand slipped around her waist, tugging to bring her closer. She slid forward in a smooth, gliding motion and her face was right there, her lips… They parted just a little as he leaned down to kiss her. Her hand gripped his arm.

He let himself get lost in their kiss.

Until the van door banged open.

She startled back, breaking the kiss, the embrace. Her hand dropped from his arm.

Gareth hunched in the doorway of the van. His dark hand gripped the cell phone so tight his fingers were blanching toward beige.

"We got a problem," he said. "Joan's not answering her phone."

CHAPTER 15

Sebastian grabbed hold of the bench beside him as Gareth took the corner fast. The tires skidded, almost screeching and Sebastian swore they were going over on two wheels. Then the van righted itself and leapt forward down the street. Buildings and trees whizzed by, blurring in the darkness.

Joan, not Joan.

His heart hammered in his chest. She'd always been supportive of him, sometimes in a teasing way, but he thought she had genuine affection for him. He sucked in a breath. Oh god, he'd thought of her like a mother. He hadn't realized that until now. She'd mothered all of them, gathering them around her like a mother hen.

No, he couldn't lose her now.

He couldn't lose a second mother now.

Gareth took a right turn. Sebastian dug his fingers into the bench but the van bucked hard and he found himself flying toward the other side. He ducked, managing to avoid smashing his head against a shotgun strapped to the wall.

"Woo hoo, better than a roller coaster!" Charlie stood near the back of the van, feet parted, one in front of the other. He spread his hands as he bent his knees, looking like he was surfing.

"Shut up," said Sebastian.

"What?" Jessica's voice called from the front.

"Nothing," Sebastian said over the squeal of the tires. Gareth took another turn, another right, pressing Sebastian back against the wall.

The blur of houses and shops outside the windows shifted into a line of grey concrete buildings as the van entered the industrial district. Gareth pulled the van to the side of the road and stopped. The engine ticked down as it cooled. The front doors sprang open as Gareth and Jessica jumped out. A moment later, the back door opened and Gareth appeared, his grim face looking blurry through Charlie's somewhat translucent form.

"Hey, watch it!" Charlie said as Gareth climbed into the back of the van, but of course Gareth couldn't see or hear the ghost. His arm reached right through Charlie's torso, grabbing for the shotgun in the gun rack opposite Sebastian.

"If you're waiting for an invitation to join us," Gareth said, "consider it given." He backed out the van, retreating through Charlie, who gave him an annoyed look.

Get out of the way. Sebastian waved a hand at the ghost and reached for the second shotgun. He climbed out of the back of the van, where Jessica was stuffing ammo into her pockets and checking on her handgun.

"Let's go," Gareth said. "Their last position was near the old Montgomery Furniture Factory."

Their footsteps shuffled over old pavement, cracked and crumbling. Sebastian could smell the river, feel the moisture in the air pressing against his skin. Several of the streetlights had been smashed, leaving few pockets of pale yellow light to light their way, but it didn't matter. Even the dimmest of light was as bright as sunlight to the In-Between. Sebastian actually preferred it this way.

The shadows gave form to the squat buildings around them, none of them more than three stories tall. He could almost smell a mix of sawdust and furniture polish in the air, as if an airborne residue of what these old factories had been years ago. In its heyday, Grand Rapids had been a major furniture market, building and shipping furniture across the country. That was before prefabricated pieces you stuck together yourself. Decades before, actually. Such smells should be long gone, even to him.

But still he smelled it. But maybe it wasn't a smell, maybe it was some kind of psychic residue that he was picking up. Would Joan have picked it up as well? She must have, she was more experienced with this than he was. Would it have led her forward to investigate? Had some presence disturbed the usual atmosphere here, brought out the past more?

His shoulders hunched up toward his ears. His stomach clenched. He balanced on the balls of his feet as he moved forward.

His body knew and it just took a moment for his mind to realize it.

Something had disturbed this area. Someone with a strong presence, a strong psychic presence.

Someone like a vampire.

Alexa?

Had to be.

He glanced to his right and saw Charlie gliding along beside him. The ghost had a grim expression. He nodded to Sebastian.

"I think she's here," Sebastian said.

Jessica who had been walking ahead and to the left, turned to glance back at him. "What?"

"I think she's here."

In the dimness, he saw a muscle jump along the side of her jaw as she clenched her teeth. She gave a sharp nod and pulled her gun out. She held it in both hands in front of her as she moved. Ahead to the right, Gareth raised his shotgun to the ready position.

Both were listening to him without any argument. A nice change from having to deal with someone like Nigel. Then he remembered how Nigel had died, how he should have been there to help them.

His fingers tightened on his own shotgun. He couldn't bring those people back but he could stop more slaughters.

He could save Callum.

He *would*.

Gravel crunched under his feet. A light breeze rose up, carrying the scent of the water and an even stronger scent of sawdust and furniture polish. He turned his head, following the trace. There, that building. Three stories, yellowish brick coated with layers of dirt and grime that dulled the yellow and darkened it to an almost brownish tinge. Boarded up windows still held a few slivers of glass. The wood door stood shut but he could see a chain lying in front of it.

Snapped in half.

"There." He pointed.

They moved forward as a unit. Gareth and Jessica split to the sides, taking up point, leaving him to approach the door head on. In the darkness, he saw Jessica's nod, her body tense and ready. He felt Gareth on the other side. Poised.

Sebastian gripped the door knob, felt the slick surface with a layer of grime slide in his palm. His fingers tightened. He nodded to them. One, two...

Three!

He yanked the door open and barreled inside, darting to the left.

Blackness. He heard Jessica and Gareth storm in after, both spreading out to present multiple targets. But nothing came at them from the blackness. It was deeper here than outside. Even the pale light from the open door did little to illuminate the inside. Sebastian blinked a couple of times and his eyes adjusted.

Empty concrete floor stretched away from them, coated with dust. But he could see the disturbance in the dust line where someone had walked recently. He heard Gareth click with his tongue and wag two fingers forward.

They crept along, following the trail. Gareth took the lead with Sebastian following. He sensed Jessica behind, her gun tracking back and forth, making sure nothing caught them unaware.

As they moved, Sebastian caught the suggestion of pillars along the way. Then to the right, a wall jutted out with a darker shape in the center. A door.

He clicked his tongue to his teeth. Ahead, Gareth gave a nod and motioned them toward it. Jessica took up point on the right and this time Gareth moved to the center, leaving Sebastian to the left.

As they drew up to it, Sebastian saw that the door was ajar a few inches, pushed inward. Stale air seemed to waft out. He tasted dust and ash, could almost feel it coating the insides of his nostrils and tickling the back of his throat. He resisted the urge to cough, but couldn't resist the urge to swallow. The sour taste almost made him gag.

Sour.

He could feel both Gareth and Jessica tense. So they felt it too.

Vampire.

Joan and Brian would have sensed it too. Why hadn't they retreated and called in?

Maybe they hadn't had the chance.

Before Gareth or Jessica could move, Sebastian stepped forward, pushing at the door. He heard a sharp intake of breath from Gareth, almost a hiss from Jessica. He ignored them and stepped through the door.

A stairwell headed down into a deeper inkier blackness. Another eye blink and he could make out the vague outline of the steel rail leading down.

His feet blurred as he hurried down the steps. The sour stench grew stronger as if leading him on.

"Sebastian!" Jessica's whispered call trailed after him, then he heard the shuffling of their footsteps as they followed.

Sebastian didn't wait. He'd waited long enough.

The stairs led to a small landing then curved down. He counted two more landings, thick with dust that billowed up into the air as he passed, itching at his nose. Then he saw the bottom of the stairs.

And a door hanging open.

An old steel door with the top hinge twisted like taffy. The bottom hinge still hung on, straining to hold the door upright as it listed inside the room beyond. The sour smell overpowered even the heavy stench of dust but as he moved toward the door, he caught an undercurrent of iron. Thick. Wet.

Blood.

Someone had spilled a lot of it.

He started when a hand grabbed his forearm. He felt the brush of soft hair across his cheek.

"Wait for us," Jessica said into his ear.

He gave a nod. A moment later he heard the scrape of Gareth's boot on the landing behind him.

"Strict formation," Gareth said, pitching his voice low. "Assume hostiles."

Jessica gave a nod and nudged Sebastian. He nodded too.

Gareth tapped their shoulders. One, two, three!

Sebastian darted through the door, aiming left. He felt Jessica peel away, aiming right. Gareth headed up the center.

They all stopped, poised, guns ready, crouched to present the smallest targets.

Nothing witnessed their impressive entrance.

Nothing still living anyway.

Sebastian spotted the bodies just ahead of Gareth. Brian lay on his face, hand still clutching a knife. When Gareth turned him over, Sebastian saw the man's face coated with blood and the wide slice across his throat.

Carotid artery. He would have bled out within a few minutes.

Just beyond him…

No, Sebastian couldn't look. He saw Jessica put a hand up to her mouth. Gareth pointed his shotgun to the floor. The end of it scraped on the concrete.

Sebastian didn't want to look, wanted to walk out the door. But Callum... He couldn't just leave.

He turned his head.

Joan lay just beyond Brian. Her arms and legs were outstretched, her face turned up to the ceiling. But her torso lay front down and her arms and legs were too outstretched. As Gareth took a step forward and Sebastian followed, as if unable to stop himself, he saw someone had pulled Joan's limbs from her body, then arranged them in place around her.

And they'd pulled off her head.

A high pitched giggle came out of the darkness beyond Joan.

Gareth's shotgun flashed up. Jessica took aim from Sebastian's right.

The giggle sounded again. Then a patter of footsteps approached.

From the darkest shadow, a thin form took shape. A waif-like girl stepped forward. Blood smeared across her mouth and down the front of her denim dress. She wore flat-soled shoes that skidded across the concrete. Her left hand pushed pale blond bangs from her eyes.

"She asked me to wait for you," she said.

"Who asked?" Gareth said.

The smile on her face dissolved into a sneer. "I'm not talking to you." She glared at Gareth, her hands tightening into fists by her sides. Her entire body grew taut as if she was going to launch herself forward at him. Then she relaxed, her body loosened. Her head turned just a fraction, dismissing Gareth from her attention.

She focused on Sebastian.

"I'm talking to you," she said. "She said you were kind of cute. We could have some fun." Her fingers twisted in the skirt portion of her dress, lifting it past her knees, past her thighs. "Want to?"

"Who said?" Sebastian said. "Who asked you to stay?"

She smiled, ducking her head coyly. "You have to ask nicely."

His fingers tightened on the shotgun. He wanted to just shoot the vampire but he had to know what she was talking about and confirm his suspicions about where Alexa had gone. Even over the overpowering stench of blood and the sourness of the vampire that wafted toward them, he could tell Alexa was already long gone. She had been here, somehow he knew that, but now she was gone.

And he had to follow.

But first this one.

And he couldn't waste time chatting.

He took a deep breath and let it out. His shoulders relaxed. His body loosened. His awareness of the room amplified. He felt the slight imperfections of the concrete floor beneath his feet. Heard the air hissing through the ventilation shafts over his head. Beneath the blood and the sourness, hung the thickness of stale air, trapped too long in the basement, now mixing with traces of fresh air that had followed them down the stairs like puppies.

Would she taste that fresh air, know that it was dark outside? She would be longing to go out, to head off on a hunt? Although they'd killed Brian and Joan no vampire would have been able to feed on them. In-Between were poisonous to vampires. So she must be hungry. She must be just dying to get out and hunt.

All she had to do was talk to him, tell him what he wanted to know. Where had Alexa gone? Had she taken the boy with her? A human boy, with black hair and a wiry frame.

Sebastian tried to picture Callum and realized he couldn't be sure of exactly what his brother looked like now. He must have grown but by how much?

Two years could have changed him so much. Sebastian felt his heart almost shrivel in his chest. In front of him, the vampire laughed.

No, stop, he was losing focus. She was pulling away…

His mind lunged forward. He felt her wail and struggle against him but he wouldn't let her go. Not without knowing where Alexa had gone, without knowing what happened to Callum.

Where was Callum?

Where was he?

He felt her scream soundlessly, an echo that howled in his mind. He pushed it aside and pummeled her.

Where was Callum? Where was he?

WHERE IS MY BROTHER?

She buckled beneath the onslaught. He almost hear her knees scrape the concrete floor as she crumbled. Her hands slapped the ground. Her body convulsed.

He felt her mind trying to hide from him, darting into corners. Racing, racing. He pursued relentlessly, asking over and over. Where? Where?

Where?

Finally he felt her mind crack and the memories tumbled outward, spilling in a flood that flowed through him. First day of school wearing white bobby socks and a brown skirt with yellow top, laughing at the television with a group of girls as they watched some nameless sitcom. Making snow forts. Riding a bike, first a small one with training wheels, and then it morphed into a ten-speed mountain bike while around him the world changed from a suburban street to a hilly dirt path.

Memories, all her memories.

He would drown in them if he didn't stop paying attention.

Focus.

Callum. Look for Callum.

But it was hard to turn away from the memories of her life. She'd been human in them and they'd been locked away once she'd been turned. Now they flooded outward and he could feel the vampire part of her shrieking to stop it.

Strange, why would the vampire want to stop this flood of memory? Didn't it have access to it anyway? Vampires knew what the human they'd been had known.

But maybe only on the surface. Maybe there was something about this flood of memory that vampires didn't like.

He wanted to know more but there wasn't time.

Callum.

He pushed the word at her, felt her mind yield. The human memories fell away.

Cold, dark. Concrete rough under her legs as she crouched on the floor. Keep her head bowed. Obedient. That way, avoid any further beating from the presence that stood before her. She glanced up and in the dimness could still make out the slim form of a woman in front of her.

"Repeat it," the woman said.

That voice. Familiar. But the tone sounded harsher than he ever remembered. Always before the voice had spoken of books and classes.

Now she spoke of death.

"Repeat it."

The crouching vampire shuddered. She bowed her head. "Come alone. He knows the place. Where it started for him and ended for Charlie."

"Good. Make sure he understands he comes alone. Kill any others."

"Yes, Alexa."

Yes. Alexa.

He stepped back, even felt his body move, left foot shifting back, carrying his weight away from the vampire. She sagged, almost stumbled.

"Your message," he said.

She lifted her head and leered at him. "You heard it."

"Say it out loud for them."

"You go alone. To the place where it started and where Charlie ended. Make sure you're alone."

His hand tightened on the gun.

"And the others?" He nodded at Jessica and Gareth.

The vampire opened her mouth.

She darted away, racing back into the darkness. Gareth started after her.

"Don't!" Sebastian said.

"She killed Joan and Brian," Jessica said.

"Not alone she didn't," he said. "And she's supposed to kill you. It could be a trap."

"All the more reason..." she started.

"Don't," he said. "Please."

He turned to her, grabbing for her arm to stop her from following Gareth, who had himself stopped ten feet away, hesitating.

Jessica inhaled sharply. Her hand came up to touch his face.

"Sebastian, you're bleeding."

He lifted his hand and swiped under his nose. It came away bloody.

"That always happens when you push too hard." Joan's voice sounded from behind him. "You're going to have to learn not to do that."

CHAPTER 16

Sebastian turned. Joan stood wearing the same business suit and heels. Her hands folded neatly in front of her. She looked poised and calm, everything normal.

Except for her own body lying just to the right of her.

"You're dead," Sebastian said.

"What?" Gareth said.

A smile formed on Joan's lips. "Yes, I am. I'm okay with that. I lived a lot longer than I expected, considering."

"Sebastian?" Jessica said. Her head turned to face where he was looking. He could tell from the way her head tracked that she couldn't see.

"They can't see me, of course," Joan said. "But you can." Her head tilted to the left. Strands of her greying hair rested on her cheek. "Grellock's book, I suppose. It affected you even more than I realized. You were always special."

"I'm not special," Sebastian said.

"Yes, you are," Joan said. "Even at the beginning, you were closer to the vampires than any of us."

He shook his head. He didn't want to hear this, didn't want another ghost following him around.

Didn't look like he had much choice.

"Sebastian." Jessica touched his arm. He could hear the uncertainty in her voice. "Your nose."

She held out a paper napkin to him. He took it and it crinkled in his fingers as he pressed it to his nose. Within moments, he could tell it was soaked through.

"The nose bleeds and the headaches get worse," Joan said. "It's part of the price you pay. Some things you can do without paying the price, just because you're more sensitive, like talking to us." Her hand touched her chest and then she waved over at Charlie who nodded to her and took a bow.

"But more than that and you'll suffer. You'll have to pay in blood."

"Callum," he said.

Joan shook her head. "They're long gone from here, Sebastian. And it may already be too late. But look carefully, Sebastian. Make sure you look carefully."

No, it couldn't be too late. He couldn't accept that. His eyes blinked rapidly to clear his vision. She was wrong. What the hell did she know anyway, she was just a ghost.

A ghost who stood beside her body that had been torn to pieces.

Alexa alone couldn't do that, couldn't take down two seasoned In-Betweens. It would take several vampires, ambushing them.

Like the ones sneaking up on them now...

He felt them surge forward, hidden behind the stench of blood and dust. Snarls filled the air. From the ceiling, bodies dropped through the air. They landed in puffs of dust, cutting the In-Between off from each other.

A large male separated Sebastian from Jessica. She dropped to her knee and fired, hitting another male in the chest. It staggered back, howling.

Gareth was surrounded by three vampires. Two of them moved to flank his back as Gareth swung the shotgun to meet them. Dust billowed up as they scurried around in an elaborate dance to stay out of range of his gun.

Too many of them. Too many.

Sebastian's fingers tightened on his own shotgun. His head throbbed. He felt blood on his lips. Blood that made him want to rip and tear. Blood that made him want to drink even though he knew he couldn't, knew their blood was poison. But still it could be spilled and splashed across the floors and walls. It could be sprayed as a warning to others.

To those other freak In-Betweens.

Sebastian's breath caught. He'd tuned into the vampires without even trying. If it was that simple...

A price to pay...

Fine. Whatever. He'd pay the price. He had to save them. He had to save Jessica.

He had to save Callum.

In front of him, the large male growled and stepped forward, arms opening, claws extending. Sebastian felt the need to rip and tear, to slice and destroy.

Do it. *Do it!*

The vampire crouched. Lips pulled back from its fangs. It snarled.

Do IT!

It spun and lunged at the other vampire beside it. Fangs tore through the other vampire's throat. Blood splashed on the floor, mixing with the dust.

Sebastian turned his attention to the three vampires surrounding Gareth. There, the one just behind, in the denim jacket and spiky brown hair. It snarled, craving. Sebastian could feel the craving.

Just a change in direction.

It spun and leapt on the blond vampire beside it. They went down in a tangle of limbs and snarls. The third vampire stepped back and stared across the room at Sebastian. He could feel its stare.

And behind the stare: fear.

It feared *him.*

It turned and ran.

A moment later, the others followed. Their footsteps echoed and faded as they vanished through the basement.

Gareth shot and decapitated the remaining vampires who fought each other, ignoring the In-Between. After the bodies lay still on the concrete, Gareth wiped blood from his blade and stepped over to Sebastian.

"You okay?" he said. "You don't look okay."

Pain created a haze around the man in front of Sebastian. He wanted to shake his head but it might fall off if he moved it too much.

"You did this, didn't you?" Jessica stepped around Gareth, moving to stand closer to Sebastian.

He tried to speak. He opened his mouth. He was sure of it. He could feel the muscles in his jaw contract, pulling his jaw down. His tongue pressed out, getting ready to form into the shape of words.

But her image swam in front of him. The darkness around her encroached. He could feel it seeping into his mind, into his soul, bringing along the images of blood and flesh swirling together, until they all melded into a rich, thick black.

A sharp sting flattened his cheek against his teeth. His eyelids fluttered. He felt his feather-thin eyelashes brush his cheeks. Were his eyes open? Opening? All he saw was darkness.

No, not just darkness. Shapes formed. Dark grey on black, edges smeared. He tried but couldn't quite focus. Keep trying.

One shape moved closer. The edges became more distinct. Chin, face, a thick flow of hair curled around her neck and down her left shoulder like a python.

Jessica.

He tried to say the words but he couldn't make his mouth work. Why? What had happened? He tried to remember. Vampires. There had been vampires. Too many for the three of them, so he'd taken care of it.

Wait. He'd taken care of it?

What was going on?

He tried to say the words, but still his mouth wouldn't work.

Dammit.

"Is he awake?"

Gareth's voice sounded from over Jessica's shoulder. She turned her head to the left. From profile, Sebastian admired the upturn of her nose and the curve of her neck. He liked to press his check against her neck, feel her soft skin against him.

"I don't know," she said. "His eyes are open but he's not talking."

"Let me take a look," Gareth said.

Gareth moved into view. From this close, Sebastian could see white in the whiskers that poked out of his brown skin. Concern deepened the lines around the man's mouth. Sebastian watched the movement of Gareth's eyes track across his face.

I'm awake. Couldn't Gareth see that?

But his gaze never stopped moving.

And Sebastian's body refused to cooperate.

"Paying your price, buddy."

Charlie's voice sounded near his ear. Sebastian tried to turn his head to the right but it wouldn't move. Instead, Charlie's ghostly face appeared behind Gareth. He frowned.

"You don't look so good, Sebastian."

Help me!

"You're asking for help? Really?"

Please.

"Would if I could," Charlie said. He shrugged. "I don't know how."

Anger burned in Sebastian. He felt his skin grow hot. Maybe it would help him move. He tried to lift his head, tried to move a hand, even a finger.

Nothing.

Dammit!

What about when you talked to Stan? You moved my body. Do that!

Charlie's head tilted. "I suppose I could try that."

Do it!

"I think his eyes are moving," Gareth said. "I think he's awake but he might have had some kind of stroke or something. We'd have to get him to a doctor to find out for sure."

"Oh god." Jessica pressed her hand across her mouth. Tears formed in her eyes.

No, don't cry for him. She'd already shed too many tears because of him. He didn't want to cause her anymore pain.

Charlie, come on.

"Okay, okay, I'll give it a try."

Charlie's ghostly form moved through Gareth, coming closer, closer, until it blurred and vanished into Sebastian.

A familiar chill spread over Sebastian's body, making all his nerve endings tingle. Before, he'd felt a strangeness, a heaviness as Charlie took over but this time, his body felt lighter. He could almost feel Charlie inside his head.

His arms moved, pressing against the concrete as Charlie pushed him into a sitting position.

"Sebastian!" Jessica said.

Gareth grabbed Sebastian's upper arm, steadying him. "Man, are you okay?"

"I'm not Sebastian. I'm Charlie," Charlie said, using Sebastian's vocal cords. His voice did sound different, even to Sebastian's ears.

"What?" Gareth said.

What do you want me to tell them? Charlie's thoughts floated through Sebastian's head.

Tell them I can't move. I'll talk through you.

"Sebastian can't come to his body right now," Charlie said. "I can give you his messages."

Stop being a smart ass!

Shut up.

"Charlie, is that really you?" Jessica said.

Sebastian felt his mouth curve into a smile, almost a leer. "You got it, babe."

"You're his ghost friend," Gareth said. "You're possessing him."

"Just until Sebastian is more himself," Charlie said. "Can you help me up? I don't quite have the full sense of his body just yet." He winked at Jessica.

Gareth's grip tightened and he pulled. After a moment, Sebastian's body stood, wavering just slightly on his feet. The coldness spread through his limbs as Charlie took full control. Sebastian felt his arms and legs tense and relax. He took a few steps forward, then back. Test driving.

Would Charlie give him control back?

The thought made his mouth go dry.

Oh relax, Charlie's thoughts floated through his head. You think I want to stay in your scrawny ass for the rest of your life?

Behind the words, Sebastian felt the affection from his friend. This wasn't just some ghost possessing him. It was Charlie, helping him out.

Sorry. I just have to get better. Callum...

I know. One step at a time, right?

"What happened to Sebastian?" Gareth said.

"I think he blew a fuse," Charlie said. "Repair crews are on the scene."

"Charlie," Jessica said.

Charlie spread Sebastian's hands. "I don't know what happened. He's still in here, if that's what you're wondering. He wants to go after Callum."

"We will," Jessica said.

Sebastian tensed, hearing the steel in her voice. No, she couldn't come along. Not if it would put Callum at risk.

But could he really do it himself in the shape he was in?

He didn't think Alexa would be understanding.

Tell her she can't come, I'm sorry, Sebastian said to Charlie. *We have to go alone.*

You really think she's going to listen?

Charlie was right. Sebastian recognized that look on Jessica's face, the stiffness in her shoulders, the clench of her jaw. She'd never listen and it could endanger Callum. Could endanger her.

He couldn't worry about everyone.

We have to get away.

"Sebastian wants to leave you behind," Charlie said. "He has to get Callum."

Dammit, Charlie, what the hell are you doing?

A huge favor, buddy.

Jessica folded her arms across her chest. "Oh really? He thinks he can dump us, does he?"

Charlie shrugged Sebastian's shoulders. "Kind of a dick, I know. But he doesn't want to endanger you. Alexa probably wouldn't be understanding."

Charlie...

Shut up, you idiot. I told you before what you have to do. You have to actually *talk* to her. Jessica's smart enough to listen, ya know. Well, maybe not that smart since she seems to like *you*.

Fuck off.

A chuckle echoed through Sebastian's head. But he noticed that Jessica had dropped her arms to her sides.

Her brow furrowed in confusion.

"It could put Callum at risk if we all show up together," Gareth said.

"We can't just let him go like this." Jessica gestured toward Sebastian. Sebastian felt his lips tug upwards into a smile, but not his usual smile. One of Charlie's. What would that look like on his face? He didn't grin wide like Charlie had.

Maybe you should try it some time.

He didn't respond. It was bad enough having Charlie in his head. He didn't want his friend getting a swelled head over it.

Because, well, maybe he was right.

There wasn't all that much to smile about in his life. Maybe Sebastian needed to take advantage when those things worth smiling over did show up.

Things like Jessica.

Like Callum.

But first, he had to get to his brother. Make sure he was okay.

"We all have to go," Jessica said. She turned to look at Sebastian. "But we'll hang behind when we get there. We'll back you up."

"Works for me," Charlie said. What do you think?

I don't have much choice, do I?

Charlie chuckled.

No, pal, you really don't.

CHAPTER 17

Ridgeview City was an eight hour drive from Grand Rapids. Alexa had a head start but she'd need to go to ground before daylight. They could be waiting for her.

Maybe.

Halfway through the trip, Sebastian sat in the back of the van, listening to the hum of the wheels on pavement as Gareth drove. The bench felt hard beneath his rump but at least he felt it a little stronger than he had a few hours ago. Was he starting to get his own feeling back? He couldn't tell. Charlie still rode shotgun in his body, moving him around and talking for him. He'd even coaxed out Jessica's story about her brother and mother.

It had taken Sebastian the better part of a year to get it out of her.

How did Charlie do it?

Try talking to her, buddy, Charlie said inside his head.

Oh shut up.

She sat across from him in the back, knees together, her hands gripping the bench as the van wavered. She turned her head toward the front, her long ponytail flopping over her shoulder and cascading down her front.

"How long?" she called out.

From the front seat, Gareth shouted back. "Three hours, maybe a little more."

Faint streaks of sunlight already brightened the horizon. By the time they reached the campus of the Ridgeview College, it would be full morning. They'd have to spend the day waiting.

Weird.

Only a few years ago he'd been a student at that college, studying business, living a normal, regular life. It felt almost alien now. All because he'd left a party early and taken a walk in the woods.

How different would his life have been if he'd never done any of those things?

Charlie and Alexa would still be...

He pushed that thought away, clenching his hands into fists so tight that his nails bit into his palms. He could regret all he wanted but it wouldn't change anything. They would still be changed and his parents would still be gone. The only shot he had was to save Callum.

Focus on that.

"We should stop for food," Jessica said.

No, we have to keep going. Tell her, Charlie.

"Sebastian's whining again," Charlie said. "I suggest we stop and shut him up."

"Did you eat today?" she said. "Well, I haven't. Not for two days. Too busy trying to catch up with you. So I'm eating. A break for half an hour isn't going to make any difference."

She waved at the windshield. The sky was definitely lightening now. Streaks of yellow glowed on the underside of distant clouds. A deeper blue was overtaking the dark.

Even with the pain it caused him, he couldn't help but feel grateful to see the sun.

Another few minutes passed before the van began to slow. Gravel clunked and jumped under the wheels as Gareth pulled off the highway. Through the windshield, Sebastian watched the brown bricked, one story building come into view. They parked and Gareth jumped out of the front seat.

Jessica moved to the back of the van and grabbed onto the door leaver. She turned back to face him. Her ponytail whipped around.

"We're just getting out to stretch our legs. Gareth will get the food. We're not going near people. Got it?"

"Sure, babe," said Charlie.

She frowned at him and pushed the door open.

Gareth was already walking toward the building. As Sebastian stepped out of the van, the stench of grease and gas assaulted him, mixed with dust and exhaust. The whine of early morning traffic hummed along the highway. The breeze tugged at Jessica's hair, brushing several wisps free that tickled her cheek and forehead.

It hissed along the gravel, ruffling the short grass near the back of the building, just behind the parking lot. He noticed the dumpsters back there, blue paint chipped and peeling. It reminded him of the dumpsters in Europe. Did all dumpsters look the same? Was there only one manufacturer of dumpsters?

His thoughts were rambling away from him. One of his symptoms of being overtired. But he couldn't sleep. Not now. Not so close.

Callum.

He had to stay awake and alert for his brother.

Besides, he was afraid he might not wake up if he fell asleep.

Instead, stay focused. Pay attention. Stay alert. Those dumpsters. They even painted them the same shade of blue. Probably got a deal on the paint…

The lids were closed, he noticed. You usually didn't see that.

The breeze brought a whiff of sourness.

His heart almost stuttered then began to pound. Vampire!

Sebastian lunged forward. His legs caught and started pounding on the pavement. He heard Jessica call him. Then her footsteps surged after him.

Man, what the hell are you doing, Charlie roared in his head.

Vampire! It could be Alexa!

His feet skidded on the pavement as he reached the first dumpster. His palm touched the side, scraping on flaking paint as he stopped himself.

Jessica reached him a moment later. She grabbed his arm and wrenched him around.

"What the hell?" she said.

"Vampires!" Sebastian's voice bellowed out of his throat.

He could still feel Charlie in there, still felt the coldness in his limbs. But he was more himself. Every minute, he gained more control again.

He needed it now.

"Smell them?" he said.

Jessica tilted her head back and sniffed the air. Her lips parted, then thinned as she nodded. Her right hand waved to the next one.

There, she mouthed.

Still in the early morning twilight, the vampire could still be dangerous. The back of the building shaded them from the rising sun. It could be just enough darkness for the vampire, if it was fast.

They had to be faster.

Jessica pulled out her handgun but Sebastian didn't have anything. They'd taken the shotgun from him. He started to turn toward Jessica. She yanked a large knife from her belt and handed it to him, handle first.

His fingers touched the handle as the lid of the dumpster flew open.

The stench of rotting orange peels and coffee grounds wafted out, still not overpowering the arching sour smell. The vampire leapt up, balancing on the top edges of the dumpster, hunching in the shadow of the building. Grime and garbage smeared the sides of her face. It was female, dressed in a now stained white flowered dress. Hands with nails decorated with chipped pink nail polish hooked into claws. Light brown hair hung in clumps around her head, pulled out of a loose bun at the nap of her neck. Her face twisted in a snarl.

No spark of intelligence in those eyes, just the wild glare of an animalistic vampire.

The most dangerous kind.

At the most dangerous time.

She snarled and leapt for Sebastian, hands reaching. He jumped back at the last minute. Her nails whooshed past his face, parting the air a mere inch away. As she landed, Jessica fired.

The gunshot echoed in the parking lot. The vampire squealed as the shot hit her in the thigh. She lunged and swung at Jessica. Jessica jumped back. Her foot slipped on the gravel. Her arms shot out to try to keep balance, but her leg was already too far in front.

She fell back, landing on her rump.

The vampire leapt.

Sebastian reversed the knife blade and threw it. The knife hummed as it sliced the air then slammed into the vampire's back. It reared up, shrieking. Hands clawed behind itself as it tried to reach the knife buried between its shoulder blades.

Jessica rolled to her right, reaching for the gun.

The vampire noticed the movement. Lunged forward. Claws reaching for Jessica.

Jessica was too far from the gun.

No!

Sebastian pushed at the vampire, felt her mind raging like a wild, molten thing, all fury and blood lust. The killing desire roared at him, flooding his senses until he thought he would drown in it. No! He pushed it away, pushed through it as if he was swimming in her mind. There had to be something else here, something he could hold on to, make *her* hold on to. Wild emotions swarmed around him, pulling and yanking at him, daring him to indulge. Scraps of memory floated past him, biting, blood, drinking. Was that all she was aware of? She was the most primitive of Grellock's legacy, not even killing for revenge, only to satiate her thirst.

But she wasn't always like this, there had to be something from before, some scrap. He dug down, searching. The blood lust hummed in his brain. So easy to just taste a little, just drink a little...

Dig down.

Summer.

The feel of cotton sheets, damp from the washer.

A warm breeze bringing the scent of cut grass and just a tinge of coolness as the evening fell.

Wood clothes pegs snapped as hands clipped sheets onto a clothes line. He felt air expand in his lungs as she took a deep breath. She'd gotten to the washing late so the sheets would have to hang out overnight. Even with the coolness, they should be dry by morning.

By the time she finished, the sun had already gone down. The breeze blew a little stronger, rustling the sheets on the line, bringing along the summer cut grass smell...

...and an overpowering sourness that enveloped her as pain pierced her neck...

Back... go farther back. Who were you before?

Remember...

The vampire inside twisted, trying to pull away but he held on, forcing her to look down, look deeper.

Who are you?

Miranda. She loved knitting, even volunteered to make booties and mittens for the preemies at the hospital. She worked part time as a bookkeeper at the church and drove her two children to school in the mornings, sharing car pool duties with two other mothers down the block. Her husband, Hal, worked as a manager as the grocery store. Sometimes he brought home extra coupons but money was still tight. She took to hanging clothes out on the line in the backyard to save the cost of the electricity to run the dryer. The white line hung from the long, thick nail Hal had hammered into the siding on the house and she strung it across the sparse, yellowed grass to tie the other end to the side of the rusting swing set that the kids hardly used.

Soon she found she loved the fresh air smell on the clothes, even with an undercurrent of exhaust fumes from the road.

If only she'd done the wash a little earlier that day...

No, stay farther back. Strengthen those earlier memories. He could feel her thoughts like threads around him and he tried to gather them together. He had to hold the picture, had to make her see who she was, who she had been...

Farther...

Meeting Hal in high school. He was a tall, gawky kid with scrubbed cheeks and bristly black hair that did nothing to hide his big ears. So shy he could barely talk to her. First date had been an old drive in, showing *Chinatown.* Hal had been all embarrassed by the ending.

As a child, Miranda loved to paint and dreamed of being an artist but her dream had been bigger than her talent. She still loved to visit museums, still loved to look at paintings, at the thick colors, the way the brush strokes mimicked and blended light and shadow into shapes and objects. The ultimate illusion.

Only now the only color that really held interest was red.

Bloody, sticky red.

And she mourned the loss of all the other colors.

He could feel her now, inside, buried deep under the rage and unquenchable thirst of the vampire. The tiniest of sparks inside. He reached out to touch that spark, to blow it into a tiny flame.

Miranda...

Help me. Let me go...

The desire burned through her and he translated into words although she spoke no words to him. The feeling blew through him like a wind. A clutching, begging need to be free. It wasn't even her mind anymore.

He felt like he had touched her soul.

Help me...

His mother had called to him that way, begged him to free her, to save Callum. And here was another woman, another mother, asking the same thing. Asking for death.

Was that all he could give?

Maybe death was the kindest gift he had.

But he remembered the ricochet, the pain engulfing him. How much more of that could he endure? Pushing that hard couldn't be the only way.

Maybe he could try something else.

Something that wouldn't almost kill him in the process.

He felt the vampire scratching at the edges of his awareness, gaining in strength even as the core of Miranda's focus weakened. The vampire was so strong in her, so animalistic. It wouldn't be long before it engulfed her totally.

He had to open the well and let it all spill out.

He focused on Miranda, focused on the threads of her memory. Every thread was a thin bind that kept her tied to the vampire. Cut the binds and she would fall away. Spiral into death. And the vampire would follow.

He hoped.

Now he had to do the reverse of what he'd done before. Forget all the pieces of her, push them away, sever the ties. One by one, he felt her memories drop away. He felt her cry out at the loss of her children, the loss of summer days and fresh air, the loss of Hal, and finally the loss of paintings swirling into a blend of color and darkness.

The tiny spark of Miranda withered, grasping.

Let go…

Sebastian gave a gentle shove.

The spark winked out.

The vampire roared.

Sebastian yanked himself back.

Pavement slammed against his back. His breath whooshed out of him. His fingers scraped on gravel. His head throbbed. Bright light pierced his eyes. The sky above him shone a light blue. A few fluffy clouds poked above the edge of the brick wall to his left.

Right. The back of the convenience store.

Memory came back.

In front of him, the vampire withered on the ground. Limbs spasmed. Her head jerked from side to side. Her eyes had rolled up so far he could only see the whites. Froth splattered her lips. After a moment, her body went rigid. Her back bent upwards, bending her into a bow. Then a sigh escaped her lips.

Her body sagged to the ground.

And lay still.

He could almost feel the final exhale.

Jessica climbed to her feet. She scooped up her handgun, pointing it at the ready. But she didn't need it. Sebastian could feel it. Even she could probably feel it.

There wasn't anything there. Not human and certainly not vampire.

Miranda was now well and truly gone.

Jessica poked her toe at Miranda's shoulder. No response.

Her eyes were wide when she turned to look at him.

"What did you do?"

He could only shrug.

Jessica wanted to leave immediately but Gareth forced them all to eat first. They all crouched in the back of van. Sunlight filtered in through the front windshield, making Sebastian's head pound. After he winced for third time, Gareth pushed past him and leaned into the front seat. Sebastian heard him rummaging around, then a black hand shoved a pair of sunglasses at him.

"Put these on," Gareth said.

Sebastian shoved them on his face.

Jessica plunked a hamburger in his hand.

"Eat," she said.

"I assume you're mostly back with us," Gareth said. He nibbled on a French fry.

Sebastian managed a bite of the cardboardy hamburger. Even doused in ketchup and mustard, it was tasteless. God, didn't he miss a good hamburger.

"I think so," he said.

"Good." Gareth finished his own burger and wiped his hands with a napkin. He folded the paper wrapping and slipped it back into the restaurant bag.

"Now, mate, I believe you need to tell us what the hell is going on with you. First you have this ability to Influence vampires, then you see ghosts, and now you're killing vampires without even touching them. Might you have some explanation for all this?"

Gareth folded his hands on his knees and leaned forward. A look of expectance rested on his face. Beside him, Jessica stared down at the meal on her lap, taking great interest in the French fries balanced on her knee.

Sebastian knew if he could smell her at all he'd be smelling fear from her right now.

She was afraid of him.

That made a part of him want to curl up, but he couldn't. Not yet.

Not with Callum still out there.

He ate two more bites of the hamburger, knowing that even if he tried to urge them to leave now, Gareth would insist on this discussion. And he would insist on Sebastian eating.

Probably a good idea.

"I think it was the book," Sebastian said.

"Grellock's book?"

Sebastian nodded. "I could feel him in it, feel the book itself. I think it did something to me."

Gareth frowned. "Other In-Between handled that book. Why can't they do any of this?"

"Sebastian's always been different." Jessica spoke still hunched over her food. She didn't look up.

"Is that right?" Gareth said.

Sebastian nodded. "I think I'm closer to... well, than most other In-Between."

Gareth nodded. "Okay. So you're more sensitive or whatever. You touch Grellock's book and that mojo in it fires up something in you. You start by Influencing a few vampires and now you can kill them. Ever tried killing more than one at a time?"

"No," Sebastian said. "I'm not really killing them."

"That vampire near the dumpster looks pretty dead to me."

"Of course she's dead but I didn't kill her," Sebastian said. "I released the woman inside."

Jessica's head jerked up. "What do you mean released the woman inside?"

Sebastian spread his hands. "Miranda. There was a little bit of her inside. I helped her let go."

Jessica stiffened. A fry dropped her from fingers. Gareth's frown deepened.

"Are you saying that vampire was still human?" he said.

"A little spark of her," Sebastian said. "They all have that. Why?"

"They're vampires," Jessica said. "They're just vampires."

Sebastian opened his mouth but she crumpled the paper on her lap. She lurched up from the seat, reaching out to swipe up the bag that sat at their feet.

"I'll toss this," she said and yanked at the door handle. Sunlight blazed in, making Sebastian wince behind his glasses as she pushed the door open. She jumped out, dragging the bag, and slammed the door shut behind her.

"Testy," Charlie said from Sebastian's left. He sat with his hands folded in his lap. He looked at the French fries in Sebastian's hand and sighed.

"What was that about?" Sebastian said.

"How many vampires do you think she's killed?" Gareth said. "If there is still humanity in them like you say, she's killed all those people."

"It's buried," Sebastian said. "Practically extinguished. It won't ever be able to come out. She still killed vampires."

"Collateral damage," Gareth said. "It's hard to accept they're a part of that."

"So are we," Sebastian said. "I'd like to make sure my brother isn't."

"Of course," Gareth said. He popped a final fry into his mouth and balled up the paper from his lap. He squeezed past Sebastian into the front of the van and settled into the driver's seat. A moment later, the engine roared to life.

The back door swung open, illuminating the interior. Sebastian blinked in the blinding sunlight. A shadow fell across his face as Jessica stepped up into the van. She pulled the door closed, cutting off the light.

She sat across from him, her hands together on her lap, her face expressionless.

How much more could he push her, how much more could he take away before she turned away from him completely?

The seat jostled under him as Gareth hit the accelerator. The van moved forward, gaining speed as they left the parking lot.

"Dude," Charlie said. "Talk to her. Don't be a dick."

Shut up! Can't you let me handle this?

"Yeah, cuz you're doing such a great job."

Can't I talk to her alone? For once?

Charlie hrmphed. "Fine. Be like that."

He vanished.

Sebastian sighed with relief. He glanced across at Jessica.

"They're still vampires," he said. "All of them. There's no coming back from that. You couldn't have done anything different."

"I don't know," she said. "I can think of a lot of things I could have done different."

She was talking about him. He could tell from the way she held her body rigid, staring at her hands, not even looking up at him.

He really had fucked it up with her this time.

"I'm sorry," he said. "I've been a walking disaster since you met me. Maybe you shouldn't have tried to help me out in the library."

Her shoulders jerked as if he'd hit her.

So she had been thinking the same thing.

Damn.

At least he could maybe stop being a burden to her.

"When I get Callum back, I'll take him somewhere far away. I'll get out of your hair."

Now her head jerked up. Tears made her eyes look watery.

"Oh really?" she said. "Running again?"

She lifted her hand and whacked him across the face.

He fell off the bench, onto the floor of the van. The van's rocking sent him back toward his seat and his head smacked into the bench seat. He tasted iron in his mouth where his cheek had been cut by his teeth.

He blinked and looked up at her.

She'd turned away, sliding down the bench toward the back of the van. Her hands covered her face.

Her shoulders shook.

With the van speeding along, regaining his feet was a tricky business. He managed to drag himself up onto the bench beside her.

But now what? What could he say to her to make her feel better? He wasn't even exactly sure what he'd said wrong.

Except that she'd accused him of running again.

But he just didn't want to burden her anymore.

"I can not believe how much of an idiot you are."

Charlie appeared on the bench in front of him. He shook his head, blond hair shimmering in the sunlight from the front of the van.

Oh yeah? So what should I say to her, oh wise one?

"Maybe actually *tell* her you don't want to burden her, that's why you're leaving."

Hadn't he said that? He thought back. He thought he had.

But had he?

"Oh jeez," Charlie said. "Say what I tell you say."

What?

"Do it! Now put your hand on her back and repeat after me."

Charlie cleared his throat. "Jessica, I'm not running from you. You're the best thing in my life."

I…I can't say that.

"You'd better or you'll never see her again."

Charlie was right. If Sebastian didn't do something, say something to convince her, he'd lose her for good, if he hadn't done so already.

He hesitated before he placed his hand on her shoulder. Her shoulder flinched but she didn't pull away.

And she didn't punch him.

Progress?

"Jessica, I'm not running from you. I just… I just don't want to screw things up for you any more than I have."

"That's not what I said," Charlie said.

Shut up!

"Right." Her voice sounded muffled. She sniffed. Her hands moved away from her face. Even turned away he caught a glimpse of the tears staining her cheeks.

"So after all the people I've lost, Joan, and even Nigel, you're just going to leave me all alone."

"That wasn't what I meant," he said.

"Will you wait for me?" Charlie said.

Shut up. I'm talking to her myself.

Charlie threw his hands up. "Oh great. Screw it up even more then."

"Charlie's trying to tell me what to say," Sebastian said, "and he is better at it than I am. I know I suck at it."

Several strands of her hair clung to her cheek. He brushed them back, tucking them behind her ear. Her skin was smooth and soft against his palm. He couldn't smell her at all, just the faintest trace of soap left over from washing. But nothing of her.

How he wished he could smell her.

How he wished he could let her know how much he wanted that.

Maybe he could.

He closed his eyes and breathed in. His hand on her neck felt warm, as if her skin was heating up, melding to his flesh. Another breath took him down deeper.

Deeper.

He felt the waves of her around him, familiar and yet strange. Pain weighed on her. Unshed sorrow over Joan. Guilt over Nigel, that she had left to follow after Sebastian instead of staying to help. Fear that all the vampires she'd killed had been people, not monsters.

You freed them, he tried to tell her, but he felt her pull away. He didn't want that. So he let it go.

Still he could feel her turn away from him. It wasn't working. He had to do more.

Help me, please.

He felt his words drop away. For a moment, nothing seemed to change, then he felt a shift, a flicker of curiosity. Her attention turned toward him.

He'd done it now.

He had to either tell her all of it now, share it all, or pull away and probably lose her forever. He wouldn't get another chance like this.

But telling her... she'd really know how much of a freak he was, how different from the others, from her.

Would she ever be able to accept it? Accept him?

He would never know if he didn't tell her.

Everything.

It isn't just Influencing vampires and seeing ghosts. There's more...

He showed her. The vampire he'd sent up to the roof. The man he'd shoved into the convenience store, the man he'd killed accidentally. Killing Bianca, which had resulted in Brent's death. The vampire Thomas. Even his mother and how he'd felt the spark of her inside, begging for freedom, for Callum's safety. He finished with Miranda.

And all the while, the effect it had on him. The pain, the headaches.

How touching the book had changed him, given him this power, and urged him to cross over, to take full control.

How tempting that was, how seductive that call.

His own fear about how it made him even more of a freak.

When he finished, he felt stripped bare.

No more defenses.

He felt terrified.

Now she knew. She knew how close to the edge he was. How freakish he was.

Now she had every reason to turn away.

He waited for her to do it.

Instead, he felt a warmth flow through him, envelope him. She turned, not away, but toward him. He felt the spark of her glow, burning so bright and strong he felt almost weak before her. And then a trickle of delight, of laughter echoed through him.

You're such an idiot, Sebastian.

Her words danced around him, bright and childlike. He could almost imagine the girl she'd been before she'd morphed into the woman she was.

You try to do everything by yourself, don't you know by now I love you and I'll help you no matter what?

Loved him? She loved him?

He felt the trickle of laughter again. It trailed off into the distance, as her presence faded.

After a moment, he felt the steady rocking of the van beneath him.

And her hand on his arm.

He opened his eyes.

She'd turned toward him. Tears dried on her cheeks, evidence of her sorrow, but now she had an amused expression on her face.

"You're such an idiot," she said.

"Um," he managed before she leaned over and kissed him.

"Well, I guess you must have managed to say something right," Charlie said.

Sebastian waved his hand at the ghost then pulled Jessica closer.

To hell with the peanut gallery.

CHAPTER 18

"Alone," Sebastian said. "I have to go alone. She'll know if you're there, you know she will."

They stood under the shade of a large maple, a block away from the Ridgeview College. The oddest sense of déjà vu flowed through Sebastian. He recognized this street, was sure he'd walked up the concrete sidewalks, admired the older Victorian style homes. From here he thought he could smell the sweat from the long distance runners that always ran the track on the other side of the campus. Different perfumes mingled with exhaust and the new buds that sprang up around the campus. Late spring heading into early summer. Soon classes would get out.

It all felt so familiar, almost as if he'd lived a parallel life here. Maybe part of him had branched off that fateful night. Was there a twin of him wandering around here somewhere? A Sebastian who had not left the party, had not been bitten by Bianca and turned into an In-Between? Had that Sebastian finished classes and continued on with his degree?

Continued on with a normal life?

He tried to imagine what that would be like.

It all seemed like grey fog to him.

"We could back you up," Gareth said.

"She'll know," Jessica said. "It's probably bad enough that we've brought him this close."

She shifted on her feet. Her hands were shoved deep into her pockets. Her eyes were lost behind a pair of sunglasses but he knew how much those sentences cost her. He could see the tiny muscle jump on the side of her jaw.

Gareth frowned. "I don't like it."

"I won't risk Callum," Sebastian said.

Gareth glanced away, down the street toward the campus. He too wore sunglasses. He slipped his hands into the pockets of his black jeans, mimicking Jessica. His head bowed.

"Sebastian…"

"Don't," Sebastian said. His hand shot up to stop Gareth's words. "Don't say it. I don't want to hear it."

Gareth pressed his lips together. "Okay. Will you at least carry a phone? Leave the line open so we know you're okay?"

"Yeah. I suppose I can do that."

"Good." Gareth stepped past him and climbed into the back of the van.

Jessica moved to Sebastian's side. Her hand slipped around his arm.

"Are you sure this is such a good idea?" She pitched her voice low.

"I have to," he said. "I wish…"

She nodded. "I know."

Her lips brushed his cheek and came to rest next to his ear.

"She'll try to pull you down, to turn you, to tempt you. Remember, I'm with you."

Her cheek felt smooth and soft against his face. Even without her scent, he could feel the warmth of her body, the steady sureness, the bright glow of her love.

His hand slipped around her waist, tightening into an embrace.

"I'll remember," he said.

Her lips pressed against his cheek again then she stepped away just as Gareth jumped out of the back of the van.

"Uh sorry," he said. "If you're done…"

He held out a small black cell phone.

Sebastian took it and slipped it into his pocket.

"I've programmed it," Gareth said. "Just hit one and hold it for a moment. That'll open the line. I'll mute us on this end so she won't be able to hear us, but we'll hear everything. If anything starts, we'll be right there."

"Sure," Sebastian said. "Thanks."

Gareth nodded and put out his hand. They shook. For a brief moment, Sebastian thought he almost caught the echo of a thought from Gareth, something mixed with worry and hope, then it was gone.

Was this how it had been for Joan? Was that why she thought she'd die sooner? Did this ability somehow burn you out faster?

He only hoped he'd be able to worry about that later.

He gave Jessica a final brief smile before turning to head toward campus.

Back to school.

Funny that he never thought he'd see this building again.

Saggon Dorm sprawled in front of him, silver siding gleaming in the late afternoon sun. Two years had done little to change it. Maybe a little more dirt around the bottom near the foundation. A few different colored blinds or curtains hung in the windows. But everything else looked the same.

The same as two years ago when he'd shared a room with Charlie, ate in that same cafeteria facing the bank of windows that looked out into the courtyard. Walked those same halls with his feet pounding those tiles just like everyone else.

The same hurrying students flocked in and out of the main door, running shoes scuffing on the concrete steps. The late spring breeze brought him a mix of perfumes and colognes, soap and body lotion all overlaying the warm scent of their bodies, of their blood.

So many people. So much blood.

Just a taste...

He turned away from the front of the dorm. The grass crunched under his feet. It hadn't rained here for a few days. Vegetation was a little brittle.

He could smell it in the air. But rain was on the way. He could feel the hint of moisture, the way the wind carried it.

It would be a good soaking.

He headed back across the lawn, following the path as it curved along, angling past the grove of trees. Those trees.

He remembered those trees.

Wandering in at night, his sense of direction getting mixed up. The wet scent of dirt. The harsh grip of her hands. The sour smell of her breath.

And the sharp bite on his neck.

His life was never the same.

Please don't let it be that way for Callum.

It would be hard enough helping him deal with their parents' deaths. Let that be the only thing he had to help his brother deal with. Let him not be too late for anything else.

He had to keep hoping. It was the only thing stopping him from curling up into a ball.

The path curved away from the trees.

He stepped off and slipped into the grove, sliding between a set of dark, brown trunks. The ground felt hard under his feet. Diffuse light spackled the dead leaves, dirt and twigs that littered the area. It reminded him so much of that same time, just a few years ago.

This would have a much different outcome.

"It was in here, wasn't it?"

Charlie's voice floated behind him. Sebastian didn't bother to turn his head. He could feel the coolness that accompanied Charlie's appearance.

"In here is where I died."

"You don't have to come," Sebastian said. "If you don't want to see..."

"No, it's okay. Just weird is all."

Sebastian glanced back over his shoulder. Charlie followed, his hands shoved deep in his jeans pockets, shoulders hunched up toward his ears. He shook his head. His blond hair waved over his shoulders but didn't catch the various pockets of light.

Sebastian wasn't the only one with bad memories.

He found a natural clearing, with no small bushes. Even the ground looked clean, with only a scattering of dead leaves. He brushed some away from the bottom of a tree and sat down.

Charlie stood in the center. "Now what do we do?"

"Now we wait," Sebastian said. "We wait for nightfall."

"Do you think she'll find us?"

"Oh, she'll find us all right."

"Hmph." Charlie sat down to Sebastian right. "Do you think we'd have graduated by now?"

"Well, I would have," Sebastian said. "I don't know about you."

They talked about school then. Classes. People they'd known. Things they`d done. Parties they'd attended, or actually all the parties Charlie had attended, which was quite a lot. And all the while, the sun moved across the sky until shadows stretched across the clearing. As they dipped lower and darkened, Sebastian took off his sunglasses and slipped them into his pocket. His fingers brushed the phone. He pulled it out and turned it on, leaving the line open.

He pictured Jessica and Gareth sitting in the van listening, themselves waiting for the sun to go down.

Waiting for Alexa.

First the colors of the leaves deepened. As the darkness spread, Sebastian found they looked more distinct, the ragged shapes of some of them, the branches twisting above his head. Besides him, Charlie even looked more solid. Somehow that seemed fitting. This was the last place he'd been alive.

The buzz of students that had been the backdrop for the afternoon, faded with the light. He caught the distant rhythmic beat of the bass from the student pub. If he focused enough, he was sure he'd be able to sense the malty aroma of beer on the air.

But even beer tasted bland to him. Nothing would ever have any proper flavor again.

Nothing except blood.

And he would never give in to that.

"I told you to come alone."

His breath caught.

She stood across the clearing, a shadow between the trees. One foot shifted and she stepped forward, letting the dim starlight from above light her.

Alexa.

She had the same pixie cut to her brown hair, just a little longer now, a little shaggier. The same glasses perched on her nose. Dark Capri pants covered her legs. A white, spaghetti strap top glowed in the darkness. Her feet pushed into wedge sandals. If she'd been carrying a book, she could have just been another student returning from a late class.

Except for the smear of blood on her chin.

"We have unfinished business, Sebastian," she said.

He pushed up from the ground. His knees cracked. He'd been sitting too long. His muscles felt stiff. Mistake. He should have been preparing for a fight.

But he wasn't sure their fight would be physical.

He straightened to his full height, maybe the first time he'd ever done that in her presence.

"You're right," he said. "We do have unfinished business. Where's my brother?"

Her lips curled into a smile, not unlike the smile he used to swoon over when they were in class together.

"He's around. He's my insurance, you might say."

"Insurance?"

"That you'll do what I say," she said. "I want to make sure you cooperate."

"I thought you wanted revenge," he said. "For Constantine."

"Oh I do. Not just for him but for the book, for the plans we had. You fucked things up pretty good for us, but I've come up with something almost as good. That's what they taught us in school, right? How to be flexible."

"Where's Callum, Alexa?"

She waved her hand off to the right. "Over there, somewhere. Don't worry. You'll see him soon. When we're finished here."

Sebastian felt something else in the darkness between the trees. Another presence. Callum? He had to keep Alexa focused on him, distract her so she wouldn't realize it was his brother.

"Finished with what here?" he said.

Her head tilted, the way it always had at a particularly difficult economic problem.

"Finished with what I have planned for you."

Her finger flicked.

Movement exploded around him. Before he could focus, hands clamped on his arms, shoving him down to his knees. Sourness enveloped him. Three, maybe four vampires, surrounded him, held him on the ground, kneeling before Alexa.

He struggled to pull away but those hands tightened, squeezing flesh and muscles, grinding against his bones. Much more pressure and his bones would snap like kindling.

A lot of good he'd be for Callum then.

He sagged, stopped resisting. Maybe if the vampires felt him relax, they would relax their grips.

No such luck.

Alexa stepped forward and stopped right in front of Sebastian. He felt a hand grab a handful of his hair and yank his head back so he stared right into her face.

She smiled, her mouth wide. He smelled the sourness of her over all the others, a twisted version of her human scent. How often had he sat beside her in class, breathing in that warm scent, intoxicated by her?

Now it just made him want to gag.

"I was going to kill you," she said. "You deserve it. I wanted to do it for the longest time but then I kept thinking about Constantine's lessons. He always talked about the long view. He didn't mean years or even decades, he meant centuries. And that got me thinking. What would be the best revenge on you that would take a really long time?"

She turned away from him and waved a hand behind her. Rustling vegetation sounded. He saw shadows move, branches shiver and start to part.

Callum?

"I decided death would be too fast for you," Alexa said. "I decided on something else."

Leaves parted. A body fell out and sprawled on the ground at Alexa's feet. She nudged a shoulder with her foot. Blond hair spilled over the sandal. Alexa reached down to grab the hair and yank the head up.

Not Callum.

A young woman, probably a student. Her eyes were sunken, half closed. Pale, gaunt skin stretched over her face, giving her a wizened look. He could see the marks on her neck. Dried blood smeared around the ragged holes.

They'd been feeding on her for a few days, taking just enough to keep her weak but not enough to kill her or turn her or make her an In-Between.

"Don't you think it's a great idea?" Alexa said.

"What?" he said.

She laughed. "Oh poor Sebastian. You were always a little slow. Don't worry, I'll train that out of you."

She gave a nod.

Hands tightened on his head, holding it in a vice grip. Another hand grabbed his chin and yanked it down, opening his mouth.

Alexa grinned. She lifted her hand to the young woman's neck and pricked at the wounds. Blood began to flow. Warm, red, delicious blood. Through the sour stench of the vampires around him, Sebastian could smell the blood like a fragrant bouquet. It called to him as it dripped down the woman's neck and splattered on Alexa's fingers. She pulled her hand away and licked the blood off.

"Hmm, seventeen, maybe eighteen years," she said. "It was a very good year."

One yank dragged the girl forward like a rag doll. This close, the smell of blood filled his senses.

"It's easy." Alexa's voice purred in his ear. "All you have to do is swallow a few mouthfuls. Then we can be together like we should have been all this time."

Her tongue licked his cheek.

She shoved the woman's neck in his face.

Wet blood coated his mouth, his lips, clogged his nose. He tried to shake his head, turn away, but the vampires held him fast. The woman's neck pressed harder against him. He felt her blood dribbled down his chin.

His heart pounded, the echo thundering in his ears. Drink, all he had to do was drink. Blood called to him all the time. If he just gave in, it would stop. He would be free.

Lies! He'd never be free again. He'd be trapped forever. A monster.

No!

He struggled, feeling their hands tightened on him. He didn't care if they broke his bones now. He had to get away, had to get that blood out of his mouth. It already dribbled across his lips, over his tongue.

All he had to do was drink...

Help!

"Right here, buddy."

The chill of Charlie's presence flooded over him. Through him. His muscles trembled, contracting with the cold. Then he felt power infuse in them, buoying them up.

He and Charlie, together.

"Let's do this!" Charlie's voice echoed in his ears.

Sebastian jerked away.

His arms lashed out, shoving the vampires back. His foot lifted and he surged up, knocking the girl away from him. She crumpled to the ground at his feet. He bent over, gagging, spitting her blood out into the dirt.

Alexa sprawled to his right. She scrambled up to her feet. Her hands clenched into fists. Her face distorted with rage. Color flushed her pale cheeks.

"You won't turn? I'll make you sorry you won't," she said.

She darted across the clearing.

Sebastian took a step to follow but one of the vampires grabbed his arm. He felt Charlie's energy surge through him. He yanked his arm away and punched out, connecting with the vampire's cheek. His head snapped back. The body flew away. It hit a tree and crumpled to the ground.

The two other vampires crawled to their feet, hunching, hands hooked into claws. They snarled at Sebastian but didn't approach.

"Come on, pussies!" Charlie shouted, using Sebastian's voice.

Uncertainty crossed their faces. From the confusion, Sebastian could tell they felt something different about him.

"Are you sure you want to fight me?" he said. "My ghost friend and I would love to kick your ass."

In an eye blink, they vanished through the trees.

Now Alexa. He had to find her. Find Callum.

He spun. He could still smell her sourness, leading a trail out across the clearing. With Charlie, his senses were even more attuned. Her scent practically glowed in the air.

He took a step forward.

He heard rustling. Footsteps in the distance. Recognized Jessica's tread. She and Gareth racing forward. Of course, they would have been listening and were trying to come to his aid.

He didn't need them.

He knew what to do.

CHAPTER 19

ollow Alexa. He had to stop her, had to get to her.

Two steps across the clearing and she stepped out from the trees again.

But not alone.

She dragged Callum.

Her hand tightened on the boy's upper arm. From the paleness of his skin, Sebastian could tell she'd fed on him. Fed on his brother. He could feel his heart shrivel. He took a step back, almost doubling over.

Callum... I'm so sorry.

The boy's black hair hung limp and lifeless across his forehead. Dullness shrouded his brown eyes. His mouth hung open, slack. His shoulders drooped, his muscles loose.

Even from here, Sebastian could feel how the boy was in her thrall. Alexa tugged on his arm and the boy moved to cross in front of her, shielding her from Sebastian.

"Are you coming after me, Sebastian?" she said. "Come on then. What are you waiting for? Maybe you don't want me to kill your little brother?" Her hand stroked Callum's head, brushing his hair off his forehead, exposing more pale skin.

"He was quite delicious," she said. "The blood of children is the sweetest."

He clenched his hands into fists. With Charlie, he could feel his rage surge through him, ready to lash out. He could strike her down from here, one big PUSH would finish her. He wouldn't even need to hold her down until morning. He could kill her right now.

He knew it.

And it would kill Callum.

He knew that too.

Just like he'd killed Brent when he'd killed Bianca.

He couldn't do that to Callum. He'd promised Mom, he'd promised to save his brother.

And he couldn't even do that.

He took a step back. Alexa laughed. She knew, of course she knew he couldn't risk it. Couldn't kill her without killing Callum.

She'd planned it all along this way.

If he wouldn't turn…

Oh god, she would turn Callum!

Her lips parted in a wide smile. Her hand pushed Callum's head to the side. Without even seeing him, Callum's gaze slid past Sebastian, unfocused. Pale light glinted on Alexa's fangs as she opened her mouth.

No! He couldn't let her!

He *pushed*.

Alexa snarled. Her hands tightened on Callum, nails piercing his thin t-shirt. Her body shuddered.

But her mouth stopped just above Callum's neck. Her lips quivered over her teeth. She lifted her face and stared across at Sebastian.

Stop. Just stop and close your mouth.

He could feel power surging inside him, as if behind him, pressing against the narrow band of his self control. It wanted to lash out and engulf everything but if he let it, it would kill her and then kill Callum.

He couldn't let it. He had to stay in control.

He stared across the clearing at the vampire that gripped his brother. Stared at her.

At her eyes.

Her eyes.

Alexa?

Was that…? Something in her eyes?

Look carefully, Sebastian, make sure you look carefully.

Hadn't Joan told him that? Was this what she was trying to tell him? To look carefully at Alexa?

At all vampires?

Was there still a little piece of their own selves in every one of them?

Could he reach that in her?

"Alexa?"

Her eyes widened. He could feel himself drawn forward, falling, falling. He tried to put out his hands to stop himself. But he fell faster and faster…

Bright light blinded him.

He tried to close his eyes but it didn't matter. The light burned all around him, all through him. He tried to turn away but couldn't feel his body. Couldn't feel anything.

What? What?

"Easy pal, take it easy. It's okay."

Charlie.

As soon as he thought the word, Charlie appeared before him, hands tucked into his jeans pockets, wearing a familiar black t-shirt. Blond hair in waves around his head. He smirked at Sebastian.

Where…?

"In your head, I think," Charlie said. "Or maybe her head. I can't really tell. It's kind of fuzzy in here."

He gestured around him and as he did so, the light dimmed or maybe the clearing took shape. Trees took form around them. Branches and leaves coalescing into shape. He felt the ground under his feet again.

He followed the line of Charlie's gesture, turning.

Alexa stood behind him.

Just Alexa.

She looked even smaller than normal, almost shrunken. Her shoulders drooped. Her head dropped to the side as if it was too heavy for her neck. Dark shadows gave her eyes a hooded look. He could almost feel fatigue coming off her in waves.

She was tired. So tired of fighting.

"Alexa?"

Her head tilted up. For a moment, her eyes lit up. The shadow of a smile crossed her face.

"Sebastian?"

Her right foot slid forward an inch. Her shoulders drooped even lower, as if that small action exhausted her. Her head dropped back down.

Sebastian wanted to move toward her but he wasn't sure how. Was he real? Was any of this? Or was he in his own head, or hers? He didn't know the rules here.

"Just try," Charlie said.

Okay, try.

He thought about lifting his foot. It moved and he stepped forward. Another step. He lurched like a Frankenstein monster. This wasn't very productive. Across from him, Alexa looked even more worn. How long would she stay like this? Would she disappear?

He had to move faster. He had to reach her.

And he was in front of her. Just like that.

Oh.

Behind her, he saw darkness, spreading out and inching forward. It blocked out the trees and ground and sky. Not shadow or nighttime, he could feel a coldness, an evil inside that darkness. It smelled sour and rotting. It pressed forward with a relentlessness, a heaviness that he could feel pressing on his soul, trying to squish him down. Devour him. Erase him.

"Sebastian, I'm sorry."

Her voice sounded small. Weak. Hopeless.

She seemed to grow even smaller.

This was the only part of her left, he realized. A tiny spark inside the evil of a vampire. Was it a monster? A demon? Was this the creature Grellock had called forth for every vampire, the price of immortality?

Behind her, the darkness deepened. He could feel the coldness wafting over him. Moving closer. Getting ready to drown the last of her completely.

"Alexa."

He reached for her. So close but he couldn't quite reach her. He had to think of something else, some way to draw her to him.

"I'm the one who's sorry, Alexa," he said. "I should have protected you from this. I should have been honest with you right from the beginning. I let my fear take over and it started all of this. I'm so sorry."

She straightened. The shadow of a smile curled her lips. She reached out to him. He felt her fingers touch his. It felt insubstantial, like smoke, but behind it, he felt emotion, the spark of her.

He tightened his hand to hold onto her.

The smile on her face faded. "I can't hang on for much longer, Sebastian," she said. "It's too strong. I'm afraid I'll hurt you, hurt your brother. I can't stop myself."

"It's okay," he said. "I won't let it happen. You don't have to worry anymore. You don't have to keep fighting."

Tears shimmered in her eyes. "Sebastian..."

"It's okay really," he said. "Let it go. Let it all go."

Tears spilled down her cheeks. For a moment, he felt the warmth of her hand in his, the softness of her skin and instead of the sourness, he smelled the sweetness of her perfume. A rush of emotion moved through him, sorrow, longing, regret, and joy. Were they his emotions or hers? He couldn't tell. Then her image in front of him began to fade, leaving a glowing whiteness behind.

Her soul? Her essence? He didn't know for sure but he could still feel her there on an even more basic level. He pulled his arms toward himself, drawing the glow forward.

All he had to do was hold onto her while he *pushed*.

But the darkness had other plans.

It surged toward him. He felt Alexa scream in his mind. The glow vanished in front of him, swallowed by a wave of black that roared toward him.

It was coming for him and he didn't know if he could beat it.

He tried to pull back, tried to turn toward Charlie, reach for help but the blackness crashed over him. He was cut off, alone. He couldn't see anything, couldn't hear anything, couldn't feel anything but the darkness.

It burned with a coldness around him that made him want to curl in on himself. It was hunger and pain and anger all raging around him. And deep inside himself, he felt the tiny part of him that had been infected, that made him an In-Between, stir and rise up, as if to join the darkness. Oh the havoc he could cause. He could usher in a new age, an age of his choosing. He would be the new prince, the new emperor, presiding over the other vampires. No one would oppose him, not with the power he wielded. No one would deny him anything anymore. He no longer had to be gawky and afraid and a freak. He could remake the world in his image.

In *His* image…

From the darkness, a clawed hand beckoned him on. All he had to do was take one step, just a small one.

Open your mouth. Bite down. Keep biting even when you feel the warm, soft flesh against your teeth. Bite down hard. Pierce the flesh. And drink. Just one little drink…

Something pressed against his mouth, something soft, warm. A familiar scent, one he'd smelled for years, young, boyish…

Just one little drink…

…Sebastian…

What was that? A voice? Something calling him? It sounded far away, like from the bottom of a well. No, he was at the bottom of a well and someone was calling down to him. Someone reaching out to him…

Just one little drink…

No, that wasn't it, was it? What was *that?*

No smell now. Nothing against his mouth. Roaring sounded in his ears, drowning everything out. A wild, howling scream raged on. Angry, something angry. What?

Then something against his hand. Warmth through fabric. And beneath it, he felt a pulsing. A regular rhythm.

A heart beat.

A heart beat that he knew. A heart beat he had listened to many times in the night, lying in bed beside her, watching her breath deepen into sleep and listening, always listening to the gentle drum beat of her heart.

Jessica…

Howling fury roared at him but he latched onto the thought of her, and it brought everything back. The vampires, the In-Between, Alexa, Charlie, his parents, even Callum.

Jessica…

A lifeline. He clung to the memory, the essence of her.

Now he remembered.

And he knew what to do.

He turned back to the darkness and caught the tiniest glimmer inside.

Good try to make him forget, to make him give in, but he wouldn't.

Not ever.

And he wouldn't give her up either.

He surged forward to engulf the glimmer. He felt the weakest flicker of Alexa inside. He wrapped himself around her, still holding on to the trace of Jessica in his mind. All woven together. Protected.

Now he could get to work.

He faced the darkness.

And *PUSHED!*

Power roared through him, exploding outward in a flash of white that blinded him. He felt the darkness howl, shrieking rage and fear. Then nothing as the whoosh of white engulfed it. Covering everything. Covering him. Leaving him sightless and deaf but with a vague feeling of pain inside as if something had broken inside him, as if this final big push had snapped a circuit in his head.

The stench of iron plugged his nostrils. The smell of blood. He felt it on his lips. His tongue wanted to lick out and taste it but he couldn't. Oh god, had he bitten someone? Had he bitten Callum?

Had he screwed everything up after all?

Something soft touched his cheek. Skin. The palm of a hand. He recognized it now, recognized the feeling of something against his cheek. A moment later, he started to feel the rest of his body and realized he was lying on the ground.

His eyes fluttered open.

"Sebastian!" Jessica bent over him. Her hand left his face and tightened on his arm. She helped him sit up.

His head pounded. Spikes of pain throbbed in his temples, making him wince. Darkness surrounded him. For a moment, he panicked. It hadn't worked, he hadn't stopped it. He struggled against the hand gripping his arm.

"Sebastian, stop! It's okay! It's okay!"

Her voice again. Jessica.

And he realized it wasn't the darkness in his head he was seeing, it was nighttime. He focused, seeing the dark trunk shapes around him, the leaves swaying just a little in the evening breeze. The earthy scent of the grass and dirt filled his nostril, cutting through the smell of blood.

Blood...

"Did I... Callum...," he said.

"He's okay," Jessica said.

He followed the line of her hand as she pointed. Just to the side of the clearing, Gareth stood with Callum, holding the boy back. Callum leaned forward, tugging to get away.

"Seb," he said. "Seb."

"Let him go," Sebastian said. He managed to push himself up to his knees as Gareth let go.

Callum flew across the clearing, arms wrapping around Sebastian's neck. Sebastian almost fell over again and would have if Jessica hadn't steadied him. The boy sobbed against his shoulder, his entire body shaking. Sebastian wrapped his arms around his brother, holding on tight.

He should look at his neck, he knew, check to see if Sebastian had bitten him but he couldn't, not yet. He couldn't bear to face that thought just yet.

"You didn't bite him, you idiot, it's a fricking nose bleed again. Geez, I don't know how you're gonna manage on your own."

Charlie!

Sebastian turned his head. Charlie leaned against a tree, arms folded across his chest. He wore a green sweatshirt with the arms rolled up to his elbows. He shook his head, making his blond hair shimmer.

You're still here!

"Not for long," Charlie said. "Just wanted to say goodbye and good luck. You'll need it."

A small hand flashed out from behind the tree, swatting Charlie's upper arm.

"Stop that, Charlie, he's done pretty well."

Alexa stepped out from behind the tree.

Sebastian stiffened, hugging Callum closer. But she wasn't... he peered closer. She smiled and he could almost see the bottom tip of a leaf through her lips.

She wasn't solid.

A ghost.

Like Charlie.

"You really are slow," Charlie said.

Alexa shook her head and swatted Charlie's arm again. "Stop being so mean. You didn't figure it out until now either. Stop pretending you were smarter about this than him."

Charlie laughed. "He knows I'm kidding. Right, Sebastian?"

"What are you talking about?" Sebastian said.

"Is that Charlie?" Jessica's voice came from behind him.

"Yeah," he said. "I have to talk to him."

He took Callum's arms from around his neck. The boy sniffed as Sebastian pulled away. His head bowed.

"Callum, I just need to do something for a minute. Can you stay with this lady for me? She's really nice."

Callum grabbed hold of Sebastian's hands. His thin fingers clutched until they bleached white.

"Don't go, Seb," the boy said. "Don't talk to those transparent people."

Sebastian's eyes widened. "You can see them?"

Callum nodded. His black hair flopped in his eyes.

"Them?" Jessica said. "I thought it was just Charlie."

"Poor kid," Charlie said. "He's weird like you. Must run in the family."

"Shut up," Sebastian said. "At least I'm not a dorky ghost."

Callum giggled, but as Sebastian rose to his feet and took a step forward, the giggle stopped. Callum grabbed his arm.

"Don't."

Sebastian pried his brother's fingers away. "It's okay. It's just for a second. I'll be right back.

He glanced up at Jessica. She moved to stand by Callum's side. She put her arm around the boy's shoulders.

"Don't worry. I won't let anything happen to him," she said.

Callum's brow still twisted with worry but his hand loosened.

"I'll be right back. I promise," Sebastian said.

Callum's hand fell away. He pressed against Jessica's side.

Sebastian turned back to Charlie and Alexa. Even in the darkness, they seemed to have a soft glow around them that illuminated the trees and surrounding clearing. Every small, shuffling footstep sent pain shooting through his head but Sebastian kept moving, wincing as he went. Finally he stopped just in front of Charlie.

"What is going on?" he said. "Explain it to me."

Charlie opened his mouth but Alexa stepped forward.

"He can't explain it, he barely understands it himself," she said.

"Hey," Charlie said.

"Well, it's true." She turned back to look at Charlie. He pursed his lips and shook his head, blond hair shaking around his shoulders.

She turned back to Sebastian. She looked just like she had before this had all happened, before Constantine, before anything. The same bright eyes, the same wide open expression, the same relaxed poise. Everything Sebastian had loved.

But he could still see the outline of leaves through her skin and he knew what that meant.

"It's not your fault, Sebastian," she said. "It's not like you did this on purpose. How many evenings did you walk outside and not get attacked by a vampire? It's not something most people expect."

The catalogue of his subsequent sins flashed through his mind, all the things he should have done, could have done, should have said, but it all seemed pointless.

What would any of it matter to a ghost?

He'd failed at that major thing. All other flaws paled in comparison.

"It wasn't your job to save me," she said. "You had to take care of yourself. I made my own decision."

"What do you mean?" he said.

"I mean he gave me a choice. It wasn't a good choice but it was still a choice. I was... I was afraid to die."

"You... chose?" he said.

"I didn't really understand, there wasn't time to consider..." Her shoulders drooped. "I tried."

"You did the best you could," he said.

Her head lifted. "So did you."

He felt her words sink into him, past the pain throbbing in his head, past the fear that still clenched at him, even past the heartache of losing his parents. *The best you could...*

She was lying to him, he realized, trying to make it easier on him. She'd never chosen. Constantine had chosen for her. But still she didn't blame Sebastian.

The best you could...

"Thanks," he said.

She smiled. "Thank you." Her smile widened. "You saved me after all, Sebastian. And brought me Charlie to guide me home."

"I brought?"

"Why do you think I was stuck with you?" Charlie said. "Something in you wouldn't let me go until Alexa was here."

"Me? I didn't do anything," Sebastian said. "You just showed up."

"He showed up when you were ready to deal with me," Alexa said. "He had to. I was the one that killed him. But you were the one who could free me."

"But I didn't... *do* anything," he said.

Had he? He couldn't remember. It was getting fuzzy. The pain in his head increased.

"It's okay, dude, let it go," Charlie said. "I think you maybe broke something in there. Don't push yourself."

"Yeah, okay."

He could feel fresh wetness on his lips. A swipe with his hand showed him his nose was bleeding again.

"You better go take care of that," Charlie said. "Better take care of all of them." He nodded back behind Sebastian.

Sebastian glanced back at Jessica and Callum. He flashed an index finger at his brother; just one more minute. The boy frowned but nodded.

When he turned back, both Charlie and Alexa looked faded, like an old black and white photograph. Even the colors looked washed out.

"Hey," he said.

"We have to go, Sebastian," Alexa said. "It's time. Thank you for freeing me. I can never repay you for that."

"But you're dead," he said.

"Some things are worse than death. Being a vampire is one of them."

"Don't worry about her now," Charlie said. "She'll be fine. I'll make sure only upstanding angels hit on her." He winked. Alexa swatted at his arm again.

"Hey, good thing I don't bruise easy." He wagged a finger at her. "Listen Sebastian, heal up good and take care of your brother. I don't know if you'll be able to do this again for any of the other vampires, you may have pushed yourself too hard. If you did, you did all you could do, man. Even for me. You gave me the chance to help you and that's what friends are for. Hope to see you again. But not for a long time."

Charlie moved forward as if to give him a hug but faded before he even reached Sebastian. It didn't matter, he felt a very Charlie-like essence tickle inside his mind, leaving him with an overriding sense of laughter and friendship.

Tears rose in his eyes. He had a Charlie-shaped absence in his life now. He could feel it.

Soon he'd have an Alexa-shaped one too.

Even faded, she looked lovely, reminding him of his infatuation. He had loved her in a puppy-dog kind of way. Worshipful, as if from a distance. Maybe it never would have worked because he'd never really seen her a regular person.

Her smile widened. "I liked being your perfect woman," she said. "But you're right. I don't think it would have been sustainable, for either of us."

She moved forward to stand right in front of him. Without the sourness of the vampire, he could almost smell a faint whiff of her sweet perfume.

"Goodbye, Sebastian," she said.

"I'm sorry, Alexa," he said. "I wish this had never happened to you."

She nodded. "I know. I wish the same thing for you. For me, it's over. For you, it's still going on. Take care of yourself, Sebastian. Take care of them."

"I loved you, Alexa," he said.

She smiled again even as she began to fade, her image thinning like mist.

"I loved you too."

And like that, she was gone.

CHAPTER 20

Gareth knew someone who knew someone with a safe house where they could hole up for a few days. It was a small bungalow a couple of miles outside Ridgeview City. Set far back from the road, it almost reminded Sebastian of his first glimpse of a farm house in France with its off white walls, dark brown shutters and the porch that wrapped around one side.

He shook that out of his head, but without actually physically shaking his head. The ache pounded away at his temples although it had faded quite a bit. Jessica fussed over him most of the time, but without the more developed network in Europe, there was little they could do for him right now.

But every day, the pain lessened a little bit, and with it, the more severe symptoms of being an In-Between. Maybe he had broken something inside himself like Charlie had suggested, and maybe that breaking would reset him to be just like the others.

Maybe he wouldn't be quite so much of a freak anymore.

Four days after rescuing Callum, Sebastian knocked on the faded, white wood door before opening it. Callum was sleeping in the small single bedroom beyond. As the door creaked open and Sebastian poked his head around, he caught a glimpse of Callum still lying in bed. He swiped his arm over his face before turning his back to the door.

"It's almost ten," Sebastian said. "You want some breakfast?"

Callum wasn't eating enough. Sebastian didn't like the gauntness in the boy's face. Although the vampire Alexa had fed on him, it wasn't enough to turn him into an In-Between, as long as he ate properly and got out into the sun. But Callum wasn't being very cooperative.

Sebastian crossed to the bed and sat down. He tugged on the boy's shoulder. After a moment, Callum turned over. He blinked rapidly, keeping his gaze low.

Trying not to let Sebastian see the tears.

Sebastian's hand tightened on the boy's shoulder.

"I had a dream about Mom." Callum's voice trembled.

"That's okay," Sebastian said. "You should dream about her. You should remember her."

"Was she really a vampire?"

Sebastian let out his breath slowly. He hadn't wanted to tell Callum but he deserved the truth.

"She was but deep inside she was still Mom. The last thing she asked me was to keep you safe."

"Really?" Callum looked right at him, eyes wide and brimming with tears.

"Really."

Callum launched himself up, hugging Sebastian in a fierce embrace.

"She was herself deep inside too, wasn't she?" Callum's voice was almost muffled in Sebastian's shoulder.

Sebastian puffed his brother's hair out of his mouth. "Who?"

Callum pulled back to face him. His hand swiped at his face.

"That girl. The one who took me."

"Alexa," Sebastian said.

Callum nodded.

"Yeah, she was."

"The rest are too, aren't they? Themselves deep inside."

"I think so," Sebastian said. "At least the new ones probably."

"And you can set them free."

"Well, sort of. I could. I don't know if I can now. My head, I might not be able to."

"Sure you can," Callum said. "You just need a rest. Teach me how to do it."

A laugh escaped Sebastian's lips. "Teach you? I don't even know how I do it."

"You can learn by teaching me."

Sebastian shook his head. "Cal..."

"Come on, Seb, you can. I saw the ghosts. I bet I could do this too. Teach me!"

Sebastian tilted his head at his brother. The boy *had* seen Charlie and Alexa, without even the benefit of being a full In-Between. Maybe Charlie had been right, maybe it was something in his family. If being an In-Between had awoken that ability in Sebastian and Callum could see them even without being an In-Between, no telling how far the boy could go. He might end up teaching Sebastian a few things.

And he might end up being better at it.

If Callum could learn to release vampires, it might just be the thing to turn this whole mess around.

Who knows, maybe together they'd be able to stop vampires for good.

The door creaked open behind them. Jessica appeared in the doorway. She leaned her hip against the frame, tilting her head to the side. Her hair spilled across her shoulders. She'd taken to wearing it loose. Sebastian liked the way it hung down, the way it moved like a curtain in the breeze.

"Before school starts, I think you both need a good breakfast, don't you?" she said.

Callum ducked his head a little. He was still shy around Jessica. Probably because he liked her. Sebastian pressed his lips shut tight to stop the grin.

"We'll be right out," he said.

"Okay. Eggs are getting cold. I'm not making more."

She stepped back, her shoes clicking on the wood floor. The door swung shut.

"What do you say?" Sebastian said. "Breakfast? Then we talk some more about this teaching thing?"

Callum nodded. "Okay."

"Okay."

Sebastian kissed his brother on the forehead. Callum squirmed away. "Don't!"

"Mom would want me to do that."

"Shut up!"

The boy's arms shoved like a piston but Sebastian caught a glimpse of a grin before Callum ducked his head down.

Sebastian got up from the bed and the flurry of arms and legs twisting away from him.

"Hurry up or there won't be any food left."

"Shut up!"

Sebastian closed the door as his brother started to climb out of bed.

He followed the shadows down the hall toward the kitchen. Bright sunlight reflected off the pale yellow surfaces. He winced, feeling his head start to throb again. Funny, he hadn't been quite so sensitive to light the last few days but it seemed to be starting up again.

Jessica stood by the stove, stirring at a pan in front of her. She glanced over her shoulder as he walked in.

"You okay?" she said.

"Yes, just the light. Where's Gareth?"

"He went to fill the van with gas and use an Internet connection in town. He doesn't want this place traced."

She knocked the spoon on the side of the pan and set it down on the stove. As she turned the temperature dial down it clicked under her fingers like a hammer. Then she crossed to him. Her hand felt soft as she touched his cheek.

"Are you sure you're okay?" she said.

"Yeah, I just need a rest," he said.

Her hand dropped away. She frowned. "Okay. Fine." She started to turn away.

Talk to her. He could almost hear Charlie's voice in his head.

He caught her arm, stopping her. She didn't look back at him.

"I'm getting sensitive to light again," he said. "I thought it was going away. I thought I'd be just a regular In-Between but it's all coming back again. I'm still a freak after all."

"You're not a freak." She turned toward him. "I don't love freaks."

"What?" he said.

"You heard me." She moved closer. He felt her soft breath on his cheek. "Yeah, I did."

He closed the inch wide gap and kissed her. Her body curved perfectly against him. Somehow, talking to her, being with her made it hurt a little less.

Funny how that worked.

"I thought there was breakfast."

Callum's voice came from behind him.

Jessica broke the kiss and stepped back. "There is. Come on in."

She turned back to the stove as the boy clomped in. The laces on his running shoes slapped on the floor as he crossed to the small, green, Formica table. His jeans hung low on his bony hips and the t-shirt looked like it was three sizes too big. None of it looked like an affected style although Sebastian could see white ankle socks poking out from under the jeans. Growth spurt? Was that maybe why Callum looked too thin?

Sebastian sat across from his brother as Jessica dished out eggs onto three plates. A plate of toast, a pitcher of orange juice and a carafe of coffee finished the meal. Callum toyed with his fork as Jessica sat down on his left.

"Don't play with them, eat," she said. "I won't let Sebastian teach you anything if you don't clean off your plate."

Callum took a tiny bite of egg and swallowed it down. "If I learn that will it make me a freak too?"

Sebastian's fingers tightened on his own fork. How could he reassure the boy that he wasn't a freak when Sebastian wasn't so sure about himself?

But Jessica's head shot up.

"What are you talking about?" she said. "I don't love freaks."

"Huh," Callum stammered. "But you don't… you hardly know…"

"I know enough," she said. "Now eat your breakfast and before you start talking about teaching and so on, we're taking you shopping for new pants. You're outgrowing those ones."

"I don't need new pants," Callum said.

"Yes, you do," Jessica said. "Eat."

Callum ducked his head and hunched over his plate but not before Sebastian saw the telltale blush color his cheeks.

Jessica smiled and winked at Sebastian. She picked up her own fork.

"I used to have a brother," she said. "The vampires killed him at the same time they made me an In-Between."

Callum's head shot up. He stared at her.

"It's nice to have one again."

Her voice sounded soft. Callum squeezed his lips together. Tears formed in his eyes.

Sebastian took hold of Jessica's left hand. "It's nice to have family."

"It sure is," she said.

Her smile looked brighter than any sunlight, and didn't hurt at all.

"Oh, shut up," Callum mumbled.

"Eat your breakfast," Jessica said. "Before I give you a big kiss."

Callum looked mortified.

Sebastian laughed. "If he doesn't want it, I'll take it."

"You already get your own," she said.

"Then I should give back."

He leaned over and kissed her cheek. He felt the muscles shift as she smiled. He breathed in the fresh scent of her hair, letting it tickle his nose. He moved his lips closer to her ear.

"I love you, Jessica," he said.

"I love you too," she said.

"Do you have to do that at breakfast?" Callum said. He wrinkled his nose in distain.

"Shut up and eat your eggs," Sebastian said. "We have to go jeans shopping after."

"Then teach me about vampires."

"Fine. Just eat."

Callum shoveled a forkful into his mouth.

"Could you teach me too?" Jessica said.

"I don't know," Sebastian said.

"Joan always said I was a little sensitive." The words came out of her in a rush. "Maybe I could learn too."

"Maybe," he said. "Maybe there's a way all of us could learn it."

She smiled and started eating.

Sebastian picked up a piece of toast and began buttering it.

Maybe he could teach her. Maybe it was possible. He hadn't really thought of it before but if he could teach the other In-Between, even a little bit of this, maybe then they could all learn to free the human within the vampire. Maybe something good could come out of all of this death.

Maybe there was a reason for hope after all.

Sebastian gazed across the table at Jessica and Callum eating their breakfast and smiled.

He'd say he had more than one reason to hope. Definitely.

About the Author

Based in Toronto, Canada, Rebecca M. Senese writes horror, science fiction and mystery/crime, often all at once in the same story. Garnering an Honorable Mention in "The Year's Best Science Fiction" and nominated for numerous Aurora Awards, her work has appeared in *Tesseracts 16: Parnassus Unbound, Imaginarium 2012, Tesseracts 15: A Case of Quite Curious Tales, Ride the Moon, TransVersions, Deadbolt Magazine, On Spec, The Vampire's Crypt, Storyteller, Reflection's Edge, Future Syndicate* and *Into the Darkness*, amongst others.

When not serving up tales of the macabre, mysterious or wondrous, she volunteers as a zombie or vampire at haunted attractions in October to stalk and scare all the unsuspecting innocents.

Find Me Online

Website - http://www.RebeccaSenese.com
Twitter - http://twitter.com/RebeccaSenese

www.ingramcontent.com/pod-product-compliance
Lightning Source LLC
Chambersburg PA
CBHW032128180726
48284CB00002B/705